"THE KING IS DEAD!
LET THERE BE NO MORE KINGS!"

So the newly formed Council of South Ehleenoee had decreed, and so it would be. But in the Council's midst were those who did not wish to join Milo Morai's Confederation or see an end to the old ways.

And as the Council raised its brave new army and prepared to reconquer its war-lost lands, the enemies of the Confederation waited—planning, forming alliances of their own, seeking the one proper moment to send Horseclans warriors and Ehleen lords alike to an unexpected and deadly fate. . . .

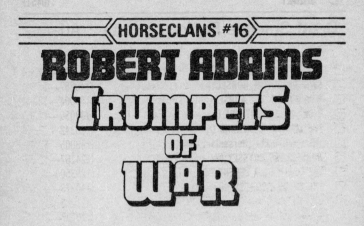

HORSECLANS #16

ROBERT ADAMS

TRUMPETS OF WAR

A SIGNET BOOK

NEW AMERICAN LIBRARY

NAL BOOKS ARE AVAILABLE AT QUANTITY DISCOUNTS WHEN USED TO PROMOTE PRODUCTS OR SERVICES. FOR INFORMATION PLEASE WRITE TO PREMIUM MARKETING DIVISION, NEW AMERICAN LIBRARY, 1633 BROADWAY, NEW YORK, NEW YORK 10019.

SIGNET TRADEMARK REG.U.S.PAT.OFF. AND FOREIGN COUNTRIES
REGISTERED TRADEMARK—MARCA REGISTRADA
HECHO EN CHICAGO, U.S.A.

SIGNET, SIGNET CLASSIC, MENTOR, ONYX, PLUME, MERIDIAN and NAL BOOKS are published by New American Library, 1633 Broadway, New York, New York 10019

First Printing, February, 1987

1 2 3 4 5 6 7 8 9

PRINTED IN THE UNITED STATES OF AMERICA

For Steven Barnes, Toni, and Lauren

Prologue

At the head of a force numbering five hundreds of thousands, the largest host ever seen upon this land in all memory, Zastros, High King of the Southern Ehleenoee, had invaded the Kingdom of Karaleenos, to his immediate north. But despite his vast force—partially, actually, because of that force's very vastness and consequent difficulty to keep always under firm, central control and keep supplied—his advance had not been either easy or inexpensive. What with green crops and forage burned where they had stood, most sources of water poisoned or foully polluted before him, while hit-and-run partisans nibbled at his flanks by both night and day, he soon was losing as many men to desertion as he was losing to enemy action or disease; furthermore, the deeper that the host penetrated into the hostile land, the larger became the percentage of loss figures, with severe malnutrition of men and beasts added into the horde of troubles, as the hyperactive partisans now closed in to his rear picked off most of the supply trains bound for the army.

Nothing that High King Zastros did or ordered done seemed to work to his advantage or that of his hosts from the moment that any of them set foot into Karaleenos. Gallopers sent back into Zastros' own lands with messages had a distressing tendency to not return; so too did the various units he sent back to organize and/or guard trains of the desperately needed supplies. When message arrows loosed by unseen bowmen rained down on camps of sleeping men promising uncontested passages and guides to potable water to any man or group of men returning south, out of Karaleenos, whole units began to desert Zastros, noble officers and all. One understrength squadron of his lancers even defected, went over into the service of his waiting enemies.

Nonetheless, the host he led into camp on the southern bank of the Lumbuh River still was formidable enough to daunt many a captain. But those high-ranking heralds who crossed over the ancient stone bridge—the only way remaining to cross the swift-flowing river short of rafting, which would have been suicidal in the face of the solidly fortified north bank—returned long of face with exceedingly bad news.

It seemed that High King Zastros was facing not only King Zenos of Karaleenos and his army, but the High Lord of Kehnooryos Ehlahs, the Lord of the Pirate Isles, and several strong contingents from as many states of the barbarian Middle Kingdoms, plus thousands of mercenaries. Altogether, said the heralds, they totaled a force almost as large as that one which by now followed Zastros' Green Dragon Banner, out-numbering the southerners, indeed, in horsemen.

Furthermore, their spokesman—Milos Morai, High Lord of Kehnooryos Ehlahs, King Zenos' northern neighbor, with whom Zastros had been more than certain that the Kingdom of Karaleenos was at war—had flatly refused to cross the river and come to battle with the southern force. Was the High King to continue his advance, he must fling his army against the well-fortified north bank, which meant that the bridge must first be taken . . . and a thick, solid stone wall had been erected entirely across it near to the northern end of the span and topped with mechanical spearthrowers, which last meant that win, lose or draw, the Green Dragon Banner was certain to have fewer men following it after the assault than before.

That had been when High King Zastros' staff had most sorely regretted having advised him to order most all of the war-elephants—which huge beasts it had been impossible to keep properly fed, anyway—killed and butchered to feed his starving troops while still on the march northward. Now, all that remained was a brace of elephant cows, draught beasts, which had been used to draw his monstrous wagon-mounted pavilion.

Nonetheless, the officers and specialists had hurriedly altered a couple of sets of war-elephant armor for the smaller—and now very undernourished—cow elephants, given them a crash course in the bare rudiments of elephantine battle training, then used them to spearhead the advance of a picked force across the bridge, one morning.

The elephants had not liked it from the beginning. Only the repeated pricking of spearpoints from behind and the fact that with the two of them abreast the space was too narrow for either to turn about kept them going for as long as they did.

When the elephants were a little beyond the middle of the bridge, the defenders had set afire the corduroy of pine logs overlaying the stones of the roadway, and as the roaring fire neared them, the two elephants went mad. Smashing down a stretch of rail—stone, wood and all—one of the cows had tumbled into the river. Thus granted the requisite space, the other had turned about and headed back south at a much faster pace than she had proceeded north, now heedless of just what or whom she knocked over or stepped on, her tender trunk rolled tight for protection and her eyes wide with fear and pain.

With one elephant either drowned or captured by the enemy and the other clear out of her head and last seen headed south at respectable speed, Zastros had set the artificiers of the army to fabricating a big wheeled tower a third again as high as the wall that stood on the bridge. He had kept them at it all of that day and through the

night, as well. But it had never been used, for the
assembled troops had not moved onto the bridge when
so ordered, stubbornly just standing in their ranks,
sullen-faced, pretending to not hear the orders. Not
even when Zastros sent mounted troopers of his
personal guard among the mutineers to maim and slay
would the recalcitrants obey the commands to proceed
against the enemy, though they had unhorsed and slain
not a few of the Green Dragon Guards before the remainder had managed to fight their way out of the
ranks.

Each succeeding hour of each succeeding day after
that shameful debacle had seen calamity piled atop mis-
fortune for High King Zastros and his miserable forces
on that ill-starred venture of conquest. So repeatedly
were their string of camps attacked by mounted archers,
boatloads of pirates and, on one occasion, even a mob
of swampers that the threatened men did the instinctive
thing, moving themselves and their camps closer and
ever closer together; true, this did make effective
defense easier, as it shortened the perimeter, but it also
made the spread of any disease or illness—and there
were more than enough of each category among ill-
nourished men in swampy camps—faster and more certain.

The High King, desperate for supplies now, sent off
the last full-strength squadron of horsemen he owned
with orders to escort back a complete train. The pitiful
survivors of the last supply train to get up to the starving
army reported that that squadron had not even paused
at the border post, but had ridden on south.

As that word passed about the sprawling camp, the
Host of the Green Dragon began to melt away like a
chunk of river ice under a hot sun. In droves, the
soldiers turned their faces south and quitted the camps
that now were filled with starvation, disease and death.
Those officers or sergeants so unwise as to try to stop
the deserters were lucky to be left beaten into mere in-

sensibility rather than dead of a swordthrust or an axe-swipe. And units ordered to pursue and kill or capture the deserters were as likely as not to, rather, join them and head for home.

Finally, the surviving peers of the Southern Kingdom met in secret council and sent a trusted man across the river in a boat by night to meet with Milos of Kehnooryos Ehlahs, King Zenos, Lord Alexandros the Pirate and the other leaders of the Northern Host and try to arrange—indeed, if necessary, beg for—bearable terms for a surrender. Of course, *Strahteegos Thoheeks* Grahvos *tehee* Mehseepolis *keh* Eepseelospolis doubted, all things weighed and considered, that even their chosen emissary could get decent terms out of the northerners, but one could always hope . . . and pray.

That had been why he had been as stunned as the rest when Captain *Vahrohnos* Mahvros had come back from across the river to repeat the words of the High Lord of Kehnooryos Ehlahs.

Mahvros of Lohfospolis looked half again as old as his actual age of thirty years, his darkly handsome face drawn with fatigue and the nervous strain of the last thirty-six hours, but his voice remained strong as he addressed this council of the highest-ranking noblemen left to his race.

"My lords, I spent most of this day past with High Lord Milo, King Zenos of Karaleenos, Lord Alexandros Pahpahs of the Sea Isles and the *Thoheeks* Djehfree of Kuhmbuhluhn . . . although Lord Milo seems to speak for all, most of the time.

"Lord Milo swears that no man or body of men marching or riding southwards from here, armed or unarmed, will be harmed or hindered, do they go in peace. Indeed, if they proceed along the main trade road, they can be certain of guides to show them to sources of unpolluted water and even small quantities of animal forage.

"Lord Milo emphasized that he wants none of our

arms, equipment or supplies, none of our animals, none of our rolling stock, not even our tents. We are welcome to bear back anything that we brought north from out of our own lands. He demands only the surrender of the persons of the High King and Queen, them and any loot stripped from the lands of King Zenos.''

"Harrumph!" interjected *Thoheeks* Mahnos of Ehpohtispolis. "This Lord Milos is most welcome to that precious pair, say I. Good riddance to exceedingly bad rubbish!"

"Yes, yes," Grahvos agreed, "we made a serious, a very costly error with Zastros, and we know that, we all know that now. But no one of us could have known away back when just how much he had changed in the wake of his catastrophic defeat at the Battle of Ahrbah-kootchee and his three years of exile. Hopefully, it is not yet too late to save our homelands from any more of Zastros' misrule.

"Well, if the High Lord of Kehnooryos Ehlahs wants the High King and his witch-wife as full ransom payment for all of the rest of us, our alternatives are few, and each one more bitter than the last: we can just continue to sit here while the soldiers desert individually and in whole units until starvation or camp fever or an arrow in the night takes us off, or we can gather what forces are left and biddable to our orders and essay another assault against that deathtrap bridge . . . although, to my way of thinking, falling upon our swords would be an easier and a cleaner and a quicker way of suiciding.

"But, my lords, our people down south don't need us all dead, they need us all alive, so I say we should just leave Zastros and Queen Lilyuhn to our esteemed former foemen and take ourselves and our warbands back home, for as God knows, we and they have more than enough to accomplish or try to accomplish there. How says the Council?"

Seven ayes immediately answered his question.

Grahvos nodded. "Agreed, then. Now that that much is settled, we must bring another thorny matter into the open. Who *is* going to rule without Zastros, eh? Each one of us here has just as much claim to the Dragon Throne as the next. But can the Kingdom of the Southern Ehleenchee survive yet another three or more years of civil war and general anarchy? I think not.

"Take a good look around this table, gentlemen, and while you do so, reflect that our Great Council was once made up of thirty-two *thoheeksee.* Including Zastros, there are now only nine *thoheeksee* within our camp. If young Vikos made it back home all right, there are still but two living *thoheeksee* in all of the lands of the Southern Ehleenoee.

"What of all the rest, gentlemen? I'll tell you what: twenty of our near or distant kin, almost two thirds of the original Council, died senselessly and uselessly while dishonorably fighting like cur-dogs over a stinking piece of maggoty offal!"

Grahvos stared each of his peers hard in the face, then went on in grim tones. "I say: no more, gentlemen, no more. If we name another of our own number king, just how long will it be before one or more of us others is tempted to enlarge our warband to overthrow and replace him?"

There were sober nods and mutterings of agreement with his hard words all round the table.

At length, *Thoheeks* Bahos grunted the obvious question in his rolling bass voice. "All right, but then just what are we to do, Grahvos? We Southern Ehleenohee *must* have a strong ruler. But another tyrant like Hyamos and his lousy son would beget another rebellion; you know that and so do we."

Grahvos once more gave his place to Captain *Vahrohnos* Mahvros, saying, "Now, lad, tell them the rest of it, that which you told me when first you returned."

"My lords, while awaiting us and even while fighting us, the High Lord Milo has persuaded King Zenos and

Lord Alexandros to merge their lands and folk and destiny with him and his in what he calls his Confederation. With his client state of the *Thoheekseeahn* of Kuhmbuhluhn, Kehnooryos Ehlahs, Karaleenos and the Sea Isles, he will rule over and command more forces and resources than even the richest and largest and most powerful of the barbarian Middle Kingdoms."

The seven seated *thoheeksee* squirmed, cracked knuckles and shot furtive, worried glances at one another and at Grahvos. With such a newmade power immediately to their north, they might not have enough time to bring the kingdom back to enough order to repel a retaliatory invasion. Perhaps . . . perhaps they should, after all, fight here and die rather than live on to see their patrimonial lands occupied by hordes of aliens?

"My lords, the new High Lord of Kehnooryos Ehlahs, Karaleenos, the Sea Isles and Kuhmbuhluhn has freely offered the thirty-three *thoheekseeahnee* full-standing memberships in his Confederation. All nobles are to retain their lands, cities, rights and titles, only their sworn allegiance will change, for there will no longer be a king, but rather a prince and three or four *ahrkeethoheeksee*, these to be chosen and appointed from among the thirty-three; the twenty-eight or -nine will be responsible to them, and they, the High Lord's satraps, will speak for the Confederation. There will never be another king.

"In practice, each *thoheeks* will act as royal governor of his lands for the High Lord. Once each year, all will meet to work out taxes and any other matters with the High Lord's emissaries.

"Please understand, my lords, the High Lord is bringing no pressure to bear, he demands no immediate answer to or acceptance of this offer. He bade me say only that Council should be told, think on the matter for as long as they wished and only then answer yea or nay. I have done his bidding, my lords."

The first to speak subsequent to the dropping of this bombshell was *Thoheeks* Mahnos. "What of our warbands, *Vahrohnos* Mahvros? What had this High Lord Milos to say of them? Does he mean to take them all into his army, march them away, leave us defenseless?"

But it was Grahvos who answered the question, prefacing his answer by saying, "I had all of this of the good Mahvros a little earlier, of course. Now, naturally, we will be expected to furnish some troops for the Army of the Confederation and to maintain a trained spear levy, as we always have done. Noblemen will not be denied bodyguards and some armed retainers, nor will cities be ungarrisoned, but the large warbands must be dissolved."

Thoheeks Bahos nodded emphatically. "Good and good, again. Give a man—any man—a small army to play with and all hell is likely to break loose. Besides, I'd liefer see my men pushing plows than pikes, any damned day. You have my aye yet again, Grahvos, on this matter. Foreign ruler or nay, no king and no war sounds more than good to me."

There had been a few, halfhearted dissenters, but within a scant hour, the matter had been talked out and settled, for the firm yet eminently fair government of Kehnooryos Ehlahs had been the subject of speculation and grudging admiration for the thirty years since its inception, and all of the *thoheeksee* agreed that almost any form of rule was far preferable to the howling chaos that had enveloped their lands during the last decade or so.

That done, the meeting broke up and the senior noblemen scattered to their various commands to order their forces, prepare to break camp and march as soon as possible. But they had agreed to meet again, each with a retinue of reliable, loyal, well-armed men, at King Zastros' pavilion at a specified time. There still was work to do before they once more became their own men.

When, gathered at the appointed time, they finally

pushed into the mobile pavilion of Zastros, it was to find Queen Lilyuhn lying dead on the floor of the audience room. Within the bedchamber, on the great bed, lay High King Zastros. He was not dead, but so stupefied with drugs or alcohol or, more likely it was felt, a concoction of both that not even shaking or slapping would induce him to even twitch or open his eyes.

After making one last try, Grahvos turned from the sleeper and shrugged, saying, "He's out like a snuffed torch, gentlemen. But it makes no difference, awake or asleep, the bastard's still deposed. Let High Lord Milos waken him. We came mainly for the jewels and the gold and the other emblems and symbols; those treasures belong to our race, and what used to be the Kingdom of the Southern Ehleenoee is going to need their value before we get reorganized. Let's find them and the pay-chests and get on the march for home.

"One of you pull off Zastros' signet and find his sword—they should go to his young nephew, Kathros. But, gentlemen, please, no obvious plundering here-abouts; if you must steal, please steal small. I don't want our prospective overlord to think ill of us . . . nor should any of you, for remember, our future now lies tied up into his new Confederation."

There was a short, sharp battle with Zastros' body-guard officers when the chests and treasures were borne out of the pavilion and men made to load them into a waiting wagon, but the *thoheeksee* and their retainers ruthlessly cut down any man who made to draw sword or level spear against them, and with their officers now all dead or dying, the rest of the Green Dragon Guards wisely slipped away, tearing off their embroidered tabards as they went, for there was nothing to be gained by support of a deposed and probably dead king.

Well aware that whatever was left unguarded would certainly be thoroughly looted by the unattached camp followers, *Thoheeks* Grahvos stationed Captain *Vah-*

rohnos Mahvros and two hundred heavy infantry to
guard the ex-king's hilltop encampment until the High
Lord's troops arrived. He also entrusted to the younger
man a large parchment package of documents—all of
them signed, properly witnessed and sealed—containing
written oaths of fealty to the Confederation from every
landholder in the dispersing army.

Within thirty-six hours after the deposing of Zastros,
all of the organized warbands were on the march south-
ward and the Green Dragon Banner atop the pavilion
waved over a scene of desolation. Outside the still-
guarded royal enclosure, precious few tents remained
erect or whole. Only discarded or broken equipment
was left, and a horde of human scavengers flitted
through swarms of flies feasting on latrines, garbage
pits and scattered corpses of men and animals.

Grahvos was the last *thoheeks* to depart, having seen
most of the troops on the march before dawn. Leaving
his personal detachment at the foot of the hill, he rode
up to the royal enclosure and, when admitted, rode on
to dismount before the pavilion.

"Any trouble so far, Mahvros?" he asked of the
captain.

The younger nobleman shook his head. "Nor do I
expect any, my lord. Oh, my boys had to crack a few
pates and wet a few blades before they convinced the
scum that we meant business here, but we've been
avoided since then."

"But what of after the rest of us are well down the
road?" asked the *thoheeks* skeptically.

Mahvros shrugged. "My lord, there're damned few
real soldiers—men trained to arms—left down there.
And anyway, none of the skulkers are organized, it's
every man for himself. No, I assure my lord, everything
will remain just as it now is here, when the
Confederation troops come."

"What of Zastros, Mahvros?" inquired the *thoheeks*.
"Has he awakened yet?"

"No, my lord." The captain shook his head. "He still
lives and breathes, but he also still sleeps. But I ordered
the Lady Lilyuhn . . . ahhh, disposed of. Her deathwound was acrawl with maggots, and it was a certainty
she'd be too high to bear by the time the High Lord
came."

Grahvos sighed. "It couldn't be helped, you know.
That guard most likely was the one who killed her.
There was fresh blood on his spearbutt, and that butt
fitted perfectly the depression in her skull. Nonetheless,
please tell the High Lord that I'm sorry.

"Also, Mahvros, tell him that I'll see the Thirty-three
all convened in the capital whenever he so desires. I am
certain that he and King Zenos will want some form and
amount of reparations—they deserve it and I'd demand
such in their place—but please emphasize to them that
some few years are going to pass before we can any of us
put our lands back on a paying basis."

Walking back over to his horse, he put foot into
stirrup, then turned back. "One other little thing,
Mahvros, my boy. The Council met for a very brief
session just before dawn, this morning. *Thoheeks*
Pahlios was your overlord, was he not?"

Brows wrinkled a bit in puzzlement, the *vahrohnos*
nodded. "Yes, my lord, but he was slain nearly two
years ago at—"

"Just so," Grahvos interrupted. "He and all his male
kin in the one battle. We're going to have to affirm or
reaffirm or replace the Thirty-three rather quickly, and,
quite naturally, we want men that we know in advance
will loyally support us and the Confederation. That's
why we chose you, this morning, to succeed the late
Pahlios."

Delving into the top of his right boot, Grahvos
brought out a slender roll of vellum and placed it in the
hand of the stunned captain, saying, "Guard this well,
Thoheeks Mahvros. When you're back home, ride to
the capital or to my seat and you will be loaned troops

enough to secure your new lands, if that's what it takes.

"Now, I must be gone." He mounted and, from his saddle, extended his hand. "May God and His Saints bless and keep you, lad. And may He bring you safely home."

Reining about, *Strahteegos Thoheeks* Grahvos rode down the low hill to where his personal retainers awaited him.

After turning over the onetime-royal enclosure and all that it contained to the High Lord, Milo Morai, Mahvros dutifully delivered the package of documents and the oral messages to the great man. That much done, he showed him the smaller document, shyly accepted the congratulations heaped upon him by the High Lord and the others of his retinue, then gave his own oaths of loyalty, in person, witnessed by all then present.

Then that night, while Confederation Army infantry guarded the hilltop enclosure in their places, *Thoheeks* Mahvros saw his retainers treated to all that they could eat from off the broiling carcasses of a brace of fat cattle, several casks of pickled vegetables, rounds of army bread and watered wine. He himself sat that night at a groaning feast-board with the High Lord and a select company.

That night saw his initial introductions to three men who were to become his lifelong friends and whose names were to be writ large upon the pages of the early history of the Consolidated Southern Duchies of the new Confederation of Peoples.

Sub-*strahteegos Komees* Tomos Gonsalos was the first. The red-haired half Ehleen, half mountain Merikan was a full first cousin of none other than King Zenos of Karaleenos himself. He was, announced the High Lord, to be commander of the mixed force of Confederation troops he was sending along with Mahvros and his retainers to be turned over to

Thoheeks Grahvos, his for as long as he needed them to help restore order to the lands of the Thirty-three *Thoheeksee.*

The second man was a Kindred chief of one of the Horseclans, the Merikan race from off the faraway Sea of Grass who had, thirty years agone, conquered Kehnooryos Ehlahs. Pawl Vawn, chief of that ilk, was typical of his ancestral stock—blond, blue-eyed, small-boned and very wiry, with flat muscles and great endurance. Under Tomos Gonsalos, he would be leading some hundreds of Horseclans horse-archers and a small contingent of the leopard-sized felines called prairiecats.

Another squadron of cavalry—lancers, this time—was to be in Tomos' force. After deserting High King Zastros' army for good and sufficient cause, Captain *Komees* Portos and his men had been taken, entire, into the Army of the Confederation; now they were all to go back to their original homeland on loan from their new sovereign. Press of duties had kept Portos from that dinner that night, but Mahvros knew of the tall, silent, saturnine cavalry leader and had even met him a few times. His reputation had been one of leadership, rare ability and, prior to his desertion from the Green Dragon forces, unmatched loyalty; indeed, such had been his well-earned name in that army that upon the disappearance of him and his force, the general assumption of his superiors and his peers had been that he and his had been wiped out by the partisans, no one even suspecting that such a paragon of faithfulness would desert, much less go over to the enemy.

The infantry force was to be a mercenary or Free-fighter unit of the Middle Kingdoms, the condotta of a redoubtable veteran Freefighter captain, Guhsz Hehluh, he and his company presently under long-term contract to the High Lord of Kehnooryos Ehlahs.

The third man "commanded" the last "unit" that would make up Tomos Gonsalos' brigade of mixed troops. Gil Djohnz was a Horseclansman, like Chief Pawl Vawn, but compared to that magnate, his "force" was minuscule—only some half-dozen mounted men, a small remuda of spare horses and a few pack mules were almost all of it. But the word "almost" was most important in this instance, for the entity that the word covered was rather large and the presence of that entity imparted a sizable addition of threat to any foes that Gonsalos' force might face. That entity was a cow elephant, self-named Sunshine, ridden and handled and cared for by Gil Djohnz.

"I was not aware, Lord Milo, that any save us of the Southern King—ahh, of the Consolidated Duchies, that is, used elephants in war, ere this," Mahvros remarked at that point.

The High Lord smiled. "We don't . . . or, rather, didn't, when all of this started. Sunshine is spoils of war, or, to be more accurate, like Portos and his squadron, Sunshine defected from Zastros and joined with us.

"On the day of the attack on the bridge fortifications, it was. When we fired the bridge roadway, one of the two elephants leading the assault, you may recall, burst through the downstream rail and fell into the river. That was our Sunshine. She came wading ashore a bit downstream from the bridge, and I was summoned to the spot along with a few Horseclansmen I had by me just then.

"I am telephatic, you know, and I instantly discovered that I could communicate—actually converse—with Sunshine as easily as I converse with my horses or with other telepathic humans. Although frightened, she was in no way vicious, and as soon as she knew that we meant her no ill, she indicated that her armor was very uncomfortable and begged us to relieve her of it. Stripped of armor and padding, she was an appalling sight. She was literally skin and bones—you could count her every rib and vertebra."

Mahvros sighed and nodded. "Yes, my lord, your partisans were all damnably effective in denying the Green Dragon Army the supplies and sinews of war we needed so desperately then. Indeed, most of the real war-elephants were slaughtered on the march because there was nothing to feed them. The two we had remaining upon our arrival were still alive only because they had been used to draw High King Zastros' pavilion."

"Well, I am returning her to the south, to the land she came from, Mahvros," stated the High Lord. "For all that she expresses unlimited devotion to me and would stay near to me, were it up to her, I think she'll be better off in a warmer, less humid environment than the lands around Kehnooryos Atheenahs, much less in the western mountains where I mean to eventually remove my capital."

Mahvros shrugged. "My lord, permit me to say that elephants seem to work as well in snow and cold as any other domestic beast, nor do mountains seem to affect them adversely; indeed, they are reputed to be almost as surefooted as goats. True, most of ours come from the flat plains of the far west, around the shores of the New Gulf, yet the *thoheeksee* of Iron Mountain have bred their own war and draught elephants for generations high in the northern mountains.

"However, I, for one, am overjoyed at my lord's decision to release this one, for elephants of any sort, if properly managed and utilized, can be invaluable to any army, and I am certain that *Thoheeks* Grahvos will be most appreciative of this kind generosity added to the other loan of trained troops. News of such unasked magnanimity is certain to go far toward guaranteeing the continued loyalty and respect and love of your highlordship's new subjects in the south.

"It has been my experience that the pattern of the reign of a new king is often set—both for ruler and ruled—quite early in that reign by acts which denote generosity or selfishness. Your high-lordship has begun his tenure well, I would say.''

Milo Morai pursed his lips and regarded the young *thoheeks* for a moment in silence, then said, ''My boy, you are wise beyond your actual years, in addition to being brave, loyal and loquacious. Continue to serve me as well as you serve *Thoheeks* Grahvos and the late Zastros and you will not remain a mere captain *thoheeks* for long, I vow. Such a mix of valuable talents in a man so young as are you is a rare and precious find for any state or ruler, and I am not known for dismissing or for wasting such talents and men.''

Chapter I

Uttering a deep, deep groan of pleasure, Sunshine gathered her thick legs under her, sat up and then stood up, streaming water back into the wide, shallow brook. Next, she lowered herself back down onto her now-scrubbed right side, that Gil might scrub the left as well. All the while that the short, wiry Horseclansman worked on the vast expanses of skin, pausing now and again to remove ticks and deposits of insects' eggs from folds and nooks and crannies in that skin, he and the elephant "conversed," mind to mind, in the silent, telepathic way that his people called "mindspeak."

"You are the best, most caring brother that Sunshine ever has had," the pachyderm had assured him over and over. "Not even Kalizos, who was my brother for as long as I can remember, understood me and cared for me as well and as tenderly as do you, Gil-my-brother. Yohnutos, who tried to become my brother after Kalizos ceased to live, meant well and was a good man, but by then he had his real sister and me as well to care for and very little to feed us, ever, so that we were always hungry. Sunshine believes that it was because he fed so much of his own food—little as it was—to us that he sickened and then he too ceased to live.

"When the life had left him, my sister and I were so very hungry that we . . . we ate his husk, all of it, even the tiniest morsel. After that, we were cared for by the men who also cared for horses, but those always stank of fear when they were around us. You do not fear Sun-shine, do you, Gil-my-brother?"

Folding one of her ears forward, Gil began to care-fully remove a line of fat white ticks from the crease thus exposed, popping them between his nails, then swishing off the blood in the flowing water.

"Of course I don't fear Sunshine, my sister," he assured her. "If life should leave me, for whatever reason, Sunshine has my permission to eat my husk, too; better her than a horde of little sharp-toothed beasts or a bushel of slimy, shiny worms. Furthermore, I am certain that this late Yohnutos must have felt just that same way, too."

After a while, he tossed the brushes onto the pile of gear on the bank, then slid from off the elephant and waded a few yards upstream to where the water formed another pool as deep as that in which she lay.

"I am done with you, Sunshine. Stay there and enjoy the water while I wash myself, then we will go back to camp. Perhaps the stores train arrived while we were away."

Sunshine did not answer him, she just rumbled another groan of pure pleasure from the cooling, soothing water gurgling around her. Idly, she filled her trunk and then sprayed the fluid onto those expanses of her body not submerged.

Once he had bathed and dressed, his clothes still damp from their washing, the pachyderm grudgingly quitted her pool and assisted him in resaddling her and hanging the equipment back in place. Then he guided her back to the upstream pool, on a bank of which he had discovered a dense growth of the plant called fen cabbage, much relished by the elephant. It was while she was using her trunk to tear out the plants, roots and all, and stuff them into her mouth that she once more mind-spoke him.

"Gil-my-brother, there is a man lying in the tall grass

just above the other bank. He has one of the long,
hollow things that throws tiny arrows and it is pointed
at your face. When I hear him take his deeper breath
and propel that arrow, I will spray him with a trunkful
of water and you must then attack him before he can set
himself to take another breath. Sunshine has heard of
these tiny arrows; the brother of one of her sisters
ceased to live after being only scratched by one.''

Across the stream, motionless in the thick grass, his
deadly blowpipe extended before him, Benee moved his
left arm ever so slowly, gradually raising the pipe,
meticulously adjusting the aim of the tricky weapon.
Although hardly more than a child by the standards of
most inland folk, among his own people—the fen
dwellers of the coasts, called swampers by Merikan
speakers and *baltohtheesee* by Ehleenoee when not
being called by cruder, more obscene names—Benee
was both a hunter of long standing and a well-proven
warrior, having taken the spears from off no less than
three inlander warriors and the head off one of those
men. This latest victim did not have a spear, but he did
have a head to add to Benee's collection that hung in the
rafters of a certain stilt-supported hut deep in the salt
fens.
True, he and all of the others had received word from
the Men of the Sea Islands that the great inland war was
now done and that they now were no longer to slay alien
warriors along the edges of the fens. But Benee and all
of the others of his kind had silently, grimly laughed at
the words, for war or no war there never had been a
time in living memory or legend when his folk had
ceased to slay any who chose to encroach too closely to
the peripheries of the salt swamps. All inlander folk
were the enemies of the fen folk, this had always been so
and would ever be so, and it was the duty, the right, the
privilege and the joy of Benee and every other man of
the fens to kill every inlander that happened to stray
within range of his blowpipe.

The long tube aligned to his utter satisfaction now, Benee drew in a deep, deep breath, for the range was a few yards farther than he would have preferred, but the best he had been able to accomplish in the particular circumstances. He drew the air in through his nostrils, for his lips already were pressed to the mouthpiece of the pipe, the fluffy down of the deadly dart only a couple of centimeters beyond his mouth.

But a split second before he released the powerful puff that would send the envenomed dart sailing at the unprotected flesh of Benee's chosen victim, a vast quantity of icy-cold brook water inundated him with some force, spoiling his careful aim so thoroughly that the dart buried itself deep in the muddy mire from which the huge singular beast had been tearing up and eating plants. And even as he dashed the water from his eyes, Benee knew that despite his caution in the stalk, he must have been observed, for his intended victim had waded or swum the width of the pool and was now clambering up the near bank, a long, wide-bladed dirk shining like silver in his right fist.

The swamp killer was wrong. Even at a distance of less than thirty feet, Gil Djohnz did not see the small, slight man—his body, limbs and head all streaks and daubs of mud, with dead leaves, clumps of grass and other vegetable trash stuck to it here and there—until he stood up from his place of ambush and drew a brace of single-edged knives from sheaths fastened to his skinny shanks.

Benee figured that his death would be quick in the coming, now, for not only was the inlander bigger and stronger-looking than was he, with a two-edged weapon that was obviously made and balanced for fighting, but surely the inlander must often have actually fought breast to breast, man against man, something that Benee never had done—fenfolk fought thus only as a last resort, as in this instance, when cornered, otherwise doing all of their man-killing from a distance with fiendish traps or with the poisoned darts from their blowpipes, the knives they carried being tools rather than weapons.

Gil knew fen-men of old, numerous families of the unsavory breed having inhabited the fens to the north and east and south of Ehlai before the cooperative efforts of the Ehleenoee and the Kindred had rooted them out, killed them or driven them farther south and north to pose an ever-present threat to other peoples. He knew that deadly as they all assuredly were at short distances with their pipes and poisoned darts, at ranges beyond the reach of their pipes they were craven, and without those pipes they posed about as much real danger to any determined fighter as so many swamp rabbits.

Nonetheless, he was a normally cautious man, so he stopped before having come within actual striking distance of the stripling-sized, mud-daubed would-be ambusher, took a renewed grip on the wire-wound hilt of his Horseclans dirk and began a slow, crouching, bent-kneed advance on the balls of his feet. He held the dirk firmly and low, with the point higher than the pommel, ready to either slash or thrust or stab as an opportunity presented itself; a hurried glance had not shown him a fallen branch or anything else that might serve him as an auxiliary weapon, so he held the empty hand out, a little below the level of his eyes, wrist, elbow and fingers all slightly flexed.

Benee slashed at the flat belly of the inlander with his pointless skinning knife. His razor-edged steel missed its mark, but the equally sharp blade of the inlander's big dirk did not; it opened the skinny left forearm to the bone in a slash that curved from wrist to elbow. Bright red blood gushed up all along the terrible wound and began to wash the clots of drying mud from off the skin, and in his agony Benee did not even feel the worn hilt of the skinning knife slip from his weakening, now-nerveless grasp.

"Little snake's only got one fang left now." Gil

grunted to himself in satisfaction. "Wonder why this breed never learned to fight face to face, like normal men?"

His mud-caked features distorted, the swamper screamed once and threw himself at Gil, the big hunting knife extended before him like a spear. It was absurdly simple for an experienced warrior: the Horseclansman swiveled his body obliquely to the left, took his opponent's right wrist in a crushing grip and allowed a portion of the skinny man's own momentum to drive his near-fleshless body onto the leaf-shaped blade of the dripping dirk.

The blade entered deep into Benee's bowels well below his navel. He gasped, and his eyes looked to burst from out their sockets. Then, as the inlander twisted his blade and removed it by way of a vicious, upward-slanting drawcut that literally gutted Benee, the boy-warrior shrieked in a nameless degree of agony. Such a noise so close to him hurt Gil's ears, so he stepped back and swung his gory weapon like a sword, all but decapitating Benee.

Back in camp, he hastened to show the blowpipe, holder of darts, two knives and a horn tube of poison paste to Tomos Gonsalos and Mahvros of Lohfospolis, with whose infantry unit—long accustomed to the proximity of pachyderms—he and Sunshine had been marching, and recount the tale of the brief, bloody encounter.

At the conclusion, Gonsalos nodded. "You were right and I was wrong, Mahvros, this clinches the fact. We're just too close to those damned salt fens and that race of murderous lunatics who inhabit them, so inbred that they don't know which end to wipe."

To Gil, he said, "Keep closer to camp from now on; find somewhere else to wash your elephant. And get rid of that pipe and those darts and that container of venom—just the sight of them makes my skin crawl. Throw them in the watchfire there."

Then, back to Mahvros, he ordered, "Best get back
to your command and prepare to break camp. We're
going to move our location a mile or so upstream. Those
baltohtheesee stick at coming very far inland, even to
avenge the execution of one of their sneak-thief
murderers. But even so, we'll be having double pickets,
overlapping perimeters and so on until we've put a
goodly amount of distance between us and this area."

The camp was duly moved, the soldiers and noncoms
grumbling, as soldiers always have and always will.
Directional markings in the code of the army of Kehnooryos Ehlahs were left to indicate to those who could
understand them where the units had gone. In the new
encampment, Tomos Gonsalos ordered a ditched perimeter, but this was incomplete by nightfall, so Gonsalos
settled for extra watchfires and an enlarged guard force
and perimeter patrol, with the prairiecats prowling to
the east and along the watercourses leading down into
the fens.

On seeing the security precautions, Mahvros doubted
aloud and in a joking manner that even a muskrat
would be able to invade their new camp without raising
an alarm that night.

But the next morning, when Gil awoke and rolled out
of his blankets, there were two elephants lying where
only Sunshine had been when he had composed himself
in sleep the night just past. Staring in silent wonderment, a bit stunned and a bit more disbelieving of the
witness of his own eyes, he still noticed details about the
newcomer—she was a cow, also, but a little bigger and
seemingly fatter than his sister.

Rather than approach Sunshine and the strange
elephant, he mindspoke her. Not until he had had the
entire story, and been formally introduced to the other
elephant and allowed her to give him a head-to-foot
trunk-tip examination (as, too, had Sunshine, he recalled, on first meeting), did he saddle his sister and,
side by side with the larger cow, cross the camp to the
central headquarters area.

Tomos Gonsalos stood up from his breakfast to gape for a moment at the approaching pair of behemoths. Turning to Mahvros, who was still seated and chewing, his back to the sight that so astounded Tomos, Gonsalos demanded, "Why did you not tell me that elephants reproduce like *ahmoeebahs*—splitting into two identical parts, overnight?"

Mahvros swallowed hurriedly and looked up, grinning. "Is that wine you're drinking, or neat brandy? Man, elephants breed just like any other beast, but it takes about a year and a half from coupling to birthing, they say." He turned fully to look in the same direction as his friend, and it then was Mahvros' turn to gape and stare.

"Her Ehleenoee name is Ohxathees, or something like that," said Gil Djohnz, after he had dismounted and accepted an offered mug of watered breakfast wine. "But she wants to be called Tulip. It seems that she was the other half of the team that drew old King Zastros' pavilion wain, and she it was that turned about and ran back off the Lumbuh River bridge after it was fired and Sunshine had jumped into the river. She says that she just kept running until the camp was far behind her. After she had rested, she searched out food and water, then began to try to get off the elephant armor they had hung and strapped and tied on her. It took her several days of off-and-on tries, but she finally shucked it all. Since then, she has been wandering about the countryside, avoiding men. Then, yesterday, she cut the trail of Sunshine, followed it first back to the old camp, then here. She came into camp sometime last night, chatted with Sunshine for a while, then lay down and went to sleep beside her, and there they both were when I awakened, Chief Tomos."

"But how the hell did a full-grown elephant get into this camp without being seen?" demanded Mahvros. "Man, Tomos had guards tripping over guards last night, a ditch halfway around the camp, and those trained cats out beyond the perimeter, too."

Gil answered, "Chief Mahvros, Tulip says that she did not want to be seen and that so she was not seen but once. On that one occasion, however, she says she thinks that they who saw her in the dark there thought that she was Sunshine."

"So, you can telepath with her, too?" said Mahvros. "Man, down south, you and your ilk will soon put the damned, arrogant, overweening Epithiseesos family out of the elephant business in short order, I vow, and none too soon, either.

"But that still doesn't make my mind any easier for the here and now. Just how safe are any of us by night if a beast that stands at least three *mehtrahee* at the withers and weighs as much as a dozen big horses can just stroll into a supposedly tightly guarded camp? Man, the mere thought of it sets my mind aboggle and my nape hairs all aprickle. What if she'd had a dozen swamp scum on her back and had ridden them in here? What if . . . ?"

Tomos sighed. "Oh, come on, friend Mahvros, we could sit here and play 'what if?' until hell freezes over solid. Look, the elephant is here, with us, this morning, and she was not here last night. As there was no alarm last night, one would assume that any who did see her thought she was the elephant they knew about—after all, recall that the beasts are not native to this country-side hereabouts, so who would have or could have suspected that a stray one was running loose around here?—and just dismissed her as a wakeful but bene-volent beast, which is just what she appears to me to be. As I recall, you were almighty pleased that you would have the one elephant to take south to this *Thoheeks* Grahvos, so you should be twice as pleased to be able to take him two, right?"

"Yes, yes, of course," answered Mahvros. "None-theless, such laxity on the parts of the sentries and guards should be, must be, severely dealt with, punished, flogged, at least."

Tomos frowned and shook his head. "What you mete out to your troops, your retainers, is your business, of course, but please bear in mind that a thorough flogging often leaves a man unable to march as fast or as far as his fellows. As regards Hehluh's unit, you can bet that he'll flay yards of skin from off them with that acid-dripping tongue of his before all is said and done in this elephant matter. Nor do I think that Portos or Chief Pawl of Vawn will be pleased at all when they are apprised that their vaunted troopers failed to interdict or even see a titan like our Tulip wandering through our guardlines last night."

Captain Mahvros seemed a bit mollified. After another draft of the wine, he advised Gil, "Taking care of one of those beasts is a full-time job, as I'm certain you know by now. Therefore, I'd advise you to find one of your people who, if possible, can also telepath to an elephant. Let him take over the new one. Saddles aren't really needed for them, you know—*feelahksee* ride them even into battle without any saddle, down south."

Not only was the ancient royal palace of Thrahkohn-polis ghost-ridden with the shades of all the rulers who had died by violence within its walls, and a bit charred from the fire set by Zastros' immediate predecessor just before he fell on his sword, but *Thoheeks* Grahvos found to his chagrin that a fair bit of it had been at least partially looted since he and the rest had followed the Green Dragon Banner up into Karaleenos with Zastros. Moreover, a goodly proportion of the career bureau-crats had left the capital city, and those few that he could have dug out and brought back indicated precious little desire to resume their previous functions under his or anyone else's aegis.

Nor could he even blame them, not really, for in the chaos of the last couple of decades in the Kingdom of the Southern Ehleenoee, such positions had become exceedingly high-risk jobs. But lacking them and

without more than a bare handful of experienced slaves
remaining, he quickly realized that there was just no
way possible to set the palace complex back into motion
and keep it running for long. So very depopulated was
Thrahkohnpolis itself become that there was not even a
pool from which he could impress workers to possibly
labor as they trained for jobs in the palace.

That was when he decided to move his erstwhile
capital to his own principal seat, the city and duchy of
Mehseepolis, lying somewhat south and west of
Thrahkohnpolis.

"I know, I know," he told the Council of *Thoheeksee*
upon his announcement of his decision, "there will be
those who are sure to say that I mean to make myself
king . . . but, gentlemen, there are those who are
already saying that and many more that are thinking it,
and only time and the actions of our Council will prove
to these ones just how wrong are their present suppo-
sitions and slanders of me, the Council and our laudable
aims."

"But, dammit, Grahvos," rumbled *Thoheeks* Bahos,
"granted, your Mehseepolis is a strong city—it's never
fallen in all of memory that I've ever heard of—and
so, rich, but as I recall from visits, it's not all that large.
Where could you put a capital complex?"

Grahvos shrugged. "Simple. I'll turn over the
thoheeks' palace to the Council and government and
move my personal seat to Eepseelospolis, my second
city."

At this, young *Thoheeks* Vikos asked wonderingly,
"Your pardon, Grahvos, but do you mean to cede all of
Mehseepolis and its rich lands to Council? That's what
it sounds like you're doing."

"If that were what it required to set things right in the
lands we all call home, I'd not stick at giving half of all I
own, Vikos," Grahvos declared sincerely, feelingly.
"But in practice, here, no. Let us say that I am granting
Council a long-term lease of as much of the city of Meh-

seepolis as they need to fulfill the functions of our new government, but the lands thereabout will remain mine.

"I had assumed Council approval of this decision—for it is clear that we cannot remain in this sprawling, damaged place, not with the ceilings falling down about our ears, vermin scuttling across rooms from every nook and cranny, the kitchen hearths drawing so poorly that all our food must be cooked outside over open fires, all of the complex wells polluted and so little furnishings remaining that we might as well be camping out in some hoary ruin. Because of my assumption, I have already put such few royal slaves and a detachment of my warband to loading the pitiful remnants of records and files as survived the looting and vandalisms, the fire and the violent turnovers this place has been seeing regularly onto some wagons and wains. If you are all amenable, we'll plan to quit this place and take the road down to Mehseepolis in two days.

"But it will not be a short trip, gentlemen. No, I think that we must use this opportunity to pause at every city and town and seat of power along the way in order to explain what happened up north and tell as many people as possible just what is now intended, make it clear to all of them that there will never be another king, despite the fact that our land will become more powerful than ever it was under any of the kings."

The noblemen who rode through the outer gate, up the passage that led through the thick walls to the inner gate and so up the ascending grade into the hilltop fortress-city of Mehseepolis were, after six weeks of riding through lands that had been bountiful, rich and very populous within very recent times, shaken, tight-lipped and silent, each buried in his own thoughts, his own impressions of the near-wasteland they had traversed since leaving the wrecked palace at what had been the royal capital, seat of the kings of the Southern Ehleenoee.

The first shock to them had been the deplorable

condition of the very roads themselves, all weedy and
overgrown with brush, the paving stones beginning to
cant, here and there, the wooden boles of the
corduroyed sections become so soft with rot that they
were now a danger to horses or mules, not to mention
riders. Cuts, for long untended, had eroded down to
cover many stretches of roadway with red mud and
rocks of all sizes. Overgrown shoulders now offered
ready-made ambush points for brigands, and even
though the size of *Thoheeks* Grahvos' party and the
presence of so many armed and armored men saw them
pass along the road unmolested, there were many grisly
evidences of others not so strong or fortunate who had
unwisely made to use the road before them.

As for the once-numerous unwalled villages and small
towns along the Royal Road, not even one remained
inhabited, all were become only charred, tumbled, well-
looted and much-overgrown ruins, lairs for vermin and
those beasts and birds for which vermin was prey—owl,
skunk, weasel, wildcat and serpent. And right many of
the walled towns, most of the smaller, weaker ones,
were in little better shape.

The larger and stronger places that had weathered the
chaos and endured were become distrustful, unfriendly
or downright hostile to armed strangers of any description. Some of these places loosed arrows and stones
and engine-spears at any attempted approach to their
walls and gates of even small parties, most heard out
what was shouted up to them and then ordered the
parties away on pain of death, a very few allowed
Grahvos and two or three of the other noblemen into
their gates, treated them at least civilly, heard what they
had to say and then ushered them out, bidding them
welcome to return if they ever really did put the land
back to peace and order.

The once-rich lands and pastures were mostly become
ill-tended or completely unworked wildernesses of
weeds and brush and encroaching woodlands; such few

kine as they chanced across or sighted from afar were
become as lean and chary as game beasts. Masterless
dogs ran in large, dangerous packs, all of them bony, on
the verge of starvation and willing to attack anything or
anyone . . . except for the mean, muscular, long-tushed
sounders of feral swine.

But hardest for the travelers to take were the onetime
seats of the minor nobility—*komeesee, vahrohnohsee,
opokomeesee*. Some few had been just abandoned and
now were tenanted by commoners who probably were
also bandits, but most had obviously fallen by storm,
and some of these were occupied by folk who claimed to
be retainers and servants of the extirpated or scattered
and absent lords. A handful of the larger or more
cunningly placed and built holds had never fallen, for
all that they showed the prominent traces of assaults
and sieges, but not even in these was the present lord he
who had been such a decade before—sons, grandsons,
cousins, nephews and more distant kin now held the
holds and the lands (such as most of those lands were
become), and a few were illegally styling themselves
with the vacated titles, as well.

It had not been until the party was within the bounds
of Grahvos' double duchy that they found a hold still
occupied by the man who had been confirmed to that in-
heritance by his overlord. *Opokomees* Eeahnos
Ehreetheeos had lost two sons and been himself crippled
while fighting for his overlord and then-*Thoheeks*
Zastros during the first rebellion, years agone, and
when High King Zastros made to commence his march
of conquest northward and into the Kingdom of
Karaleenos, the *opokomees* had been too infirm and
aged to join and his two grandsons too young.

But they had not been incapable of fighting to retain
their own from the hosts of would-be plunderers that
had plagued the land in the absence of the monarch and
so many men of fighting age. Not only had the crippled
dotard and the two barely pubescent boys and their

scratch-force warband repeatedly held their seat against
hordes of bandits and escaped slaves, they had early on
had the men of the hold-village erect a strong timber-
and-earth ditched palisade around their hilltop homes,
had shown them how to fashion weapons and then
taught them how to use them; and the peasants had used
those homemade weapons very well, too, for the village
still stood, most of the folk still lived and worked their
fields and watched from the top of their gradually
strenghtened palisade.

Opokomees Eeahnos wept, openly and unashamedly,
when he set eyes to *Thoheeks* Grahvos astride his tall
horse. Even after the *thoheeks* had dismounted and
warmly embraced the old man, kissing him on both his
scarred cheeks, the tears continued to flow down those
furrowed cheeks and the still-powerful body shook with
sobs.

But when a brace of log drums began to boom in-
sistently from the palisaded village, the oldster gasped,
"Pahteeos, send a galloper to Komos and tell him that
our dear lord, *Thoheeks* Grahvos, has at last returned to
his lands and us, his people. He must have seen the
warband below, and thought the hold to be under attack
again."

"At once, my lord Grandfather." The boy spun on
his heel and raced away, the crossguard of the sword
slung across his back clanking rhythmically against the
nape-piece of his helmet. Both dismay and pride of race
sprang up in Grahvos when he saw that the twelve-year-
old child already bore the scars and exuded the bearing
of a veteran warrior. This boy's youth was yet another
thing that greedy, grasping, selfish *thoheeksee* had
robbed and stolen from the land and the people, and it
must not ever happen again, he and the others must do
all within their power to see that the land never again
became ripe for such, nor was Grahvos the only one of
the *thoheeksee* in that party to make similar vows to
himself during that terrible journey from Thrahkohnpolis to Mehseepolis.

The detachment of lancers that Grahvos had sent out ahead had delivered his messages, and the way was prepared for the Council before its arrival in the new capital. The Mehseepolis ducal palace was roomy enough for most functions and lodgings, and more room was provided by the adjoining citadel. Grahvos' family and household were already on the way to his alternate seat, well guarded by their retainers and the lancers.

Inside the thick, high walls, the councillors found the steep ways of the city in a riotous tumult of celebration of the return of their *thoheeks*. If any of the noblemen had before doubted that Gahvos' people loved as well as respected him, such doubts could not have survived all that they saw and heard that afternoon.

By the time that Captain *Thoheeks* Mahvros and his warband arrived at Mehseepolis in company with the loaned Confederation troops, work had already been begun, on marginal land below the city, on permanent installations to house and otherwise provide for an army of modest proportions. Mahvros made the thirteenth affirmed *thoheeks* for the new council, but the welcome addition of the trained, well-armed men he had brought with him assured that he would not be the last nobleman to appear at Mehseepolis for affirmation of his titles.

As the months rolled along, a succession of *thoheeksee, komeesee, vahrohnohsee, mahrkeeseeohsee* and even *opokomeesee* came from near and from far—from very far, in some cases—all of them with sizable and well-armed retinues in these unsettled times, all of them seeking to ingratiate themselves with this new government and to be granted confirmation or reconfirmation of titles and lands and cities they had inherited or assumed or conquered.

In some cases, there was more than just a single claimant to a few of the richer holdings, and the disputations over these gave more than a few sleepless nights to the Council until, finally, they came up with a formula for most decisions of this nature:

Sons, grandsons, brothers and nephews, in that order, were to have precedence over adopted sons, the husbands of daughters, granddaughters, sisters or nieces, but in any case, no claimant would be confirmed or reconfirmed to any title or holding unless he was willing to accept and to serve the new order (in the case of *thoheeksee*, swearing most formally to never seek to make himself or any other *thoheeks* king) so long as he should live. Immediately upon returning to his lands, a confirmed noble must assemble those men whose overlord he was and take from them written, witnessed oaths to the Council and the Confederation, it being made abundantly clear to each that his own confirmation would not be considered as final until Council was in receipt of said oaths.

The wealthier magnates were persuaded by fair means and foul to make "loans" to the new government—in gold, silver, grain, wine or whatever they just then had the most of—the value of which was to be deducted from their future taxes along with the sizable interest.

Thoheeksee were all urged to set their home affairs in order, then return to sit on Council with their peers, that they might be certain that their particular interests and desires were served. They and all of the others, save only those presently threatened severely or the *mahrkeeseeohsee*, were urged to send any surplus troops to Mehseepolis to fill out the ranks of the army that Council was building to safeguard them all.

But it was pointed out that the lands were not to be stripped to provide spearmen, for it was considered imperative by Council that an orderly agricultural cycle be reestablished as soon as possible and that all arable land be put back into production, orchards and vineyards be replanted, herds be built back up, towns and villages be rebuilt and made safe for repopulation, outlaws and bandits be exterminated, roads be laid again and maintained.

And slowly, fitfully, it began to come together, after a fashion. Sitheeros, *Thoheeks* of the triple duchy of Iron Mountain, returned to Mehseepolis with enough troops to scour the countryside along his route for bandits, arriving with sack on sack of decomposing heads and two wainloads of weapons, armor and other assorted loot taken from those bandits so unlucky as to be swept up by him. He also contributed to the army a third elephant cow which had had a modicum of war training, but which had proved difficult to manage since her *feelahks* had died of a summer fever.

Nor was this service and the elephant the last or even the least of Sitheeros' generosity. He brought for the army a full and fully equipped regiment of pikemen, a half-squadron of lancers, some three thousand *keelohee* of cornmeal, several wainloads of the famous and fiery Iron Mountain brandy, additional wainloads of cured pork, barrels of pickled vegetables and not a few pipes of a middling wine. To the Council, he presented some twelve pounds of gold and two hundred of minted silver *thrahkmehee*.

"Ten pounds of the gold, the soldiers and the elephant are my personal contribution, gentlemen," he told the council. "The silver—well, the most of it—the bulk of the corn, the pork and the wine and vegetables are from various of my vassals. The brandy is from my brother-in-law, *Ahrkeekomees* Kohnyos. All of the folk of Iron Mountain are most pleased that there never will be another kingship to breed squabblings and usurpations and ruinous civil wars. Now, true, save for creating endless and rich market for our manufactories, our farms and the like, the chaos that has so torn this land has had little effect on us, for all of the other combatants rightly considered us too tough a nut to crack, but we would all as lief see and live with a slower, steadier market and a land in peace than with all that has gone before of recent years."

In his retinue, *Thoheeks* Sitheeros had brought along skilled master weaponsmiths, along with their specialized tools and a goodly amount of semiworked metal, and these were quickly put to work to properly outfit the army, allowing the long-overworked local smiths to get some sleep and then return to more mundane tasks for the nonmilitary populace of the duchy.

A year after the capitulation of what was by then left of Zastros' host in Karaleenos saw a council of twenty *thoheeksee* ruling a bit over two thirds of the onetime Kingdom of the southern Ehleenoee, all but the very largest of the bandit and outlaw bands extirpated within the lands under Council's sway, roads being relaid, towns and villages here and there being rebuilt by their new occupants, crops ripening in reclaimed fields, the ferocious packs of wild dogs mostly eradicated and the cattle rounded up and fattening in reclaimed pasture-lands.

There had been much work for the army, often bloody work—fights, real battles, interdictions and sieges, forcible evictions of squatters and unconfirmed claimants to disputed holdings. But as the army of the Council was now the largest and best equipped still extant in all the land, they had as yet to see a defeat. The most distressing lack was that of a real, first-rate *strahteegos* or overall commander for this army.

Aside from that troubling matter, however, it was beginning to appear that the efforts of Grahvos and the rest would see their desperate gamble actually succeed.

Chapter II

Captain of Elephants Gil Djohnz did not care much or think much of the title that Tomos and the rest had hung upon him, but with no arguments affecting them, he had had to just learn to live with it. He routinely and deliberately ignored officers' calls, and when a runner was sent to summon him, he would brusquely snap that taking proper care of elephants was a full-time job and that, in consequence, he lacked the time or the inclination to sit around a table, guzzle wine or brandy, gossip and listen to some blowhard announce the latest set of asinine pronouncements dreamed up in the feather-stuffed heads of soft-headed captains of desks, up in the citadel of Mehseepolis.

Of a day, he was summoned to Sub-*strahteegos* Tomos Gonsalos' new office in the but recently completed headquarters building. Once he was there, in working clothes devoid of any indication of rank and powerfully redolent of the elephant lines, Tomos greeted him warmly, seated him and, with his own hands, poured him a large mug of fresh, frothy milk—still warm from the cow and yellowish with rich butterfat—then went back to his own chair and goblet of spiced, watered wine.

Gil tasted then drained off the mug gratefully, wiped off his lips with a soiled, sweaty sleeve, refilled the mug from the pitcher, cut himself a hefty chunk of cheese from the small wheel on the officer's desk, then settled back into the chair, smiling.

"Tomos, you should've been Kindred. You don't look like a damned Ehleenee and most times you don't think like one, either. No real Ehleenee would've ever thought of calling me over here for fresh milk and sharp cheese, not ever, for no reason."

He chuckled. "Not that I don't know damned good and well you've got you a damned good reason for doing it; it's that sly, devious Ehleenee part of you coming to the surface.

"So, my sharp-eared friend, what's the reason?"

Tomos squirmed in his chair, then said, "All of you Horseclansmen exercise a disconcerting bluntness that is often difficult for us more effete, civilized Ehleenoee to bear. We'll get to my reasons in a bit, but first, how is our fourth elephant coming along?"

Gil smiled. "Growing like a weed; he's already near to my waist at his withers. And he keeps young Bert Vawn hopping trying to keep up with him, too."

"Has he decided on a name he likes yet? We need one for army records," said Tomos.

The captain just shook his head. "The little scut changes his mind every other day, it seems. Over on the lines, we just call him Tulip's Son . . . when we aren't calling him Bert's Brat or some less complimentary things. He needs to learn discipline, that one."

Tomos looked down into his goblet for a moment then, swirling the purplish liquid about. When he looked up, he said, "Gil, my friend, armies need and must have discipline, too, in order to function, to even exist. Soldiers are not required to like the orders and routines of army life, but they are required to live their lives by those very routines and to never fail in following those orders; to not follow orders, to break routines, these are crimes in any army, crimes known under the general heading of insubordination, and they are and must be dealt with most harshly, lest discipline break down completely and an ordered army become only a mob. Rulers establish armies so as to have a force upon which they can depend to maintain peace and order within their realms, and a trained, tightly disciplined army can always be depended upon by those who raised it and maintain it. A mob, on the other hand, cannot be depended upon to do anything or to be anything other than an ever-constant danger.

"Now, in order for a stringent discipline to work properly and smoothly, it is important that the lower-ranking members of an army be constantly made aware that all those of higher rankings are also bound by the strictures of army discipline and routines and orders. Any soldier, of whatever rank, who makes it clear by his attitudes or actions that he considers himself to be above playing the old army game by the ancient rules immediately becomes a weak, rusting link in the chain that binds the army together; moreover, that rust is very contagious to other links, so it cannot and will not be allowed to remain and spread, it must be eradicated, no matter what the cost."

Pausing for a moment, the overall commander of the Confederation force lifted his goblet and took a draught of the spiced wine before looking Gil dead in the eye and saying, "You, friend Gil, are such a weak link in my army, and therein lies a problem that seems almost insoluble. Were I to send you away, back to Kehnooryos Ehlahs, as I have been advised to do by members of my staff, then I most probably would be well advised to send the elephant Sunshine with you, for I seriously doubt that she would be good for anything here without you.

"On the other hand, however, Gil, I—and we, the army, the staff, the command structure and the Council of *Thoheeksee*—cannot any longer afford to abide your flagrant insubordination, for although loss of you and thereby Sunshine would weaken our army, loss of discipline would weaken it far worse."

Now become aware of what Tomos was getting at, of why he had sent for the captain of elephants this day,

Gil was on the verge of making a reply, but the commander held up a hand, palm outward. "No, I know exactly what you mean to say, Gil. You did not and do not want to be made an officer. Why, Gil, I never could've imagined that a man of the pure water that I know you to be could be guilty of such a form of stubborn and arrogant selfishness."

Gil spluttered, his face darkening with anger, his hand unconsciously seeking the hilt of the dirk he was not just then wearing.

Tomos ignored the appearance and movements of his subordinate and spoke on. "Gil, I hold a county near as large as a duchy, two cities, seven towns and a fine hall. I've not seen my lands or my family save for all too brief snatches in six years, yet when my overlord's new overlord—High Lord Milo Morai—placed the weight of this command upon me and ordered me to march it down here for who knows how long, I did so with as good grace as I could muster and with a smiling face, for it would've been most insubordinate to have behaved otherwise to one of my superiors in both civil and military rank, don't you see.

"I desired this awesome and onerous responsibility, this protracted absence from my personal responsibilities and my family, every bit as much as you desired to become our army's captain of elephants, but I accepted because of loyalty to my overlords, and even if I should never again see my ancestral lands, my home hall or my family, I would do the same again.

"Gil, your three war-elephants are no less an important unit of this army of ours than are Chief Pawl's horse-archers, *Komees* Portos' lancers, Guhsz Hehluh's heavy foot, Lord Bizahros' light foot or *Komees* Mahrtios' pioneers and artificiers. Because we knew you to be a steady, reliable sort, you were selected to become the officer in command of the war-elephants. Reflect on the facts if you will, Gil. Your own High Lord it was who ordered you to bring Sunshine down here and serve with her in our army. Not so? He placed you and all the rest under my command; therefore, when you disobey me and my staff, when you openly flaunt your disobedience to my orders, you are actually disobeying the orders of your own High Lord. Understand? I would imagine that High Lord Milo will be most wroth if I do find it necessary to send you and Sunshine back to him, as I must do you not mend your ways immediately and begin to act and comport yourself in the manner of a unit commander.

"Were there an experienced war-eleplant officer about, I would be more than happy to give him the command post and responsibility and let you go back to being what you were, just another *feelahks*, but we have thus far not discovered any elephant officers who survived that debacle in Karaleenos and no one of our messengers has as yet come back from the source of most war-elephants, the triple duchy of Meelohnhohra. You have my word of honor, Gil: the moment that a trained and experienced elephant officer enters this camp and this army, you will cease to be captain of elephants, but until then, please do me and your High Lord the great favor of cooperating with us and helping to win over this vast, rich land for our Confederation.

"Will you do that for us, my friend?"

Newgrass, the Iron Mountain elephant, unlike the other two cows, Sunshine and Tulip, had a pair of thick, eighteen-inch tusks. She was as much larger than Tulip as Tulip was larger than Sunshine, yet she unquestioningly accepted Sunshine as leader of the small herd. There were enough differences between Newgrass and the others to make Gil certain that they were of two different strains of elephant.

The most readily obvious distinctions were that where Sunshine, Tulip and Tulip's Son customarily carried their heads low so that the arch of their backs was the highest part of them, Newgrass' back was almost

concave from withers to rump and her head was therefore the highest part of her. Nor were the ears the same
as those of the other elephants, being significantly larger
and rounder; her head did not bulge out into domes at
the temples, as did the others, either. And there were
other, less readily apparent points of difference, such as
Newgrass' total lack of the protective flap of skin over
the anal opening.

But the bigger cow's mindspeak was just as good as
that of the smaller cows and she seemed to be every bit
as intelligent. Her new Horseclansman *feelahks*, Sami
Skaht of Vawn, had never had any trouble or disagree-
ments with her since the first day that Gil had made the
introductions between them.

Newgrass had been fully war-trained at Iron
Mountain, which state used both bulls and larger cows
for such, and watching her perform her maneuvers told
Gil what he needed to know about the training of Sunshine and Tulip, whose primary function had always
been that of mere draught animals.

When the bright, willing animals had learned all that
Newgrass had to show for her training, Gil asked
Tomos Gonsalos to seek for him an appointment to
speak with *Thoheeks* Sitheeros of Iron Mountain.

To Gil, who like all his Kindred had been virtually
born in the saddle, it seemed distinctly strange to be
riding a horse after so long of riding only his elephant.
At fifteen-two, the gelding was sleek and powerful, yet
he seemed tiny and very delicate to his rider.

Gil's officer's garb passed him easily and quickly
through the gates of Mehseepolis, and the small folded
square of vellum with its impressive gold-wax seal saw
him duly admitted to the outer courtyard of the ducal
palace, where a liveried groom was quick to hold the
head of his horse while he dismounted, then lead the
beast away. At the entrance to the citadel, a courteous
but firm junior officer of the Council Guards relieved
Gil of saber, dirk and both daggers, hung the weapons

carefully on a wall hook among a host of other edge weapons, then waved him on to a functionary who unfolded and read the pass.

"The *Thoheeks* Sitheeros' office is adjacent to his suite, Captain. His grace's suite is in the palace proper, but you would likely be wandering half the day before you found it. Wait a few minutes and I'll send a man who knows his way with you."

This much said, the functionary did nothing, said no more, just stood, a slight smile on his lips. Gil had been told in advance by Tomos what to expect, so though it went against his Horseclans grain, he dug a silver *thrahkmeh* from under his belt and placed it in the soft palm of the outstretched hand, only to see all trace of a smile disappear and become an incipient frown. He dug out another silver coin to place beside the first, and the frown became a bit more nebulous. But it was not until four *thrahkmeh*-pieces were upon that palm that the trace of a smile returned to the dark, slightly greasy face of the functionary.

The boy who arrived shortly to lead him to *Thoheeks* Sitheeros' office, though looking to Gil just about old enough to begin warring, had he been a Horseclansman, already bore visible scars that could only have been made by sharp steel and moved as if he had spent much time under arms; moreover, there was an honest, no-nonsense air about him that was far more mature than his body.

Gil made to dig out a couple of silver pieces, but seeing this, the boy shook his head vigorously. "My lord Captain, I am not like unto these larcenous, bureaucratic swine, always rooting for silver. No, it is my great honor to serve my most puissant lord, *Thoheeks* Grahvos, who provides all my needs and more. Come, I will take you to *Thoheeks* Sitheeros, captain."

When the lad had knocked, introduced Gil by name and rank to a pair of armed guards, then handed the letter to one of them, he bade Gil a courteous goodbye and went back down the hall at a brisk walk.

Gil rendered the gray-haired *thoheeks* a military salute in the classic Ehleen fashion. He liked the look of the middle-aged nobleman—firm jaw and chin with a spiky, gray-streaked chinbeard, the scars of a warrior on his face and hairy arms, expressive black eyes and lips whose corners showed the clear traces of frequent smiles; the *thoheeks'* body was thick and powerful-looking, all big, round muscles, loaded shoulders, hips almost as wide as his shoulders, but with the legs of a horseman, for all.

The *thoheeks'* garb was very like that of a Horse-clansman—short boots of tooled leather, tight leather breeches, an embroidered shirt of heavy silk, broad tooled belt with a massive silver buckle. He wore large rings on one thumb and three fingers, and up close the flat gold chain held onto his shoulders by brooches and hanging down onto his broad breast could be seen to be fashioned of little golden elephants, all joined one to the other at trunk and tail.

Although two braziers were glowing with coals, the marble-walled chamber was decidedly chilly, and Gil was glad to accept the steaming spiced wine proffered by a servant.

As the manservant was padding out, the *thoheeks* ordered, "Hohfos, tell my man Drehkos to bring a hooded velvet robe for me and one for Captain Gil here, too."

Then he waved Gil to a padded chair. "Sit you down, Captain. Our Hohfos will be back shortly with cheeses and other oddments. Not only am I ever glad to meet another admirer of elephants, your visit today gave me a rare chance to get away from the boring details of Council. I tell you, Captain, had I not pledged to stay here until planting time . . ." The big man sighed gustily and shook his close-cropped head.

"But tell me, Captain, how do you people stay warm in winter in simple hide tents?"

"We don't, Lord *Thoheeks*," Gil replied. "We don't live in tents at all, except on hunting trips. Our homes are yurts, made of wood and hides and canvas and many layers of felt. So warm are they that even in the most bitter weather, a mere lamp will often render them so hot that vents must be opened to maintain comfort. Such winter warmth is unknown to you Ehleenoee, Lord *Thoheeks* . . . but then of course we barbarians have never attained to full many of the wonders of your sophisticated civilization."

The *thoheeks* stared hard at Gil for a long moment, then his lips began to twitch, then they bent upward into a grin, and when the man knocked, then entered with a tray of foods, followed by another man bearing two long, thick robes, Sitheeros was laughing uproariously, his face red and tears squeezing from out his eyes.

With visible effort, he sobered in the presence of the servants, though the stray chuckle still escaped him now and then, while the smaller trays were laid out on the table, brandy and smaller goblets fetched from a cabinet, the two of them helped into the warm robes and their chairs moved to opposite sides of the table.

To the departing servants, he said, "Tell the guards that if the city should suddenly be attacked, they may disturb me; otherwise, I am not available to anyone for any reason.

"May I call you Gil? 'Captain' is so formal, and I truly like you." At Gil's nod, he went on. "Good, then call me Sitheeros, Gil . . . when we two are alone, of course; one must keep up appearances, otherwise. Yes, rank indeed hath its privileges, but its full weight of firm responsibilities far outweighs its few middling privileges, I've always felt.

"Although you gave me the first good laugh I've had since I came to Mehseepolis by your manner of cool, politely phrased insult, you were completely right, completely justified in saying just what you did say. We Ehleenoee have always boasted and bragged to everyone who would or could be compelled to listen of our civilized and progressive culture. At one time, there was assuredly a reason for such boasting, but most Ehleenoee of the recent past and of today have scant reason to boast of anything, although it pains me to say it, it's true.

"We're most of us a static culture, really less civilized in certain important ways than many of those peoples we slander with the name 'barbarian.' For too long, we have been of the firm mindset that our way must be better because it was the way of our ancestors who conquered these lands hundreds of years ago, and so we have been too proud to try to learn ways that might be new and better and easier and more efficient that the old ones.

"Take this ducal palace, for an example, Gil. This is your classic Ehleenoee palace, and a blind man could see that it was never designed for comfortable, year-round housing in a climate like this one. No one now alive knows whenever and wherever this design originated, but I will guarantee that it was not here, not in the onetime Kingdom of the Southern Ehleenoee, but in a clime that was far warmer."

The *thoheeks* pointed a finger up at the plaster mouldings that decorated the ceiling and held the chains of the brazen lamps.

"Gil, there is no room in the living section of this palace that is lower than three full *mehtrahee*, and some are far higher, and this is fine and cool and breezy in hot weather, but in winter, there is no earthly way to adequately heat such rooms, especially when those rooms have cold stone walls and floors. Believe me or not, the rooms in the citadel yonder are far more comfortable in cold weather than are any in this palace. And the reason why is simple—they have lower ceilings, hardwood floors mostly, few and narrow windows, they're generally smaller, and many contain hearths built into the walls which will burn logs as well as coal or charcoal—and I am moving into a suite over there immediately it is prepared and furnished to my taste."

"Is that what you did back at Iron Mountain, Sitheeros?" asked Gil. "Did you move into your citadel of winters?"

The burly man shrugged. "I don't know how they made out there back in the bad old days, just suffered through it, I'd guess, like the folk here do. But we of Iron Mountain have always been somewhat different from your average lowlander Ehleenoee, Gil. We've always been willing to try new things and see if they might work better than our traditional things and ways.

"When, during the Great Disaster of three hundred-odd years ago, our palace first shook down, then burned, my many-times-great-grandsire—for, you see, unlike the case with most of the lowlander Ehleenoee, the title and lands have never left my family since first we wrested Iron Mountain and the other lands from the folk who then held it—sought out certain ancient ruins he had recalled seeing in travels and on hunts, studied the principles of the smokehouses and the barns wherein tobacco is cured, then drew up plans and saw to it that his new palace was built just as he had envisioned it.

"Since then, Gil, the entire central wing of our palace has been heated by fires burned in huge iron *kahmee-nohsee* in the cellars."

Gil wrinkled his forehead and asked, "Your pardon, Sitheeros, but that is one Ehleen word I've never heard before. What is a *kahmeenos*?"

The *thoheeks* smiled good-naturedly. "Of course you haven't heard the word; I don't know of any other Ehleenoee who use anything like it. Look you: imagine if you will a mighty iron caldron, far higher than a man big enough around to fit six or eight standing men into; imagine a thick iron grill fitted into it as a platform on which to burn fuel—mostly earth-coals, of which our mines produce a plentitude—with an iron door just above it to feed in fresh fuel, then imagine an iron sheet some foot or so beneath to catch the ashes and cinders and another iron door at that level to allow them to be pulled or shoveled out. That is a *kahmeenos*, Gil."

Gil shook his head. "But I still don't understand how this device can heat an entire palace."

"That was the true genius of my ancestor, coupled of course with his willingness to try new things, think ideas no Ehleenoee had been willing to think before him," replied the *thoheeks*. "Look you, Gil, when a fire is burning, the smoke usually rises. Do you know why?"

Gil looked puzzled. "Hmmm, I never really thought on it, it was just something that happened because it had always happened. Why?"

The *thoheeks* grinned maliciously. "Keep up that line of thinking, Gil, apply it to everything, and before long you will be the true equal of any sophisticated, civilized Ehleen. Heat always rises, Gil, and smoke rises because of the heat it contains. My ancestor had hollow spaces built beneath the floors and inside the interior walls of the new palace he built. Inside those spaces he had installed wide tubes of thin copper and iron and brick clays all leading up from one or the other of the *kahmeenohsee*. The heat rises up from them into the tubings, you see, and the heat radiates upward and outward from them to heat the rooms and chambers, even the corridors. In the worst of the cold times, the stables of both horses and elephants are heated by more recently built *kahmeenohsee*, as too are the barracks of the Iron Mountain Guards."

The *thoheeks* took a sip of his brandy, then said, "How I do carry on, Gil. But surely you did not seek a meeting with me to talk on such matters as these. What did you want of me?"

"Sitheeros," began Gil, "the elephant you gave to the army, the cow who now calls herself Newgrass, has imparted to us all that she can remember being taught of elephant behavior in battle, but . . ."

Looking and sounding excited, the *thoheeks* leaned forward. "So, it's really true, then? You can actually mesh your mind with those of beasts? I had thought the tale but another of these things told by craftsmen to shroud certain of the tricks of their trades.

"Then please tell me why that cow refused to accommodate herself to a new *feelahks* when her original one died of fever. Why she stamped the new *feelahks* into blood pudding."

"Yes, I asked her that, Sitheeros, and she told me. It was because the man who died did not die of fever, he was murdered by his wife and his brother, who was her lover. He was also the replacement *feelahks*, and Newgrass' killing of him was understandable revenge. Her only regret now is that she was never able to get at that murderous widow.

"Newgrass has a *feelahks* now who is, like me, a mindspeaking Horseclansman, and she has never given him the slightest trouble.

"But back to my reason for asking you to see me today. Are our three elephants to be an effective addition to our army, they will have to be as completely trained as possible, and as matters now stand, I have no way to do that. You have done a great deal, given a great deal, already, but let me ask you to do a bit more, Sitheeros. Please loan us the skills of your elephant master from Iron Mountain. Newgrass has no memory of his name—elephants' minds, like those of horses, just don't work along those lines—but she says that he has fairer skin than most folk up there."

The *thoheeks* shook his head in wonderment. "Now I truly believe, Gil, there is no way I now could disbelieve your talents. True, someone of my retinue just might have given you a description of Master Laskos, who trains the Iron Mountain elephants. But there is no one down here at Mehseepolis with me who could possibly know of the foul murder of the *feelahks*, months agone. It was quite by accident that the business came to light, and that very soon before I left Iron Mountain.

"The widow had been given a menial job at the palace, you see, after her husband's demise, that she and the children might eat and be sheltered and clothed. She took a fall down the full length of a steep staircase and ended it, injured unto death, almost at my very feet.

To me she admitted her guilt in the death of her husband and swore that it was his ghost had pushed her from off the top step above. She lived only moments after that fall, and I alone heard that confession, you see. One of her children is quite bright and promising, so ere this I have told no one of the fact that his late mother was a confessed murderess.

"So, all right, I'll send for Master Laskos. He can be easily spared at Iron Mountain just now, though he must return in the spring, with me. He was captain of elephants for the late King Hyamos, was in large part responsible for the famous defeat of Zastros' first rebellion at the Battle of Ahrbahkootchee; King Fahrkos, who succeeded King Hyamos, declared Master Laskos outlaw and put a price on his head, and he fled to the northern mountains and, eventually, came to work for me. Fahrkos lacked either the will or the force of loyal, dependable troops to go to Iron Mountain and take him from me, and Zastros had no interest in him. Mayhap you can teach him how to mesh his mind with those of elephants, eh? That's a knack I'd like to know myself, for that matter, Gil. Not only would it be a useful talent to have, just think of what the having of it would mean for a ruler such as me: people will often say things in front of what they call 'dumb beasts' that they never would mention around other people, so I could have an internal intelligence-gathering apparatus that would put those of my peers to shame . . . and all for the price of elephant feed, which I'd have had to provide anyway."

However, long before the elephant expert could arrive from Iron Mountain, a trumpet of war was sounded. Summoned to the command center with the other captains, Gil and the rest were briefed by Sub-*strahteegos* Tomos Gonsalos and certain members of his staff.

"The Ahndros family was almost wiped out in the

last two decades, gentlemen; only two of that blood remain extant now. One is a grandniece of the last *thoheeks*, the other is a son of his half brother. This man, one Hahkmukos, was recently confirmed *Thoheeks* of the Duchy of Ahndros by the Council, yet when he journeyed down there to take his place, they threw him out of the palace and city and chased him and his party clear out of the duchy; a number of his retainers were slain, and Hahkmukos himself was sliced up a bit here and there.''

"Hmmph,'' growled Captain Ahzprinos, commander of a regiment of light pikemen. "I know that Hahkmukos of old. Too bad the bastards didn't slice him a bit deeper . . . say, just under his pocky chin.''

Captain Bizahros, who commanded the other regiment of light pikes, nodded. "Yes, the Ahndros wine was always the best, but Hahkmukos is—to be most charitable—the stinking dregs of it, and I can't say that I fault the folk of Ahndropolis; I wouldn't want him for my overlord, either.'' He turned to the tall, spare, saturnine man seated nearby and asked, "You had some trouble with the bugger, as I recall, didn't you, Portos?''

Captain *Thoheeks* Portos' dark face turned even darker, his strong, hard hands clenched at the memory, and he nodded. "Yes, that I did, and I voted against his confirmation, too. But such are matters within that duchy that my civil peers felt the pig to be the lesser of two bad lots, and he was more than willing to trade oaths to the Council and the Confederation for the titles and lands . . . though just how much sworn oaths mean to a creature like him is a matter that only time will tell.''

"If you three gentlemen are quite finished your gossiping and name-calling and death-wishing of *Thoheeks*-designate Hahkmukos,'' said Tomos sarcastically, "I will say this: Your likes, dislikes and opinions do not, in this case, own the value of a bucket of horse

piss. A brand-new government simply cannot afford to
allow an instance of this sort to pass, nor do they want
Hahkmukos to do it the old way—raise a private warband and try to take the duchy and city by raw, brute
force—that is precisely the sort of personal warmaking
that must quickly pass out of fashion is the rule of the
Council to prevail.

"Therefore, *Thoheeks* Grahvos, speaking for the
Council, has ordered this day that a powerful force be
sent back into his new duchy with *Thoheeks* Hahkmukos, nor is the force to return to Mehseepolis until
the new *thoheeks* sits installed in his new buildings and
has gathered a modest number of armed retainers to
insure his safety.

"Any of you who feel that you could not do a
soldier's job, could not follow orders and give support
to this man who owns the support of Council, may say
so to me, either now or in private, later, and I'll brevet
one of his subordinates to command his unit until it is
once more back here. But, for now, please leave off the
insulting comments and hear us out, for I have
promised that the force will be on the march before the
end of the week."

Captain *Komees* Theodoros' now-deceased overlord
had held a duchy which had shared a long stretch of
border with the duchy in question, and so he was
familiar with the land and the people against whom they
would soon march. He was a staff officer in Tomos
Gonsalos' headquarters.

Peering nearsightedly at a sheaf of notes he had
brought to the briefing, the gangly, snubnosed man
finally brushed his thinning hair back from off his
forehead and said, "Gentlemen, the lands of the House
of Ahndros provided well for centuries. The principal
exports were maize, some wheat, tree fruits, cider and
cider vinegar, swine, cheese, freshwater pearls and some
cotton and cottonseed oil. As is to be expected, of

course, the exports during the . . . ahh, disturbances of the last fifteen or twenty years have been negligible to nil, but the potential and the lands still remain.

"There is but one real city in the duchy, although there are, or rather used to be, quite a number of towns—some walled, some not—and villages, most of the latter abutting the holds of noblemen. The lands were marched over, overrun and sacked repeatedly during the bad times, there as everywhere else, naturally; I would assume that all the villages and unwalled towns fell and were burned, or were abandoned and later burned—that's what happened elsewhere.

"At least one of the walled towns, which happened to be fortunately situated—defensively speaking—held out through it all, never falling to any assault. Ahndropolis, however, was not so lucky. Bare months before Zastros marched through, headed westward, showing his strength and garnering more, a ragtag collection of broken noblemen, sometime soldiers, gutter-scrapings, rural bandits and the like besieged the city, finally undermined part of a wall, then stormed and almost took it. They finally were driven out, but it was, I understand, a close and a very chancy thing, and the survivors were still skulking about the duchy when Zastros came marching through. He killed some and dragooned the others into his force, then marched on.

"It was during that affray that the then *thoheeks* and most of his near relations died, either of wounds or starvation or disease. After Zastros was gone, the city folk asked the husband of their late *thoheeks'* grandniece to come and be their city-lord, and he left his hold and walled town and did so. He has held it ever since, it and the duchy, too, though he has never come here to be confirmed in either his actual civil rank or that he has assumed.

"Now, the city of Ahndropolis is but slightly smaller than is this Mehseepolis; however, it is not so naturally defensible, being built on lower ground and protected by the river on only two sides. Those who have recently been there say that the undermined section of wall has been rebuilt—the foundations sunk clear down to bedrock, this time, so the townsfolk aver—and that the defenses have been made somewhat stronger in other small ways, too. Engines of several sorts are said to be evident upon the walls and defensive towers.

"This all could bode ill for an attacking army, save for one thing: The losses of people in the last twenty years have been stupendous, and unless soldiers are hired on and brought from beyond the lands here in question, that young would-be lordling simply will lack the armed men to defend so long a circuit of walls and other defenses. Therefore, it is my considered opinion that, seeing the force brought in against him, he will make to treat rather than simply slam his gates and fight."

Chapter III

Tomos Gonsalos was as good as his word, the force was ready to march by the end of that week . . . but it was nearing the end of the next week before *Thoheeks*-designate Hahkmukos and his virtual caravan of wheeled transport, pack animals, retainers and servants were sufficiently organized to join the column of troops.

Tomos Gonsalos raged and swore, then sought out Hahkmukos himself. "My lord," he began as calmly as he could force himself to do, under the circumstances, "surely there has been an error somewhere along the line. No less than nineteen wagons have drawn up outside my camp—one of them being a pavilion-on-wheels almost as large as that one of the late Zastros and drawn by a full score span of oxen—a pack train of half the size of my forces' remuda, nearly a hundred armed retainers and God alone knows how many menservants, boy servants, cooks, grooms, oxmen, drivers and catamites."

Hahkmukos smiled languidly and sipped at a goblet of hot spiced wine. "Oh, there is no mistake, my good Sub-*strahteegos*, I only am taking along enough for my basic comfort, this time. I can send for everything else when once your troops have killed all my enemies and I am safe within my city and duchy, you see."

Tomos bit his sometimes intemperate tongue, hard, and took several deep breaths. "My lord, whether or not you travel comfortably is truly of no consequence to this purely military movement, the planning of which is solely my province. A good proportion of Council's army is being tied up in emplacing you in your city and duchy, you know, and the less time it is so tied up, the better for all concerned.''

Hahkmukos sighed, his smile departed. He shoved the barely pubescent boy who had been lying beside him on the couch off onto the floor and swung his legs around so that he sat on the side of the couch. Sourly, he said, "One would suppose that there is a point you will get to eventually, Karaleen . . . ?''

Tomos gritted his teeth. "There's a point, right enough, my lord. The point is this: Satan will be chipping ice to cool his wine from out the main streets of Hell before I allow you to retard the march of my force with your huge excesses of baggage, transport, animals and retainers! You may place *a* wagon with my trains—not your pavilion, either, just a normal-sized wagon drawn by no more than three pairs of mules. You may bring your troop of mercenaries, but only if you are willing to place them whenever the need arises under the command of Captain *Thoheeks* Portos, who is to be overall commander of this force.''

Hahkmukos suddenly went as white as his ruffled silken shirt. "P . . . *Portos*? No, please, my lord Tomos, not Portos! The man *hates* me. I . . . *never* have I done aught to him, you understand, he . . . he just hates me irrationally.''

The red-haired Karaleen officer smiled grimly, feeling an amused contempt for the man and his obvious funk. "Oh, no, you flatter yourself, my lord. Captain *Thoheeks* Portos does not consider you to be worth hating . . . no, he simply despises you. And there is nothing at all irrational to that feeling, not that I can see, not after he told me just why he feels as he does.

"However, he is a good soldier, an obedient and most loyal officer. Despite his rather strong feelings about you, despite his misgivings, despite his presentiments that Council may have erred in your case, might have confirmed the wrong claimant to the duchy, he will follow my orders and force the folk of that duchy to accept you as their new overlord. After this meeting this morning, I am beginning to believe his presentiments, my lord. I agree that perhaps Council did err in the case of your confirmation; you clearly are just not of true *thoheeks* caliber."

He spun on his heel and had strode almost to the door before he half turned and said, "Good day . . . my lord." His tone, the longish pause and the accompanying near-sneer were the closest he would allow himself to come to actual insult.

He had been back in his headquarters for some two hours when none other than *Thoheeks* Grahvos himself came pounding up on a lathered horse, to rein up, swing down out of the saddle, throw the reins to a soldier and come stamping up the steps and into the building, his face dark and worried-looking.

Alone with the sub-strahteegos in his office, the *thoheeks* waved away the proffered goblet of wine, declined to sit and demanded, "Now what in hell did you say to *Thoheeks* Hahkmukos that got his bowels into such an uproar, boy? Were I you, I'd take care to guard my back and hire a food-taster—men in the mood he's just now in often seek out and retain assassins, you know. He seems to think that you and Portos are conspiring to get onto Ahndros lands, hire away his troop of mercenaries, then just turn him out and let his enemies butcher him."

"He has a very vivid imagination, my lord *Thoheeks*," said Tomos, "though how he twisted what little was said into such a scenario is a matter I cannot fathom."

"All right, what was said, then?" snapped Grahvos. "Let's hear your version of it."

Tomos told it, he told it all. The *thoheeks* stood for a long moment after Gonsalos had ceased to speak, then he slowly shook his head, sank into the chair, picked up the filled goblet and took a lengthy pull of the wine it held. At last, he began to speak.

"Hahkmukos was among the first to rejoin Zastros when he returned from his years of exile in the south, in the Witch Lands, whence he got his wife, the Lady Lilyuhn. Both she and Zastros liked Hahkmukos, and so he gained preferment, going from one high post on Zastros' staff to another. During the invasion, he served as chief quartermaster of the army, and in that capacity he became very wealthy, so wealthy, in fact, that he alone knows the full extent of that wealth."

"Yes, my lord," remarked Tomos, "and *Thoheeks* Portos is of the firm belief that gift or promise of some of those ill-gotten gains went far toward assuring *Thoheeks* Hahkmukos confirmation by Council."

Grahvos made a face and sighed, squirming a bit in his chair. "I sincerely wish I could say that I owned full faith in the incorruptibility of all my peers on Council, Tomos, but I must be realistic and candid. Even *thoheeksee* have their price, especially must this be so of men who just now own their rank, lands that are not yet fully productive and cities, towns and holds that are a shambles, where they still stand at all.

"*Thoheeks* Hahkmukos is arrogant and not very likable; moreover, he seems to have made an enemy with every *thrahkmeh* he ground out of his various sinecures under Zastros, so the first vote went heavily against his confirmation, and there never would've even been a second hearing and vote had he not suddenly and miraculously acquired some active and very vocal partisans on Council. It is not only possible but very probable, to my way of thinking, that ounces of gold had vast influence on his acquisitions of 'friends on Council' to argue his case and to, eventually, vote in favor of his confirmation. Wisely, he and his agents never committed the cardinal error of approaching me or my closer associates—the *Thoheeksee* Bahos,

Mahvros, Sitheeros, Iahkovos and Vahsilios—and it is significant, perhaps, that none of us championed him or cast positive votes on either occasion.

"So, yes, *Thoheeks* Portos is almost certainly correct in his assumption that *Thoheeks* Hahkmukos bought his title and lands, paid for them in specie and by most dishonorable means. But, still, I wish that Portos would be careful to whom he tells this dirty little secret, for nothing must be allowed to stain the Council; our sway is not yet sufficiently secure to be able to assuredly weather any really big and open scandal, not yet."

"To the best of my knowledge, Lord Grahvos," Tomos assured him, "I am the only officer that *Thoheeks* Portos has seen fit to take into his confidence in this smelly matter."

Grahvos nodded and growled, "Good and good again, boy. Let it stay that way; a lot may be riding on it.

"Now, that matter aside, what of *Thoheeks* Hahkmukos' complaint to me that you refused to allow him to take more than an absolute minimum of personal baggage and attendants with the army on the march?"

Tomos simply called for a horse, led the way to where the wagons, pack train and retinue still waited and said, "My lord *Thoheeks*, I but thought this a bit excessive, besides which, ox-drawn transport would slow the rate of march."

"And that is what you told Hahkmukos, Tomos?" asked Grahvos in a tight voice.

"Yes, Lord Grahvos. I told him that he might add one common-size wagon to the force trains, plus, of course, the baggage for his own troops."

"Sounds generous enough," said Grahvos. "I've set off on campaign with far less, many's the time. And if he wanted more servants, he could just mount them on mules. I don't suppose you would object to that, eh? Of course not. Then I can't say that I understand his flurry of objections on this part of the matter; he's had fully enough experience with armies to know that speed and flexibility are quite often important factors and that military commanders must always have the final word regarding the sizes of their trains, consequently. The way he told the tale to me, you were denying him everything save a canvas fly, a blanket roll and a pisspot. I'll go back and have a few words with him.''

The *thoheeks* first made to rein about, then turned back. "My boy, do you think you might be able to get Hahkmukos' mounted force away from this train for a few hours on some pretext or other?''

"Easily, my lord," said Tomos. "*Thoheeks* Portos had mentioned that were they to march with us, he wanted one of his officers to inspect them, their mounts, their weapons and their supplies.''

"Very good, very good, Tomos." Grahvos smiled. "You see, I had not ere this been aware of just how much Hahkmukos had brought out of Karaleenos. There will shortly be a detachment of Council Guardsmen and some others from the citadel down here to off-load those wagons and examine the ladings; they will have authority to seize anything that resembles loot from Karaleenos or property of Zastros' army, the former to be returned to King Zenos and the latter to become property of our government, as it rightfully should be.''

"One thing, my lord," said Tomos. "Hahkmukos made mention during my brief meeting with him that this"—he waved an arm along the lines of wagons and pack animals—"is but a part of his holdings, and that he would send for the rest when he is installed in his place.''

"Thank you, Tomos," replied Grahvos gravely. "I'll have that matter checked out, too. I've the idea that this *thoheekseeahn* will end being far more expensive than our Hahkmukos ever dreamed.''

The encampment was set up just out of easy engine

range from the walls of Ahndropolis. Cavalry ranged out in patrols, but no attempt was made to interdict the city and no entrenchments were begun. None of this pleased Hahkmukos, *thoheeks*-to-be, but only his sour looks and a few petulant low-voiced whines announced the fact; he had learned on the march to keep a low profile and to do so in silence.

Thoheeks Grahvos, shivering despite the heavy fur-trimmed cloak wrapped about him, growled at the *thoheeks*-designate, "All right, damn you, we're arrived and you're still alive, so do you still harbor the asinine notion that everyone from Tomos Gonsalos on down is out to kill you? Not that that seems such a bad idea to me, here and now. I'm getting too old, too full of aches and pains, for winter warring or campaigning, and it's only because of you that I'm here, you sad, sniveling specimen."

As they stood there, the huge gates cracked enough to allow for the exit of three mounted and armored men, one of them bearing a headless lanceshaft to which had been attached a rippling banner of snowy-white silk.

"Hmm," grunted *Thoheeks* Grahvos. "Our herald's bringing back some company, it would seem. I mean to go and meet them. You may go where you wish . . . should you choose hell, let me know, I'll help you gladly." So saying, he mounted his mule and rode off, leaving only Hahkmukos and the servant who held the reins of the showy palfrey atop the low hillock.

By the time the slow but comfortably gaited mule arrived before the command pavilion, the herald and the visitors were already inside with the commanders and a strong guard stood all about the enclosure, but *Thoheeks* Grahvos was, of course, passed with alacrity and without question.

Waving over a guard officer, Grahvos ordered, "Should *Thoheeks* Hahkmukos arrive, let him in . . . but be certain to first disarm him, and search him, too, but courteously, mind you."

"My lord Grahvos," said Captain *Thoheeks* Portos gravely, "this is *Komees* Klaios Kelaios, who presently holds the city. He avers that he has sent no less than six messengers to Mehseepolis to bear messages to Council, but that none ever have returned, and . . ."

Seating himself near a glowing brazier, his booted legs stretched out before him, Grahvos said, "Tell it again, Lord *Komees*, from the very beginning, please."

While the city-lord talked, Grahvos studied him carefully. He saw a man of about average height and medium build, heavily scarred about the head, face and hands, scarred in ways that the warrior *thoheeks* had seen often before. His age could have been anywhere between thirty and forty years, but if the former, then he was prematurely aging, for he bore the lines and wrinkles of care and worry. Save for a severe limp, he bore himself well and expressed himself even better, clearly born and bred a gentleman of the old, Ehleen strain, a *kath'ahrohs*, and no mistaking the fact.

Grahvos liked what he saw before him far better with every passing moment of time. Should Hahkmukos live to twice or three times his current years, he would never, could never be of the like of this one. He put the aging warrior much in mind of his own sons, all dead in the long-lasting disturbances which had rent and racked the lands during the two decades now past.

When, finally, *Komees* Klaios ceased to speak, Grahvos turned to *Thoheeks* Portos and asked baldly, "He told you the same story before I arrived, then?"

"Yes, my lord," replied the officer. "It was the same tale, though the second recounting was in more depth and detail."

Before he questioned the next officer, Captain Sub-chief Rahb Vawn, he told the city-lord, "Lord *Komees*, the officer with the unusual armor there is a Horseclansman from Kehnooryos Ehlahs. Like many of his ilk, he owns the proven ability to read minds."

Then, of Captain Rahb, he asked, "Did he lie, Captain?"

The short, slender, reddish-blond man shook his head. "Not once, Chief Grahvos; all that he told you and us before was the plain, simple truth. Were it all up to me, I'd take his oaths and march back to Mehseepolis, for his mind tells me that he would find it as hard to lie as that other one does to tell the truth. You asked, Lord Chief, I have answered."

Grahvos steepled his fingers and rested his blunt chin atop the forefingertips, staring hard at a point where a sidewall of the pavilion joined the roof. "Six noble messengers and their retainers ride out of Ahndropolis bound for Mehseepolis in a span of fifteen or sixteen months. Men trained and experienced in arms, Lord *Komees*? Yes, of course, in these times, else they'd not have still been alive to undertake such a ride.

"One, maybe even two of the earlier ones, might have fallen prey to bandit bands, but most of those were eradicated by our army some full year agone, so what chanced with the other four, eh? It does give one to pause and wonder, gentlemen."

He turned back to Portos and said, "Captain, send for Hahkmukos. I want the distinguished Sub-chief Vawn to delve into that cesspool mind when he hears the testimony of *Komees* Klaios, for Hahkmukos is the only person of whom I can think who might have thought he would gain from buying off or waylaying messengers from Ahndropolis."

An officer was dispatched, but he returned alone. "My lords, the *thoheeks* refused to speak with me. He is in his tent, but he sent word by way of one of his guards that he did not care to speak with *Komees* Klaios and that all that he wished to see of him is his severed head."

Portos growled like a lion, and before he could speak, Grahvos had ordered, "Lieutenant, assemble a detachment double the strength of Lord Hahkmukos' guard and return with them to his tent. You are to go into his tent this time, and if any man tries to stop you, you and your detachment bear my witnessed orders to put steel into them.

"You are to tell Lord Hahkmukos that he is to come here immediately, escorted by you. If he still will not, you have my leave to have him dragged here, just as he is."

As the officer was saluting, Sub-chief Rahb, grinning maliciously, commented, "It might be wise, Lieutenant, to take along a crowbar, so's to pry the bastard from off his catamite."

As the officer departed, Rahb Vawn commented to no one in particular, "Long's I've lived among you Ehleenee, and that's all of my life, I've never been able to fathom your kind's fascination for little slave boys; you can't get children on them and so it seems like such a waste."

Thoheeks Grahvos shrugged. "There has always been a significant minority of our race here who have declared that women exist only for breeding purposes, boys and younger men for sexual pleasure. I, personally, never subscribed to the philosophy, but some of my peers back at Mehseepolis do, Captain Rahb."

Thoheeks Portos said gravely, "I think that that subculture dates back to the days of the conquest of this land, before the conquerors had sent back to their homelands for women of their blood. They did not wish to pollute the racial strain through fraternization with the women of the conquered, some of them, so they made do with each other. I dabbled a bit in that direction when I was younger and still held my original lands, but no more, for it truly is a waste of precious seed for a man who needs to breed heirs and is getting no younger. But, even so, when I did so indulge myself, it was invariably with men not much younger than myself, not with the barely pubescent children that Hahkmukos keeps."

Captain *Opokomees* Gregorios of Dahnpolis put in, "It's rarer in Karaleenos than here or in Kehnooryos Ehlahs, and, I have been given to understand, rarer still in Kehnooryos Mahkedohnya. Of course, up in Karaleenos, we Ehleenoee have interbred with the indigenes from the beginning, or almost; you will find damned few *kath'ahrohsee* among us.

"And, you know, my lords, although one might expect just the very opposite, I had a drinking bout and some very long conversations with one of Lord Alekhsa-hndros' bireme officers up on the Lumbuh River during the late unpleasantness and he averred that such conduct is looked down upon in the Pirate Isles and is, therefore, almost an unheard-of thing, for all that there exist there far more men than women."

Sub-chief Rahb nodded. "Yes, true, women are scarce there, but then the Pirate Isles folk practice polyandry—each woman having two, three, four or more husbands at the same time, reckoning descent through her, as too do the Horseclanners, rather than through the sire, like most of you Ehleenee."

"Is it true, then?" asked *Thoheeks* Grahvos wonderingly. "Why, that is passing strange. It seems completely at odds to the very nature of men to willingly share one's wife with other men. Legal adultery is what it sounds like to me."

"Even so, my lord Grahvos," said *Thoheeks* Portos, "we may very well have to promulgate something of the sort in our realms, are we to see a rapid repopulation of these lands of ours, wherein far too many of the males still extant after so many years of warring are either too young or too old or, like Hahkmukos, just not inclined in the direction of breeding."

Rahb Vawn grinned broadly. "Lord Portos, I've got the answer for you. Just turn us Horseclanners loose down here; we'll ride from one duchy to the next one getting younguns on any poor Ehleenee woman as is willing. We'll charge you lords not a thing other than our food and bait for our horses, either; it's the very least we Horseclanners can do for to help you out, down here."

The assembled officers, nobles and heralds still were

laughing when the guard-lieutenant tramped in with a
dark-visaged and very enraged *Thoheeks*-designate
Hahkmukos in tow, followed by two grinning guardsmen with leveled spears held at waist level, their
glittering points a bit downslanted to threaten
Hahkmukos' rump area.

"My lords," announced the guard-lieutenant, "as
you ordered, here is Lord Hahkmukos."

"Did his guards try to impede you, Lieutenant?"
asked Portos.

The junior officer smiled slightly. "Only one of them,
my lord. When the rest saw that we meant bared-steel
business, they recalled urgent business elsewhere, all of
them."

"Bright lads, those," grunted *Thoheeks* Grahvos,
adding, "Our thanks, Lieutenant. You and those two
may retire to the outer room, the wine and the brazier,
but stay within call, eh?"

Immediately the three had saluted and left, Hahkmukos burst out bitterly, "Was it not enough, Lord
Grahvos, that you and our peers saw fit to rob me, to
seize two thirds of my possessions from out my wagons
and packs and warehouses back in Mehseepolis? Was it
not more than enough that you and Captain Portos and
even the barbarian scum from the north have treated me
with contempt and contumely all of the time on the
march? Why was it needful to humiliate me before my
proven enemy, this usurper, this *Komees* Klaios Kelaios,
who had me driven from the city Council gave me and
had me harried from off the lands of my duchy by
armed and mounted men?"

"Had you come when first we whistled you up," said
Portos coldly, "it would not have been necessary to
send men to force compliance to our orders."

"Whether you like me or the fact or not, Lord
Portos," snapped Hahkmukos, his anger and resent-
ment overcoming his fears, "I am, by act of Council,
your equal in civil rank, so you have and had no right to
force me to come here or anywhere else."

"Sweet Christ!" swore Portos. "If I thought for one minute that I was the equal of such as you, I'd fall on my sword from pure shame!"

"As regards action of Council," grated Grahvos, "you're no more than a designate until the third and final vote, and now that you're somewhat poorer, now that other facts have come to light with regard to this other claimant to the duchy, I cannot but begin to doubt that that third vote will be so favorable to your claim as was the last one.

"And whilst we are here discussing claims, what know you of six noblemen of this duchy sent toward Mehseepolis and Council by *Komees* Klaios within the last year and a half, Hahkmukos?"

The man suddenly went from rage-lividity to the color of fresh curds, and Captain Rahb Vawn frowned, saying, "He's guilty as sin, Lord Grahvos, that's as plain as fresh horse biscuits on a winter snow. Such a whirl is his mind in just now, though, it's hard to sift out facts. Can you delve any deeper, Gil?"

Captain of Elephants Gil Djohnz closed his eyes for a moment and then spoke. "I get the impression that while he himself did none of the killings, he paid others to do them, especially a stout, thickly bearded man called Yohseefos . . . something like that, anyway."

"Lieutenant . . . ?" called Grahvos.

When that worthy stood before him, the eldest *thoheeks* returned his salute and ordered, "Take a detachment, go back to the camp of Lord Hahkmukos and seek out a stout man with a thick beard and a name on the order of Yohseefos."

But before the young officer could even answer, the miserable *thoheeks*-designate barked a harsh laugh. "If all you had by way of proof of these groundless charges against me was the unsupported word of that bastard, then know that your man here killed him outside my tent before he forced his way in and brought me here. Other credulous men may believe in these barbarians who are said to be able to read minds and commune with dumb beasts, but I do not, nor does any rational, civilized man.

"With this usurper in the camp, in your power, why not just kill him and get it over with? With the army camped out in plain view and with his head on a lance, I doubt that any or many would offer fight to my guards as I ride into my city."

"For one thing," answered Grahvos, "it never has been my habit to dishonor myself or a sacred truce with murder, though I would assume you hold a different philosophy. For another thing, after these last weeks of closer association with you than I could ever have desired, I am far from certain that Council would want such a thing as you in power of any description within our realm."

"Like it or not," sneered Hahkmukos, "I *am thoheeks*, and by your oaths you and this army are required to put me in power in this duchy, for I am, after all, my father's son and my father was the half brother of the sire of the last *thoheeks* of direct descent of the House of Ahndros."

Komees Klaios snorted. "If you truly believe that statement, then you're the only one in this duchy who does! Although your late father was a decent, hard-working man who did the best he could by you and your brothers, his mother was widely known as an arrant whore, such as my wife's great-grandfather used to cart to his palace in troops to entertain his guests at drunken brawls several times each year."

"You lie!" snarled Hahkmukos heatedly. "My father was recognized the half brother of the late *thoheeks*."

"Not so!" replied the *komees*. "When the boy was four or five years old, the sire of the late *thoheeks* chanced to see him, noted his face and remarked only that he clearly was come of *an* Ahndros man; he then ordered that when the boy came of age, he should be given enough gold to set himself up in a business or a trade. He was a most generous and kindly *thoheeks*; he

did as much for full many a commoner in his lands
during his lifetime. That your sire and his mother chose
to take the largesse of the old *thoheeks* to mean an
acknowledgment of his paternity was known for long,
hereabouts. She was laughed at by other whores and by
everyone else, but because he was liked, people only
smiled behind their hands whenever he mentioned his
supposed close relationship with our late *thoheeks*.

"You know, gentlemen, if this thing's father still
were alive, I doubt not but that many of the older folk
of all stations would be willing to accept him as a city-
lord, if not as *thoheeks*, but not his eldest son, not this
creature. Force me out, kill me, if you wish—for—as he
just pointed out, I am within your power—but even
without me, you will find to your chagrin that neither
the nobles nor the commoners will accept Hahkmukos
as *thoheeks* in peace. All of them remember how
Hahkmukos left Ahndropolis, years agone, and they
will never supinely submit to the rule of a parricide, nor
will all of your armies of armed men be able to place
him securely in Ahndropolis until all its folk are done to
death!"

With a scream, Hahkmukos ripped the lieutenant's
sword from its sheath and, brandishing the blade high,
hurled himself at the unarmed *komees*, the cloak sliding
from off his shoulders to show his body naked save for
a pair of soft ankle boots and his golden jewelry.

He did not get far in his impetuous attack, however.
Captain of Elephants Gil Djohnz thrust out a leg and
tripped him neatly, then quick-moving Portos planted a
heavy booted foot athwart the downed man's neck
while bending to pry the beringed fingers loose from the
swordhilt.

"You want to see blood, do you, Hahkmukos?"
Icicles hung from Portos' words, and his tone was frigid
as a mountain blizzard. "Then I suggest that we settle
this business of claimants in the ancient Ehleen custom,
gentlemen: let Hahkmukos meet the *komees* at swords'

points in a death match, winner to take all. Will you
fight him, Lord Klaios?"

"Gladly, my lord," Klaios said, grim-faced. "Return
my sword and loan me a panoply and shield and I'll
fight him with great pleasure."

"No need to be so precipitate, gentlemen," said
Grahvos. "A man fights more comfortably in his own
panoply. Let the other gentleman return into the city
and fetch back your gear, Lord Klaios. You two can do
your combat on that little plain just beyond the main
gates of Ahndropolis—that way, more of your folk can
watch it and so be witness to God's decision in the
matter at hand.

"It was a very good, a very fitting suggestion, Portos.
My wits must be slowing with age or I'd've thought of it
myself."

Turning to the lieutenant, he said, "Help the
thoheeks-designate up, drape him in his cloak again,
and escort him back to his tent. There help him to dress
and to arm, then bring him back here. Oh, and fetch
back a brace of his guards to be his arming-men for the
fight, for I doubt if any gentleman in this pavilion
would care for that 'honor.' You might bring him back
mounted, for we'll all have to ride out to the site of the
fight."

When they had gone, Grahvos seated himself again
and called for ewers of wine to refill the goblets and
mugs. After they all were again brimming and the servants padded out, he asked, "Lord Klaios, what is the
story on this parricide business? That's a weighty
charge, as I'm certain you are aware. A claimant to a
title or to lands must swear powerful oaths that he never
has done such, save accidentally, in the heat of a large
battle, and Hahkmukos so swore before the assembled
Council. If he perjured himself, then we must know."

The *komees* set aside his goblet and shrugged. "No
one ever proved it, my lord, Hahkmukos was never
declared outlaw, you understand, but the late *thoheeks*
did make it clear to him that he would assuredly be

made to suffer for it if ever he returned to this duchy while still he was lord here.

"When she who had been Hahkmukos' mother died, his sire remarried; of course, this was while Hahkmukos was away being given a gentleman's education at his sire's expense. When he returned, his sire put him to work in his shop. Then, of a day, his new young wife apprehended her stepson in the act of forcibly abusing one of his little half brothers in the way of his kind, whereupon Hahkmukos clubbed her down, all but slew her on the spot.

"Her screams brought her husband and a brace of his customers from the shop into the living quarters, and after the raging young man had been subdued and the wife revived, and her story and that of the child had been heard and witnessed, the sire became enraged and made a sincere effort to kill or at least do serious damage to his eldest son, but his customers—both of them old friends of the sire—restrained him from doing more than beating the miscreant within an inch of his life.

"In the wake of it all, Hahkmukos left the home and shop and he repaired to and lived for a while in the most disreputable section of Ahndropolis. A few months later, of a night, someone burglarized the shop, entered the home behind it, and slew the man, his wife and all of his children by her.

"Naturally, in the wake of all that had happened before, Hahkmukos was immediately under suspicion, but the *thoheeks'* investigators were unable to place him anywhere near that section of the city at the date and time of the murders and robbery. Nonetheless, lest certain folk be tempted to do him to death on strong suspicion, the *thoheeks* saw to it that Hahkmukos left the duchy for good and all. And no one here had seen him again until he came riding into Ahndropolis to gloat that he now was confirmed as our *thoheeks* and was looking forward to settling a number of old scores within his duchy."

Chapter IV

"Get out of here, you little shoat!" Hahkmukos snarled at the young slave boy still squatting in the corner of the tent. Having suffered his master's anger before, the child bundled his garment under a skinny arm and ran out into the drizzly cold.

"Will you grant me privacy to use the pot, Lieutenant?" asked the *thoheeks*-designate.

But upon the officer's departure, it was not the brass chamberpot that Hahkmukos sought; rather did he depress what looked like just another stud set in the lower corner of a traveling chest. Out of the secret drawer that then silently opened, he took a leathern belt, the pockets of which bulged with weighty contents. When he had buckled the belt around his waist, he quickly covered it with a shirt of soft cotton, then a longer one of silk, which he stuffed into silk drawers.

Seating himself on the side of the sleeping couch, he pulled off the ankle boots, swathed his feet in two thicknesses of cotton cloth, then wrapped his lower legs in similar cloth, cross-gartering them before pulling on padded trousers that tied in place a few inches below each knee.

When the lieutenant reentered the tent, Hahkmukos had stamped into a pair of jackboots and was buckling the sides of a padded arming shirt. The officer helped finish the buckling, then his nimble fingers did up the leathern points that held on the sleeves of the garment. That done, the armor chests were opened and, one

sitting, the other squatting, Hahkmukos and the officer
inserted the steel splints into the sheaths let in the legs of
the boots for the purpose, buckled on spurs, then knee-
cops and plate cuishes above them.

The lieutenant grunted approval upon seeing the
hauberk. Though decorated to the point of gaudiness, it
was good, thick, first-quality, all-riveted rings that went
to make it up, triple mail, split at front and back for
riding, as well as on either side for ease of movement
afoot, and with sleeves that descended to a bit below the
elbow.

When Hahkmukos had wriggled into the mail shirt,
he donned a padded coif—cotton inside, thick, sturdy
silk outside—and the officer lifted out of its fitted place
in the chest the backplate, whistling softly through his
teeth as he recognized the rare quality of it. While he
held the plate in place, the *thoheeks*-designate did up the
straps and buckles crisscrossing shoulders and chest,
then he held the breastplate secure while the officer
matched the halves of the hinges and inserted the
hingepins on the one side, then snapped closed the
catches on the other.

Elbow-cops were buckled below brassarts which
themselves were overlapped by spauldrons of steel scales
riveted to thick leather. When he had cinched the waist
with a studded swordbelt, the officer fitted the cased
sword and a broad-bladed battle-dirk to it, then handed
Hahkmukos his armored gauntlets and the battle-helm
—a fine, Pitzburk-made helm, with hinged visor and
gorget and feeling to be of a weight of eight or nine
pounds.

But when he inquired, Hahkmukos told him, "I don't
have a shield with me. I'll have to take one from one of
my guards. Where are the two you brought to be my
armingmen?"

The lieutenant made a wry face. "Lord, the camp of
your guards is deserted. The picket lines are empty, and

have been stripped of anything usable or small and valuable. Your servants say that the guards hurriedly packed and rode off with their pack train at a hard gallop while we were at the headquarters pavilion. However, your own horses are left, and the servants should have two of them outside the tent by now. I'm certain we can get a shield from one of my men."

Outside the tent, two saddled horses had been tied, but not one servant or slave was within sight. "Lieutenant, it's been some time since I tried to mount while wearing armor and weapons. Give me a leg up," said Hahkmukos blandly.

The young officer shrugged and obliged him. But no sooner was the *thoheeks*-designate firmly in the saddle than he smashed his muddy bootsole full into the officer's face, grabbed the reins of the second horse and spurred his own into a fast canter out of the camp, not galloping solely because he did not wish to attract undue attention.

"The fools," he thought, "I saw right through them from the very start. No, they had no plans on my life, that mewling old bastard of a Grahvos swore. No, *they* didn't, not that pack from Mehseepolis, no, they just meant to rob me and humiliate me, then to let that damned usurper of a Klaios cut me down. They must have known that I'm not a fighter, that my armor and weapons were bought only for appearance and because in the grades of Pitzburk I bought, they are damned good investments, just as these blooded horses are."

Not until he was completely out of sight of the camp, only the more lofty reaches of the city of Ahndropolis still barely visible in the drizzly mist, did Hahkmukos rein up long enough to throw the hooded cloak he had grabbed off a hook as they had left the tent over his gaudy panoply, remove the devilishly uncomfortable helmet and hang it from his pommel and fold the hood up so that the cold water would no longer drip and run down his face. Then he set the horse to a gallop, heading

northwestward, away from both Ahndropolis and Mehseepolis.

In the spartanly furnished little office, *Thoheeks*
Grahvos finished his perusal of the sheaf of witnessed
oaths of Klaios, the surviving landholders of the Duchy
of Ahndros and those of the men that the acting-
thoheeks had carefully picked to fill the many
vacancies. As the elder man tucked the documents into
first a waxed-parchment folder, then a waxed-leather
tube, he said, "The Horseclanners will be in the saddle
at dawn and I with them, so these should be in
Mehseepolis by the end of the week. Never you fear, my
boy, you'll be confirmed, for you're just the sort of
thoheeks we want in these lands. When you've set things
in order hereabouts and can do so, come to Mehseepolis
and take your place on the Council. Until then, I'll vote
your proxy as we discussed.

"Save for the troops we're loaning you and Ahndros,
all Council forces should be on the march back by noon-
day tomorrow. The order is set for dawn, but I've never
yet seen an army set out on time and I doubt that I ever
will." He chuckled ruefully. "Yes, the Horseclanners
always leave on time, but then they are barbarians and
can't fathom the senseless and inevitable delays of
civilized armies. I like them and respect them, they're
probably the finest, the most dependable and effective
troops Council just now owns, and I mean to persuade
some of them to stay down here, take lands and breed
up more of their race."

As he stood and hitched his light dress sword around
to make for easier walking, he admonished, "But, son
Klaios, you'll be wise to keep some sturdy, faithful
bodyguards by you and the Lady Ahmahleea and the
children at all times, hire a food-taster or two as well,
and make constant use of their services. Hahkmukos is
a coward—he would not fight anyone breast to breast,
not if that opponent was armed—but he is highly

dangerous, I feel, nonetheless. I doubt not that that
empty drawer that gaped from the side of his travel
chest contained gold, so you can be certain that he
doesn't lack the hire of an assassin or three.''

"You feel then that he and his troop of hired bravos
will not be back to openly harass the duchy, Lord
Grahvos?" asked Klaios, looking a bit worried.

The *thoheeks* chuckled and shook his head again.
"No, I don't. They didn't leave together, you know.
When Lieutenant Bralos slew their captain, then
dragged their employer off almost naked and at the
points of spears, they at once elected a new captain,
looted everything that could be speedily grabbed up,
then rode off headed northeast, while Rahb Vawn tells
me that Hahkmukos' trail veers almost due west. So far
as the troop are concerned, I'll not be surprised at all are
they in the camp under the walls of Mehseepolis trying
to enlist in our army . . . and I'll probably recommend
taking them on, for they seem to be good, experienced
fighters, survivors, and such types Council can always
use.''

"How goes it with the young officer?" inquired
Klaios, with patent and sincere concern. "When last I
set eyes to him, he looked as if a herd of cattle had run
over him.''

Grahvos smiled. "Yes, he was a mess when he
staggered back to the pavilion—all mud and blood and
bruises, and barely able to talk coherently or even see
where he was going. He almost brought the roof down
atop us all when he walked into that main post.

"But he'll live. His nose was broken, of course, and a
few teeth loosened, but the swelling has subsided
enough for him to be able to see and drink broth and
wine easily now.''

Klaios nodded. "Good. However, I feel that I owe
him suffering-price, since he was, in effect, injured in
service to me and to the Duchy of Ahndros.''

Grahvos reached over and gripped the *komees'*

shoulder firmly and said in a grave tone, "You, Lord
Klaios, are a true gentleman of the old school, and I
thank the good God that He sent us such as you to rule
these lands.

"But worry yourself not in this matter. Lieutenant
Bralos has been paid in full for his injuries. I awarded
him Hahkmukos' tent, baggage and furnishings, plus
some of the pack mules that the bravos didn't lift to
bear his new possessions back to Mehseepolis. I also
gave him to understand that his name is now high on my
personal list of young officers deserving preferment."

Sub-*strahteegos* Tomos Gonsalos greeted *Thoheeks*
Grahvos warmly when he rode into camp with Captain
Sub-chief Rahb Vawn's clansmen. The older man
staggered up the steps and through the anterooms, then
virtually collapsed into a chair in Tomos' office,
looking to be utterly drained, thoroughly exhausted.

Deep concern on his face and in his tone, Gonsalos
filled a mug with watered brandy and asked, as he
proffered it, "Are you quite well, my lord Grahvos?"

"Oh, I'm not ill, Tomos, not really," groaned
Grahvos. "But one more week of hell-riding with those
Horseclanners would have seen me dead. Man, those
little bastards ride day and night, they stop only long
enough to unsaddle their mounts, slap the saddles onto
remounts from the remuda, perhaps have a quick piss,
then they're mounted and off again, both eating and
sleeping in the saddle—at a fast amble, most often, at
that."

He grinned tiredly. "But by Christ I kept up with the
bastards. It became a point of personal and racial honor
to me that they not be able to boast that they rode an
Ehleen nobleman into the ground."

Tomos shook his head. "My lord, you are perhaps
the most valuable man the Confederation has, our
strongest and most faithful supporter in these southern
lands, and you are no longer a young man. You could

have burst your heart, killed yourself, at such foolishness. Please say that you'll not again be so
stubbornly . . ."

Grahvos waved his hand. "Oh, never you fear, my
good Tomos, I've had a crawful and more of cavalry
marching for a good long while. But I also now have
even deeper respect for those damned Horseclanners of
yours. Lord God, what a weapon they make for our
arms. Give them enough of a remuda and I don't doubt
but that they could cover the full distance from east
coast to west of this onetime kingdom within three or
four weeks . . . and like as not fight and win a battle
when they got there."

The older man drained off his mug of brandy-water
and, while his host refilled it, inquired, "Have you seen
anything of a stray troop of Ehleenoee mercenary horsemen about in the last few days, Tomos?" Then he
recounted all that had transpired with the wretched and
craven Hahkmukos in Ahndropolis, ending with the ad-
monition, "So, if they do ride into camp, I'd accept
their enlistments, but I'd also break them up, spread
them out as far as possible among existing units of our
cavalry; otherwise they just might decide to bolt in a
tight place, and leave us with a gap in our battle line
when and where we least can afford one."

As he stood to leave for the city, he remarked, "By
the way, I have hired away one of your officers, Captain
Rahb Vawn, to be my personal bodyguard; he's even
now explaining his decision to Chief Pawl of Vawn. I
pay well for service; besides, I'm hoping that Rahb will
learn to like it well enough to stay here, marry and breed
more of his kind among us. There are still rich lands
lacking lords within my and many another
desmesne . . . which is something that all of you
northerners might take into consideration when you
plan for your futures.

"Now, I'm off for the palace, a hot bath and a soft,
warm bed."

* * *

Four days later, Captain *Thoheeks* Portos marched the rest of the cavalry, the infantry, the elephants and the trains into the permanent camp below Mehseepolis —men, animals and vehicles all mud-caked, half frozen and miserable. Even the sturdy, uncomplaining elephants were showing irritability bred of the exhaustion of pushing and pulling wagon after wagon out of mudhole after mudhole day after day in icy rain or clammy mist.

"That abortion of a so-called road," Portos told Tomos after the troops had been formed up and dismissed, "has got to go to the top of the repair list. All the logs are rotted out; the only bridge that is still there, even, is the old, narrow stone one over Yahlee River; to cross the rest of the streams we had to send out patrols to seek fords. In one place there was no ford to be found, so the artificiers and pioneers had to swim a treacherous and powerful current with lines in their teeth, haul over and set cables, then set the elephants to stand upstream in six feet of rushing water to partially break its force while men and horses were swum and wagons were floated across. That had to be done twice—once on the march down there, once on the march back—and that is what cost us our only deaths—nine men, two horses and two mules.

"If I hadn't believed fully that those barbarians can really talk to those elephants, Tomos, I'd have to, after this campaign. They can get those beasts to do things that I've never before seen either a draught elephant or a war-elephant perform, not in all my years of warring with and against armies that utilized them.

"And the efforts of those three elephants is all that got our trains back up here over those quagmire roads, too. Without them, we'd have been putting down draught animals right and left; as it was, when a wagon mired too deeply for the animals and the men to drag and pry it out, one of the elephants would put her forehead against the back of it and pop it out like the stopper from a bottle, then the team would be rehitched and so proceed to the next impassable stretch of slimy road.

"We didn't get to better roads and slightly drier weather until yesterday. Did the barbarian cavalry and *Thoheeks* Grahvos make it back yet?"

Tomos nodded, smiling. "Four days ago."

Portos hissed between his teeth. "And how many horses did they kill and founder?"

"None," the sub-*strahteegos* replied, adding, "I know, I know, it sounds impossible, but it's true, nonetheless. Their secret, so *Thoheeks* Grahvos avers, is that they never push any one mount too hard for too long. That's what their oversized remuda is for, you see. They change horses several times each day; they seldom ride really fast, but they stay in the saddle and moving for eighteen and twenty hours a day, every day, until they get where they're headed."

The tall captain shook his head. "Oh, they're all tough little bastards, I'll be the first to grant you that much. High Lord Milos chose well when he chose such as them. I'm told that they went through the best that Kehnooryos Ehlahs could field, years agone, like shit through a goose. And they went on to clobber you Karaleenoee pretty thoroughly, too, didn't they?"

Tomos sighed and nodded soberly. "That they did, friend Portos, that they assuredly did, over and over again, year after year. We kept on fighting . . . and losing men and lands and battles, for we of Karaleenos are as stubborn and as proud as any other people of the Ehleen race. Hell, we'd probably still be fighting them had not your late and unlamented High King Zastros poised so great a threat that King Zenos decided to make stand with High Lord Milo, Lord Djefree, Lord Alexandros and the rest against a common foe.

"But back to the here and now, Portos. Did you see on your march aught of the mercenary cavalry troop formerly employed by Hahkmukos? Grahvos seemed to think they might be headed back here seeking an employer."

"Oh, yes, I'd meant to mention that matter earlier, Tomos," Portos answered. "They're with my cavalry column, what's left of them as can still sit a horse, that is. About two thirds of the original troop are alive or were this morning, but most of them are wounded to one degree or another. We came on them camped and licking their wounds three days' march out of the Duchy of Ahndros."

"They ran into bandits, did they?" asked Tomos.

Portos pursed his lips. "In a manner of speaking, yes. But, no, just another rendition of the same sad old story: their newly elected captain and a brace of his close friends tried to sneak away one night with the best of the loot of Hahkmukos' camp, they were caught and killed, and then a general melee ensued. A day later, we came across them. We put down the ones who were clearly death-wounded, of course, and stuffed the ones who couldn't ride into the ambulance wagons. Our *eeahtrohsee* have done the best they could for them, but even so, two or three a day have died on the march. What disposition do you want made of them?"

Tomos shrugged. "Well, Grahvos wanted to hire them on for our army, but parcel them out to various existing units. I'll tell you, take the ones you want of them, if any, and funnel the rest into that squadron of light cavalry that's being raised. That's the best I can figure, just now.

"By the way, while the force was down there, *Thoheeks* Sitheeros brought over an officer from Iron Mountain and introduced him to me. He's the *thoheeks'* war-elephant trainer, one Master of Elephants Laskos. What's wrong? You know him or something of him, Portos?"

"I've never met him, no, Tomos, but, yes, I surely do know of him," replied Portos, "and I wonder just who

twisted just what tails to get him down here. Sitheeros
treasures him, and rightly so, too. That man was King
Hyamos' captain-general of the war-elephants. He
developed ways of using elephants that no one had ever
before known or thought about.

"But he and the usurper, Fahrkos, couldn't get
along. He was declared outlaw and disappeared; for all
that Fahrkos had the lands scoured over and over, he
never could catch him. Now we know that most of the
years he was missing, he was holed up at Iron Mountain
with *Thoheeks* Sitheeros.

"He's not an Ehleen, you know."

Tomos nodded. "Yes, I'd thought he didn't look like
one, and he owns a singular accent in his speech, too;
I've never heard one like it, I don't believe. Where did
he come from?"

Portos shrugged. "Maybe Sitheeros knows, but I
don't. There're tales about him, though; some say that
he came south from the Black Kingdoms, up near
Kehnooryos Mahkedohnya, others aver that he is from
some land beyond the Eastern Ocean and came by way
of Lord Alexandros' Pirate Isles, long ago, then there
are those who think that he came from some place far to
the west, beyond the Sea of Grass. I've never given
much thought to it, any of it.

"What would you, who have at least seen him, say is
his age?"

Tomos knitted up his weathered brows. "Oh, I don't
know, fifty, sixty, maybe. Why?"

"Because," said Portos, "not only was he King
Hyamos' elephant trainer, he also served Hyamos'
father, old King Vitahlyos, which means that the
man—who was a man grown, they say, when first he
came to these lands of ours—must be in his eighties
anyway, if not looking back at his ninetieth year."

Tomos' dark eyes widened perceptibly. "You
think . . . ? Could it be possible? Might he be one such
as High Lord Milo and the High Lady Aldora, then?

But surely, sometime over the years he has dwelt in Ehleen lands, some *kooreeos* or other has put him to the Test?''

Portos shook his head. "Maybe, in Karaleenos or Kehnooryos Ehlahs or some other land where religion, the old religion, has maintained a stronger hold than here, in the south. But the last dynasty—that of which Hyamos was the last king—had little use for the church and did much to weaken it, strip it of its onetime wealth and power over the nobles and commoners.

"At one time, a century or more back now, *kooree-ohsee* were high noblemen in all save name or title, alone. They held lands and great wealth—supposedly for the Church, of course—they traveled about the kingdom in retinues that included hundreds—sub-*kooreeohsee*, priests, all manner of servants, fully armed retainers, female concubines or male catamites or both together depending upon their tastes, cooks, servers, all manner of artisans, grooms, entertainers, professional torturers and executioners, scribes, too many others to recount. They owned and right often exercised the power of life and death over commoners and the lower grades of nobility, and they made of extortion a fine art.

"But then, in the time of King Vitahlyos' great-great-grandfather, Hyamos the First, they overreached themselves. They first tried to wring more concessions from him who was to be second of his house to rule, and when that failed, they refused to take part in his coronation, then plotted a rebellion against him. But he and his father before him had a broad base of support amongst the nobility, the gentry, even the commoners, and he rode out the troubles.

"Now the Church of that period had for long ruled by fear, and fear breeds hatred, so people supported King Hyamos *Kooreeos*-bane even more than they had before the Church tried to deny him his father's throne and have him killed for refusing to become their tool.

"None of that first King Hyamos' successors ever
forgot, and all of them openly persecuted the Church
and the *kooreeohsee*, encouraging all other folk of all
classes to emulate them. King Fahrkos, however, was
far too busy most of his short reign trying to keep the
crown from wobbling off his head, the lands under his
control and the life in his body to worry about the
Church, but the disturbances of the period between the
defeat of the first great rebellion and Zastros' return
from exile affected and afflicted the Church as much as
they did all other people of the kingdom.

"We *thoheeksee* of the Council are not in any manner
of means persecuting the Church and the *kooreeohsee*
. . . but, then, we're not going out of our way to help
them or give them power, either. We're making certain
that lands and cities and wealth and power rest in the
hands of lay nobility of the proper mindset; if some of
them want to give lands or wealth to the Church, that's
their personal business. That's the way most of us feel
about it, though there are a few old-fashioned
types—*Thoheeks* Bahos is an example—who would
grind the Church down much farther and far finer.

"But back to Master Laskos. I would be surprised to
hear that he ever was put to that brutal, painful,
degrading test, not whilst he dwelt here, for under the
last dynasty and since, the Church has consistently
maintained a very low profile and the *kooreeohsee* have
run scared; they would no more have suggested the
testing of a man in service to the king or a powerful
thoheeks than they would have suggested testing the
king himself."

"So then," mused Tomos, "it might be entirely
possible that this young-appearing very elderly man is
really an Undying. Hmmm. I think that I must send a
galloper to the High Lord at Kehnooryos Atheenahs at
tomorrow's dawn; I'd be remiss in my responsibility to
both my king and his overlord did I do less."

Portos squinted under his brows at Gonsalos. "You

truly believe, then, that this High Lord Milos is what he and his aver?''

"You do not?" asked the sub-*strahteegos*.

"Look you, Tomos," replied Portos evenly, "the man is a fine ruler, an honorable and a generous man, he is a superlative military leader—warrior, tactician and strategist, all rolled into one—and I am much beholden to him personally, but I cannot bring myself to believe him to be an Undying, some seven centuries old, no. His clans all firmly believe in him, yes, but then they are not at all a very sophisticated lot, I think you'll admit."

"Then what do you think him to be, Portos?" demanded Tomos.

"I've yet to make up my mind," said Portos flatly, but added, "Physically, he looks very much like one of us, and his Ehleenokos is almost accentless, but what accent remains is that of Pahlahyos Ehlahs—the homeland of our ancestors—or of Kehnooryos Mahkedohnya, whose speech most resembles the archaic patterns and usages. He was clearly born and bred a nobleman and trained to war, whatever his actual place of origin.''

"Think hard before you answer this question, Portos," said Tomos in warning. "Will your doubts, your distrust of the High Lord's age and point of origin, affect your military or civil service to the Council and the Confederation?"

Portos snorted. "Of course not! As I said earlier, be he what he is said to be or be he something else entirely, he still is probably the best ruler between here and the Great Northern Sea, and, also, I am beholden to him. I swore him and the Council oaths, and I mean to keep my word and my honor."

Tomos Gonsalos smiled and nodded. "Fine. Here, have some more of the brandy."

Captain of Elephants Gil Djohnz, although he had

been constrained to give the appearance of being a
"good officer," still harbored an abysmally low
opinion of military routine. Taking full advantage of
the special status of his war-elephant command, he
simply peeled his unit off from the returning column
and headed for the river shallows whereat it had become
customary to wash his huge beasts in garrison.

By the time that he and the other two *feelahksee* had
laved their charges, their mounts, their dear friends, of
an estimated ton of the sticky, gooey red-clay mud and
had arrived back at the lofty building that housed both
them and the elephants, it was almost dark and the three
cow-elephants were yet to be fed, which would entail Gil
organizing enough elephant-barn hands to make certain
that he and the other two did not get stuck with doing it
all.

It was for this reason that he was shocked to the point
of utter speechlessness to find the full staff, even the
ones who had been on the march with him and had
returned here while the elephants were being bathed and
whom he fully expected to have decamped to the
Kindred horse lines in the interval, waiting and ready to
unharness the three massive beasts and lay their food
before them. Stunned, it was only on her third attempt
that he realized that Newgrass was trying to range him
mentally.

"Yes, sister of my sister," he finally beamed in
response.

"The master of elephants from home, he is here,
brother of my sister, I can smell him," she announced.

Peer as he might into the deepening gloom which was
only partially dispelled by the light of the wind-blown
torches, Gil could not spy a strange Ehleen. Deciding
that the long-awaited Master Laskos must be somewhere inside the cavernous barn, the Horseclansman
slid easily down to the ground and began to work at
loosening the buckles of Sunshine's harness, his lead
being at once followed by the other two *feelahksee*, the

waiting men moving forward to lend a hand at the tasks.

He was approached by a stranger, but he noted that this one was assuredly no Ehleen, either. Though darkly weathered, his skin tone was as fair as that of a Horse-clansman, his lips were thin, his close-cropped hair was either blond or white, and in the tricky light of the torches his eyes looked light, too. His clothes were more of an Ehleen cut than Horseclans, but the frame that they swathed was in no way Ehleen-like, being slender, flat-muscled and wiry, no more than a finger or so higher than Gil's own height.

Gil said, "You can get the buckles on her off side."

But the stranger just stood looking at Sunshine for a moment; he made no move to help with the work. Finally, he spoke, his Ehleenokos sounding almost pure to Gil, to whom it was not a native language. "Very good, young man, very good. You keep her clean, and that is a something of great importance as regards the proper management of elephants. However, you do not really need a heavy, clumsy, bulky war-saddle like that; a simple pad of folded wool would suffice."

"Not that it's any of your affair," blurted out Gil, a bit peeved that the man still had made no move to help him unharness Sunshine, "but I prefer a saddle, and she doesn't mind. Why should you? Who the hell are you, anyway, and what are you doing here? You obviously are not come to work, to care for my elephants."

A fleeting smile creased the stranger's thin lips. "Oh, but you are wrong in that assumption, Captain of Elephants Gil Djohnz. I am come here for precisely that purpose and, I am given to understand, at your expressed request. I am Rikos Laskos, summoned from Iron Mountain by my patron, *Thoheeks* Sitheeros. I arrived while still you were out on campaign.

"This is your personal elephant, then, the cow called Sunshine? Yes. Well then, will she allow others to do for her? Fine. Then let us go to a place wherein we can converse privately, eh?"

In the cluttered tack room where Gil maintained a sometime office, Laskos seated himself upon a folded barding, such as was draped over war-elephants before mail and plate armor was attached. He flexed a leg, clasped his hands on the knee and leaned back. "Now, tell me the complete truth—what is this business about you being able to talk to elephants and horses, man?" All at once, he mindspoke, very powerfully, "Are you a telepath, then?"

"Yes," beamed Gil, "and so are you. So why cannot you mindspeak elephants and horses, too?"

"I can mentally communicate with equines, mules, dogs and, to some extent, camels and a number of other animals. But, for some reason, I have never been able to reset my telepathic patterns to those of elephants . . . and I have been trying for more years than you could imagine," replied Laskos. "How did you learn, Gil Djohnz? Did someone teach you?"

Gil frowned. "Well, not exactly. On the day that Sunshine came out of the river, God Milo approached her and mindspoke her. I and a fellow clansman were with him and helped him and her to take off the armor that was hurting her. I don't clearly remember just when I started mindspeaking her, but I did. Then, God Milo had me ride her back to our great camp and feed her all of the hay and other foods that she could eat, and after that day, he had my chief free me from all other tasks to allow me to devote all of my time to feeding and otherwise caring for her.

"But I have taught several other Horseclans mindspeakers how to mindspeak elephants, so I can easily show you how, if that is what you and *Thoheeks* Sitheeros want of me. But what I want of you, in return, is to teach me and the elephants and the other men how to do the things it is necessary for elephants to do in war. Newgrass, the cow that the *thoheeks* brought down from Iron Mountain, has imparted to us all of her own war training, but she says that there is more that she was never taught or that she now does not recall.

"For instance, she has told us of elephants she has seen hurl spear-sized darts and boulders the size of a man's head, and wield swords with six-foot blades."

Laskos flitted another smile, shrugging. "It's true, some few elephants can be taught to throw oversized darts and big rocks with a fair degree of consistent accuracy, but most cannot, and it is an utter waste of time—yours and theirs—to try to teach them the knack. As for the massive sword business, I suppose that it would work in battle, for a while, though as you've no doubt noted, it is the natural inclination of elephants to roll up and safeguard their precious and sensitive and vulnerable trunks in any time of danger.

"Gil Djohnz, there are two major purposes for elephants in warfare, if we disregard their frequent and most sensible roles as draught animals. One use of the two is to armor them heavily and use them to smash through formations of pikemen, spearmen or shield-walls; the other is to use them as moving platforms for dartmen or archers or slingers—fast-walk them along the enemy's front that the missile-men may bleed the enemy a bit and so soften them up just prior to one's own lines moving forward in the attack. All other maneuvers of elephants on the field of battle are but variants of these two basics.

"I'll willingly teach you and the others elephant warfare, but you must understand from the very onset that these beasts have some very definite limitations and a host of weaknesses and vulnerable points; in some ways, indeed, they're more delicate than horses.

"But first"—he abruptly stood up—"let us go outside and talk to your elephants, you and I."

Chapter V

The Mehseepolis to which *Thoheeks* Grahvos
returned from his brief campaign was a crowded,
bustling swirl of activity. More than merely adequate in
size to have for long and long been the capital and the
principal city of a double duchy, the ancient city was
proving to be simply too small to house and to office the
needs of a Council of noblemen ruling a vast, sprawling
land which was becoming known as the Consolidated
Duchies of Southern Ehleenoee. Everything and every
place within the grim circuit of walls was become or
becoming overcrowded, packed to the bursting seams,
with the heterogeneous host necessary to administrate
and to serve.

So heavy was the traffic wending up into and down
out of the city become that the tall, thick gates seldom
were closed anymore and the repairs and restrengthen-
ings of the drawbridge that spanned the deep gorge that
had for so long so protected the principal approach to
the ancient city had rendered it too weighty to anymore
be raised by the chains and windlasses, so it was now
permanently lowered.

That gorge, which had received the drainage of the
hilly city's sewers and drains since first the present city
had been built where once, in ancient times, had stood
only a stronghold, had with the present overpopulation
been metamorphosed into a stinking mess, an ever-
constant affront to eyes and nose, wherein vermin of
every sort fed and bred among the faeces, garbage and

slimy pools of wastewater and above which clouds of
noxious insects as thick as the nauseating miasma rose
up to greet everyone who crossed the bridge or walked
the walltops. Grahvos longed for the spring cloudbursts
that would flush the foetid cesspit down into the plain
and river.

The hordes of workmen—carpenters, joiners, stone-
masons and the like—added to the overcrowding but
were every bit as necessary as the *thoheeksee* themselves. The palace complex had been quickly outgrown,
and now the workmen were hard at work converting
and connecting onetime private homes and other nearby
buildings into a spreading, mazelike complex. In order
to render the space of the old citadel free of other
pressing uses, all activities and offices of a military
nature had been transferred out onto the lower plain
and into tents and thrown-together temporary buildings
making up an enclave between the spreading camps of
the army and the foot of the steep road that led up to the
city.

Of a day when the plants and shrubs of the palace
garden were showing off their first green leaf and flower
buds, in Nature's eons-old announcement of the new
growing season, called by men the spring, two men
sought an audience with the Council of *Thoheeksee*.
There was a vast disparity between these two—one
being a graybeard and the other a far younger man,
almost a stripling—but at one and the same time, it was
obvious to any who saw them that they were very closely
related by blood. The old man was the tallest of the
pair—about six feet from soles to pate; his physique was
big-boned and still looked very powerful, with the scars
indicative of a proven, veteran warrior. A few of these
scars looked to be fairly new.

Lord Eraldos of Elsahpolis, one of the assistant
chamberlains and harried to distraction that day, knew
that he had seen the old man or someone very much like
him before, but he could not just then place the who or

the where or the when, and the petitioner flatly refused
to state his name or his rank, only stating that he was a
nobleman who had been most unjustly treated and he
was, therefore, seeking redress of this new government,
the Council of *Thoheeksee*. The only other words he
deigned to send in to Council were exceedingly cryptic,
to Eraldos' way of thinking.

"Ask the present lord of Hwailehpolis if he now
recalls aught of a stallion, a dead man's sword and a bag
of gold."

But then code words and phrases were fairly common
(though less so at this than at certain other courts Lord
Eraldos had served in his lifetime, he was happy to say),
so he dutifully jotted it down on the prompting pad he
kept in his mind and then continued with seemingly
endless routines. With one occurrence and another,
however, it was not for some two hours that he remembered to pad around the table to the mentioned
thoheeks and diffidently put to him this singularly odd
question, to then be scared nearly out of his wits.

Thoheeks Vikos of Hwailehpolis sent his heavy chair
crashing over as he leaped to his feet and clamped his
big, hard hands on both the startled assistant chamberlain's shoulders with crushing force.

"Where is this man, Eraldos?" he demanded. "What
would you estimate his age? Did he come alone of his
own will or did others bring him?"

When he did not get an immediate answer, *Thoheeks*
Vikos' eyes flashed fire and he shook the chamberlain as
a terrier shakes a rat. "Well? Well, man, will you
answer me?"

Lord Eraldos' lips moved but no sounds emerged. As
Vikos set himself to another round of shaking,
Thoheeks Portos gripped his forearm, admonishing,
"Have done, Vikos, have done! Between shaking and
terror, you've rendered the poor man dumb with
fright."

When the trembling functionary had scuttled out of
the chamber to fetch back the petitioner, Vikos made to

explain his atypical actions to his peers at the council table. "It was after that gory debacle at Ahrbah-kootchee, in the early days of the war against Hyamos' son, Prince Rahndos. I had fought through all of that black day as an ensign in my late elder brother's troop of heavy horse, and in the wake of the main army's rout by the war-elephants, I and full many another poor nobleman found myself unhorsed, disarmed and hunted like some wild and desperate beast through the swamps of the bottomlands.

"Near to dusk, I was wading across a broad pool when I heard yet again the crashing of brush and the shouts of horsemen. They sounded almost atop me, so I broke off a long, hollow reed and went under the water, as I had had to do right many times that terrifying day. But this time I knew that if they came at all close, I was done for; unlike all the other pools that had hidden me, the water of this one was clear to the sandy bottom, nor was its deepest part very deep, perhaps three feet, perhaps less.

"All at once, as I fought to hold myself underwater, I became aware that a man had ridden into that pool; the legs of his horse loomed close to my body, and, not liking the idea of a lance pinning me to the bottom to gasp out my life there, I resignedly surfaced, that I might at least die with air in my lungs. I looked up into the eyes of none other than *Komees* Pahvlos Feelohpoh-lehmos himself!

"In a voice pitched so low that even I could but barely hear, he growled, 'Keep down, damn fool boy! Keep down, I say, else I'll have to slay you.'

"Then he shouted to his troopers who were riding nearer, 'You men search that thick brush up there where the creek is narrow and murky. This pool here is clear as fine crystal; nothing to be seen in it save fish and crayfish. I'll give my stallion a drink of it, then ride up and join you.'

"Then the *komees* deliberately set his horse to roiling the bed of that pool with its hooves, while he did the same with the butt of his lance, stirring up sediments and clouding the water. He dropped upon me a sheathed, bejeweled sword, and when I once more brought my face up to where I could see, he dropped a small, heavy bag with a crest embossed in the soft leather.

"He said then, 'Your late father was my battle companion of yore, young Vikos, and after this sad day, you may well be the last living man of his loins. So there is a bit of gold and a good sword taken off the body of a dead man. Stop moving about blindly and go to ground until it's full dark, then head northwest. What's left of Zastros' rebel army is withdrawing southeast, and we'll be pursuing them. If you can make it up to Iron Mountain, you'll be safe with your cousins there. And the next time you choose a warleader, try to choose one who owns at least a fighting chance to win, eh? God keep you now, my boy.' Then he rode through the pool and led his men away through the swamp."

Thoheeks Grahvos nodded. "Yes, Vikos, it sounds exactly of a piece with all else I know of the man. For all of his personal ferocity and his expertise in the leading of armies and the waging of wars for the three kings he served during his lengthy career, still was he ever noted to be just and, when it was possible, merciful to his defeated enemies.

"Strange, I'd just assumed him to be dead, legally murdered by Fahrkos or Zastros, as were the most of his peers. It is indeed good to know that at least one of the better sort survived the long bloodletting. Who was his overlord, anyway? Does anyone here recall? If he'll take the oaths, I can't think of anybody who would make us a better *thoheeks* then *Strahteegos* Pahvlos the Warlike."

"And so," concluded old *Komees* Pahvlos, "when it was become clear to me that these usurping scum, these bareborn squatters, were all determined to not only deny young Ahramos here his lawful patrimony, but to take his very life as well, were they granted the opportunity, I knew that far stronger measures were required, my lords."

He sighed and shook his show-white head. "Could but a single man do it alone, it were done already. Old I assuredly am—close on to seventy years old—but still am I a warrior fit for the battle line, and my good sword is yet to become a stranger to my hand. But only a strong, disciplined, well-led force will be able to dislodge that foul kakistocracy that presently holds Ahramos' principal city and controls his rightful lands, and due to reverses, I no longer own the wherewithal to hire on men, to equip and mount and supply them with even the bare necessities of warfare.

"The two of us, Ahramos and I, were able to fight our way out of both the palace and the city, but far more than a mere two swordsmen will be required to hack a way back in and see justice done the now-dispossessed son and heir of the late *thoheeks*. This is why I come."

"I would wager pure gold, *Strahteegos Komees* Pahvlos," said *Thoheeks* Grahvos thoughtfully, pinching his chin between his thumb and forefinger, "that nothing—neither adversity nor your venerable age—has robbed you of a whit of your old and rare abilities to lead armies, plan winning battles and improvise stunning tactics on the spur of the moment any more than those same forces have taken away your skills of swinging sharp steel hard and true.

"I'll be candid: I had meant to hear you out, then ask you to take oaths to the Council and the Confederation and then confirm you the lord of one of the still-vacant *thoheekseeahnee*, for I trow you'd make a better *thoheeks* than many another candidate for that rank. I still mean to see you so installed, too.

"But now, fully aware of how vital you still are and how great is our need, I have in mind a better, far more useful task for you, at present."

* * *

Pawl Vawn, Chief of Vawn, sat at a table in the camp quarters of Sub-*strahteegos* Tomos Gonsalos; with them around the scraps of the just-eaten meal sat Captain Guhsz Hehluh and Captain *Thoheeks* Portos.

As he filled his cup with the honey wine and passed the decanter on to Portos, the Horseclans commander demanded, "If this Pahvlos is such a slambang *strahteegos* and all, Portos, how come he didn't tromp you all proper for his king and end it all before it got started?"

"Oh, he did, he assuredly did, my good Pawl," replied Portos in his grave voice, "in the beginning, years ago. I was there, I was a part of that rebel army then, I and my first squadron of horse, and I am here to tell you that he thoroughly trounced us. He nibbled off all the cavalry and the light troops, then smashed the main force with a charge of his war-elephants and his heavy horse, crushed it like a beetle, virtually extirpated a force that had begun the day a third again larger than his own and had drawn itself up on the best stretch of ground with the most natural assets available in that part of the country.

"It required years of effort, after that, and the then-unknown help of the Witchmen to reassemble an army for Zastros to lead against *Strahteegos Komees* Pahvlos Feelohpohlehmos. That, in the end, we did not have to face him again was an inestimable relief to many a one of us, believe me, my friend."

"Well, why didn't you?" asked Pawl Vawn.

Portos shrugged, toying with his winecup. "By that time, all of the ancient royal line was become extinct and *Thoheeks* Fahrkos, who seized the crown and the capital, had dismissed the *strahteegohee*, as they all were hostile toward him. Most of the royal army as then remained had chosen that point to march away with their officers, so that all Fahrkos had when we brought him to bay was his own skimpy personal warband."

"Well, even so," put in Freefighter Captain Guhsz

Hehluh, as he doodled with the tip of a calloused forefinger in and around a pool of spilled wine, "before I'm
going to put me and my Keebai boys under the orders of
some whitebearded doddard, I'll know a bit more about
him, if you please . . . and even if you don't, comes to
that.

"You Kindred and Ehleenee, you can do what you
wants, but if I mislike the sound or the smell of thishere
Count Pahvlos, why me and mine, we'll just shoulder
our pikes and hike back up north to Kehnooryos
Atheenahs and I'll tell High Lord Milo to find us some
other fights or sell us our contract back."

But within the space of bare days, Captain Guhsz
Hehluh was trumpeting the praises of the newly
appointed Grand *Strahteegos* of the Confederated
Thoheekseeahnee of Southern Ehleenohee. *Komees*
Pahvlos and his entourage had ridden out and found the
Freefighter pikemen at drill. For almost an hour, he sat
his stamping, tail-swishing horse beside Hehluh's in the
hot sun, swatting at flies and knowledgeably discussing
the inherent strengths and weaknesses of pike
formations and the proper marshaling of infantry. At
length, Pahvlos had actually dismounted and hunkered
down in the dust of the drill field to sketch with a horny
finger the initial positions and movements of an
intricate maneuver.

"I'd been led to believe he was lots older than he
actually is," Hehluh declared to his officers. "He's
really not that much older than me, and he's not one of
these hidebound bastards that so many Ehleenees are,
either. He flat knows the art of war, by damn! Hell,
after only the one meeting, I've already learned things
from that man."

The Freefighter captain drained off the dregs of his
mug and said, "Frahnzwah, you go find us some more
beer or cider or wine to drink. The rest of you, clear off
the top of this table and I'll show you some of the things
our new Grand *Strahteegos* showed me. Never can tell

when I might not be around and one of you may have to take over in the middle of a battle."

After he had watched and evaluated the heterogeneous units which Council had assembled and called its army, Pahvlos closeted himself with Tomos Gonsalos. To begin, he said, "It's basically a good unit you command here, Lord Tomos, these northern troops. I'd take you on with them just as they are now were you not a mite shy of infantry and a mite oversupplied with cavalry for good balance. In order to rectify the deficiency, I'll be brigading your pikemen—Captain Hehluh's unit—with two more regiments of equal size—all veterans, too, no grass-green peasants and gutter-scrapings more accustomed to pushing plows and brooms than pikes.

"I'm of the opinion that both you and Hehluh will get along well with Lord Captain Bizahros, who commands the reorganized Eighth Foot, from the outset; however, Captain Ahzprinos, leader of the Fifth Foot, also reorganized, is another dish of beans entirely.

"Please understand me, Lord Tomos, Captain *Vahrohnos* Ahzprinos is a superlative warrior and a fine commander in all ways, else he would not be serving under me in any capacity. But he also is loud, brash, bragadacious and sometimes overbearing to the point of real arrogance. Nonetheless, I can get along with him and I expect my subordinates to do so too."

And so, in the ensuing weeks that stretched into months, the Confederation troops and the two regiments of once-royal foot of the Kingdom of Southern Ehleenohee drilled and marched, drilled and marched, shouldered pikes, grounded pikes, presented pikes at various heights and angles, sloped pikes. They drilled by squad, by file, by platoon, by company. The regiments formed column, they formed lines of battle of all descriptions, from schiltron to porcupine, propelled always by the roll of the drum and the hoarse, savage shouts of their officers and sergeants. When felt to be

ready, they were assembled as brigade in battalion-front
line-of-battle and put through even more and more
intricate drills under the critical eye of Grand
Strahteegos Komees Pahvlos the Warlike himself.

Old Pahvlos had sent, early on, messengers to old
friends in the far western lands, requesting that they
send fully war-trained elephants, *feelahksee* and
elephant-wise officers, but as yet none of the messengers
had returned and no elephants had arrived; therefore,
he still was perforce employing the three cows that had
been there when he first arrived and took over the army.

Of course, these three were not those huge, looming
bull elephants to which he was accustomed and which
now were—hopefully—on the march from their western
breeding and training grounds, but rather the smaller,
usually tuskless beasts that his previous armies always
had used only for draught purposes. That the old man
had consented to their use in battle at all was a
testament to the truly extraordinary control of them
exercised by their Horseclans *feelahksee*, Captain of
Elephants Gil Djohnz and the other two northern barbarians.

The old officer had been astounded at his witnessing
of the first drill he ordered for the elephants, that he
might judge their degrees of capability. Before his
wondering eyes, the three cows rendered performances
such as he never before had seen in all his many years of
serving with and commanding elephant-equipped
armies. Certain of his staff, indeed, had been set to
mumbling darkly of sorcery and barbarian witchcraft
until he dressed them down in disgust at their un-
sophisticated superstition.

Still not quite certain that he actually believed that
this lot come from off the Sea of Grass by way of
Kehnooryos Ehlahs really were capable of mind-reading
and telepathy with animals, nonetheless, the *komees*
would freely admit that he was greatly impressed with
the Horseclansmen in general, for it had never before

been his pleasure to own the services of so splendid and versatile a mounted force as the small squadron of armored horse-archers commanded by Captain Chief Pawl Vawn of Vawn.

Traditionally, Southern Kingdom horse had come in three varieties only—the heavy horsemen who were fully armored, usually noblemen or gentlemen and their personal retainers, and fought with sword or axe or similar edge weapons; light horsemen or lancers, who wore half-armor, carried lances and sabers, and rode smaller, lighter, faster and more nimble horses; and irregular cavalry, who were mostly hired barbarians from the borderlands, who equipped, armed and mounted themselves and had often proven far from effective and dependable, save as horse-archers operating from a distance only.

But he was assured by Tomos Gonsalos and by his own instinctual judgments that these Horseclansmen had been, were and would be both dependable and murderously efficient. True, their horses were not so striking of build as those of the traditional heavy horse, but neither were they as modest of proportions as those of the light horse, either. Both Gonsalos and Hehluh—who had served both with and against these Horseclans cavalry—averred that the short, slight men were noted for both their uncanny accuracy with their short, powerful bows and their ferocity in breast-to-breast encounters with their broad, heavy sabers, their axes and their spears.

Due to the horse sizes and the amount of armor that the Horseclansmen wore, Pahvlos classed them in his mind as medium-heavy horse. And it comforted his mind no little that he now possessed a reliable mounted force that could both lay down a dense and accurate loosing of arrows, then case their bows, draw their steel and deliver a hard, effective charge against whatever unit their arrow-rain had weakened.

After talking with various of the older Horseclans

warriors and observing them for some weeks, Pahvlos
thought he could understand much of how these men
and their forefathers had so readily rolled over the
armies of Kehnooryos Ehlahs, the Kingdom of Karaleenos, assorted barbarian principalities of the farther
north and numerous tribes of mountain barbarians.

As he thought on his mounted troops, Pahvlos could
not consider the reinforced squadron of Captain
Thoheeks Portos just a normal unit of lancers, either.
Equipped and mounted as they all were, they were
become, to the old *strahteegos'* way of thinking, true
heavy horse, and he utilized them as such, requesting
and eventually receiving of the Council a squadron of
old-fashioned Ehleen light-horse lancers to assume the
scouting, flank-guarding and messenger functions of
the traditional light-horse usage.

To Portos' questions regarding the reassignment of
functions of his squadron, Pahvlos replied, "My lord
Thoheeks, in my mind, if you dress man up in steel
helmet, thigh-length hauberk, mail gauntlets and steel-
splinted boots, arm him with lance, saber, light axe and
a long shield, then put him up on a sixteen- or seven-
teen-hand courser all armored with steel and boiled
leather, then that man is no longer a mere lancer. He is
become at the very least a medium-heavy horseman.
That force you continue to call lancers differ from Lord
Pawl Vawn's force only in that his are equipped with
bows rather than lances and carry round targes instead
of horseman's shields."

Although inordinately pleased with all of his cavalry,
both the native and the barbarian, *Komees* Pahvlos
found himself to be not quite certain just what to make
of or do with the most singular pikemen of Captain
Guhsz Hehluh.

Unless they chanced to be the picked foot-guards of a
king or of some other high, powerful, wealthy nobleman, Southern Kingdom pikemen simply were not and
had never ever been armored, save for a light cap of

stiffened leather and narrow strips of iron, a thick jack
of studded leather and a pair of leather gauntlets that in
some rare instances had been sewn with metal rings, and
only the steadier, more experienced and more
dependable front ranks were provided with a body-
shield to be erected before them where they knelt or
crouched to angle their pikes. And, also traditionally,
they had always died in droves in almost all battles
whenever push came to shove, and this had always been
expected.

But such was not so in the cases of the big, fair-
skinned, thick-thewed barbarians commanded by
Captain Hehluh. Only the cheek-guards and chin-slings
of their helmets were of leather; all of the rest—the
crown-bowls, the segmented nape-guards, the adjustable bar-nasals—were of good-quality steel. Their burly
bodies were protected to the waist and their bulging
arms to a bit below the elbow by padded jacks of canvas
to which had been riveted overlapping scales of steel.
Both their high-cuffed leather gauntlets and their canvas
kilts were thickly sewn with metal rings, and, below
steel-plate knee-cops, their shins were protected by
splint armor riveted to the legs of their boots.

Moreover, each and every one of these singular
pikemen bore a slightly outbowed rectangular shield
near two feet wide and about twice that length. On
command, each man could quickly unsling that shield,
fit it to his arm and raise it above his head in such a way
as to over- and underlap those about him and thus
provide a covering that would turn an arrowstorm as
easily as a roof of baked-clay tiles turned a rainstorm.

Nor were these the only differences in the arming and
equipage of the barbarian foot and those of the onetime
Southern Kingdom. Aside from his fifteen-foot pike,
your traditional pikeman bore no weapons other than a
single-edged knife that was, in practice, used mostly for
eating purposes. In contrast to this, not a one of
Captain Hehluh's pikemen but also bore a heavy

double-edged sword that was almost two feet in its sharp-pointed steel blade. Other weapons and the numbers of them seemed to be a matter of personal choice; knives, dirks and daggers of various lengths and sizes were carried, sometimes even short-hafted axes or cleavers, such as could be utilized as tools, hand weapons or missiles.

Even their pikes were different. Ehleen pikes ran thirteen to fifteen feet in the haft, the steel point usually being six to eight inches long, narrow and of a triangular or a square cross-section; ferrules were never of iron or steel, rarely of brass, usually of horn. The pikes of Hehluh's men, however, were much longer to begin—some eighteen feet in the ashwood haft—with a reinforced blade point that was single-edged (so being capable of being used to cut the bridles of riders, for one thing) and a foot or more long, with iron-strip barding that was riveted along the haft from the base of the point for a good two feet to prevent swords and axes lopping off pikepoints. Ferrules were of wrought iron and nearly as long as the points; however, the overall weight thus added to the weapon was compensated for somewhat by the added balance imparted and by the availability of a last-ditch weapon to be afforded the pikeman by reversing his haft and making use of the blunt iron point.

Burdened as they thus were, Grand *Strahteegos Komees* Pahvlos had at the outset entertained fully understandable doubts that these overprotected, overequipped, overarmed pikemen would be capable of maintaining the needful pace on the march or in a broad-front pike charge; but those doubts had evaporated after he had put them to it. Those doubts had evaporated to be replaced in his open mind with an intensely troubling set of other doubts.

These new doubts began to breed in him changes of his formerly rock-hard opinions. He began to wonder just why so many generations of his forebears had care-

lessly, needlessly sacrificed so many other generations
of common pikemen with the excuse—now proven
patently false—that proper armor and secondary
weapons would significantly decrease mobility. Moreover, Captain Bizahros agreed with him and had
initiated formal requests for at least basic pieces of
armor, real helmets and shortswords for his reorganized
Fifth Foot. On the other hand, Captain Ahzprinos did
not agree with Pahvlos—flatly, loudly, unequivocally
and at very great length citing all of the old, traditional
arguments as well as some new-thought ones of his own.

Slowly, the force began to become a true, almost
complete, field army as certain specialist units were
assembled, trained or hired on. One of Council's
traveling recruiters found and sent marching back to
Mehseepolis two battalions of light infantry—one of
dartmen, one of expert slingers equipped with powerful
pole slings. *Eeahtrohsee* came with their ambulance
wagons, bandages, little sharp knives, bone saws and
ointments. Artificier and pioneer units were organized
and assigned and fully equipped. An experienced
quartermaster officer was found and—miracle of
miracles for his breed—proved out to be a relatively
honest man! They all trickled in—the cooks, the
butchers, the smiths, the farriers, the wagoneers and
muleskinners, the herders, the bakers and all of them
with their assistants and/or apprentices and/or servants
and/or slaves. And still no war-elephants arrived.

Under the overall supervision of the Grand
Strahteegos and his new quartermaster, vast mountains
of supplies began to be amassed and needed to be placed
under guard in such manner as to prevent or retard
possible spoilage or damage or pilferage. But there was
no trace or word regarding elephants from the west.

A vast herd of cattle—rations on the hoof—now
grazed around and about the forming army of the permanent camp, along with steadily increasing numbers of
horses and mules. When the treasury ran low, *Thoheeks*

Sitheeros and *Thoheeks* Grahvos contributed more
ounces of gold for the common weal. But not even then
did more elephants arrive, nor would Sitheeros part
with any more of his own small herd.

The army drilled, drilled and drilled some more.
Long, hot, sweaty route marches shook down the units
and accustomed them to reforming at a moment's
notice from the column to a whole plethora of line-of-
battle formations. Under the Grand *Strahteegos'* critical
eye and patient dedication, the infantry—the three
regiments of pikemen and the two of light foot—and the
cavalry—the reinforced squadron of heavy horse, the
medium-heavy horse-archers and the half-squadron of
light horse lancers—began to coalesce and behave and
appear to be a whole rather than several parts. But even
still, the three elephant cows, astounding as their
performances of intricate maneuvers were, were the
only probiscideans available for the army's use.

At last, feeling that he had waited and had kept his
army waiting quite long enough for the pachyderms,
Pahvlos sought audience with the Council of
Thoheeksee and announced that he intended to start the
campaign immediately, with only the three cow
elephants.

"Look you, my lords," he had said, "the city that is
our objective does not lie any short distance away from
Mehseepolis, so the army is going to be on the march for
some weeks, and I would much prefer a march in dust to
a march in rain and mud. The weather at this time of
year has always been rather dry, but if we delay for
much longer, the autumn rains will commence. In all
other ways than war-elephants, our army is ready,
honed to a fine edge, as it sits. We possess enough
supplies, weapons, transport and mounts for about
three months of campaigning, which should be enough,
in my considered judgment."

"Not if you get tied down besieging the place, it
won't!" growled *Thoheeks* Bahos, in his contrabass

rumble. "What will you do then? Forage, live off the land and despoil young Ahramos' heritage? Or send back to us for more supplies to be bought with money we don't have?"

"I have very strong doubts that it will ever come to a siege, my lord *Thoheeks*," replied Pahvlos. "That precious pack are squatting on the lands and in the city, at best, holding them by brute force, with little popular support, if any; they would not dare to shut themselves up within a city filled with citizens who all hate and fear them. No, they'll come to battle, most likely, quite soon after I arrive with the army, of that I am certain."

Thoheeks Penendos of Makopolis, barely twenty years of age, spoke up. "In your considered judgment you believe," he said in a cold, mocking tone. "In other words, *Strahteegos*, what you are saying is that you want us to approvingly seal your traipsing off with the bulk of our effectives and thousands of *thrahkmehee* worth of supplies and equipment on your unsupported, unsubstantiated word, isn't that it?"

Before Pahvlos could frame an answer, *Thoheeks* Vikos burst out, "Wipe the mother's milk off your mouth before you so bespeak and question a man who was marshaling armies and leading them to victories while your father still was shitting his swaddlings! What manner of supercilious young puppy has Council raised up in you, Lord Penendos?"

"Puppy, am I? Dog, am I?" shouted the offended man, pulling a hideaway dagger from someplace in his clothing and lunging across the breadth of the table at Lord Vikos. "I'll make worm meat of you, you *pooeesos* of turd-eating boar hogs!"

It did not go far, of course, for the most of Council were warriors, first and foremost. Vikos tumbled back from the slender, winking blade, regained his feet and secured a good grip on the younger man's wrist with one hand, applying painful pressure to force him to drop the weapon. Meanwhile, *Thoheeks* Bahos hurled his massive bulk atop the would-be killer's lighter and more slender body, effectively pinning him in place to the tabletop. Gasping foul curses, Penendos used his free hand to draw out another hidden dagger, only to have that wrist secured by *Thoheeks* Sitheeros well before he could bring it into any dangerous proximity to either Vikos or Bahos.

"Gentlemen, *gentlemen, GENTLEMEN*!" roared *Thoheeks* Grahvos with a volume that rattled the goblets and crystal decanters on the sideboard. "Stop it this instant! Stop it, I say, else I'll call for the guards and give you all pause to cool off and reflect the error of your ways in a dank, dark cell down belowstairs.

"Bahos, get off that fool's back before you collapse the table. You and Sitheeros search him thoroughly and take any more sharp toys you find on his person, then put him back in his chair. And if he makes to rise again, you'll both know just what to do, eh?"

"My lords," he said finally in a harsh voice, "are we all here an aggregation of civilized, orderly inheritors of our ancient Ehleen culture? After the last few minutes, a non-Ehleen would doubt such, deeming us but another lot of brawling, blood-mad barbarians or overgrown and ill-reared children, which is the same thing, really."

Turning to Pahvlos, who still was seated, he bowed low and said, "My lord *Strahteegos Komees*, please accept my apology and that of the Council of the Confederated *Thoheekseeahnee*. Please believe me when I say that such regrettable behavior as that to which you have just, unfortunately, been witness is not the usual way in which Council meets and conducts business."

Sensing that an answer might be embarrassing to Grahvos and certain of the others and was not expected, anyway, Pahvlos gravely and slowly nodded his head, once, in acknowledgment of Grahvos' formal courtesy.

Then, addressed again the men ranged along the sides of the table, Grahvos' voice lost any hint of warmth. "Lord Penendos, you are come of good stock, out of

loins of decent, honorable noblemen. You've
dishonored both yourself and the memory of your
forebears, this day, here. One might think from your
disregard of Council's rule that all weapons must be
deposited upon that table there by the door before
business commences and from your willful weaponed
attack upon the person of a peer you knew to be
unarmed that you were bred in the mountain hut of
some barbarian or in a tent out on the Sea of Grass.

"You owe apologies both to the lord *strahteegos* and
to *Thoheeks* Vikos. Since all your misdeeds were said
and done before Council, then these apologies must be
delivered before Council, also. Let us see if you can
speak more like a gentleman than you act."

He maintained his fixed stare until *Thoheeks*
Penendos dropped his gaze to his shaking hands held in
his lap. Then the elder man turned to stare just as hard
at Vikos. "Lord Vikos, you owe an apology to Lord
Penendos. You should not have named him dog or
spoken so harshly to him. Remember, he is too young to
personally recall much of the exploits of *Strahteegos
Komees* Pahvlos. And although his manner was most
assuredly and needlessly insulting, his question was
quite proper from one whose memories hold no
knowledge of the reputation, the many victories of Lord
Pahvlos. We will expect that apology to be delivered
before Council, too.

"But before we get to those matters, I think that we
should vote on the quite reasonable request of the lord
strahteegos. I vote yes."

Chapter VI

Mainahkos Klehpteekos and Ahreekos Krehohpoleeos had risen fast and high from their origin as common irregular troopers in the first, almost extripated army of then-*Thoheeks* Zastros. That both men were incredibly savage and completely unprincipled had helped them to so rise, that they owned an ability to organize and lead men like themselves and were often inordinately lucky had helped even more.

During the long years of howling chaos in the Kingdom of the Southern Ehleenohee, they and their heterogeneous packs of deserters, banditti, unhung criminals, shanghaied peasants, city gutter scum and stray psychopaths had signed on as mercenary forces to quite a few warbands of the battling lords. Occasionally, they had actually given the services for which they had been paid, but more often they either had deserted en masse or had turned their coats at a crucial point of a battle, especially so if such ongoing conflict showed signs of being a close contest.

At length, so odious had their well-earned reputation become that no lord or city—no matter how desperate—throughout the length and breadth of the sundered realm would even consider hiring them on in any capacity. At that point, they proceeded to follow their natural inclinations, becoming out-and-out predatory ruffians, the leaders and their lawless followers at war against all the world.

Then, at long last, *Thoheeks* Zastros returned from

his lengthy period of exile in the demon-haunted depths of the deadly swamps that surrounded and guarded the sinister Witch Kingdom. He brought with him a witch-wife from that land of dragons, magicians and sorcerers and marched back and forth across the lands, raising as he went an army much larger than the one he had led to defeat, years before, on the bloodsoaked field of Ahrbahkootchee.

With King Fahrkos and all his family dead in their gore in his blazing palace, the returned Zastros had had himself declared High King—a new title for the Kingdom of the Southern Ehleenohee—and crowned, then his forces had begun to scour the lands for warriors and men of the proper ages and degrees of soundness to serve in the huge army he was forming for the invasion of the Kingdom of Karaleenos and points farther north. At length, he led out his half-million and more on a path of supposed glory that would lead finally to a muddy, unmarked grave on the banks of the Lumbuh River for him and no grave at all for the bodies of the untold thousands of men and animals the bones of which would litter his line of march.

With the new High King, all of the nobility of warring age and a large percentage of both city and rural commoners on the road of conquest behind the Green Dragon Banner, Captains Mainahkos and Ahreekos had found themselves in a pigs' paradise. Now they were able to prey not only on travelers and villages, unwalled towns and isolated holds, but on walled towns and smaller cities, as well.

They descended upon these now all but defenseless smaller cities like a pack of starving winter wolves upon so many sheepfolds; they behaved in their usual fashion—conduct that might have been called bestial, save that it would have shamed any wild beast. With all the onetime garrisons gone north with High King Zastros, the old men, women, boys and assorted cripples seldom held out behind their walls and gates for

long, and when scaled by the forces of the bandit warlords, those walls shortly enclosed a slice of veriest hell
on earth for all who had dwelt therein.

No female above the age of six was safe from the lusts
of the marauders, nor did the perverts spare boys. The
elderly and the very youngest were generally cut down at
the beginning of an intaking with callous strokes of
blades and stabbings of spears, and thus were they the
luckier citizens, for it was after the first flush of
bloodthirst was sated that the true horrors commenced.

After all visible wealth and goods had been
plundered, then were the luckless inhabitants savagely
tortured to extract possible hiding places of more loot,
and torture for definite purpose often led to torture,
maimings and indescribable mutilations for no purpose
at all save the satisfaction of causing agony and hearing
screams and pleas. Some of the pack delighted in such
atrocious obscenities as forcing hapless sufferers to
imbibe of unholy broths seethed of portions of their
own bodies or those of spouses and children. Brutal
men would gouge out eyes, rip out tongues, slice off
breasts and sexual organs, noses and ears and lips,
smash out teeth, sever leg tendons, then leave the
bloody, croaking, flopping things to roast in the blazing
ruins of their homes.

Of a day, however, a broken nobleman who had
joined the bandit army to avoid starvation had words
with Mainahkos and Ahreekos and slowly convinced
them of the sagacity of those words. For all that they
and most of their followers were now become wealthy
beyond their former wildest dreams of avarice, each
succeeding victory had cost and was costing them at
least a few men, while men of fighting age or strength or
inclination were become almost as precious as emeralds
or rubies in this land stripped of warrior stock by High
King Zastros' strenuous impressments and recruitings
atop the civil war and its years of carnage. Moreover,
the few scattered survivors of witnesses to the intakings

and occupations and burnings of the stinking charnel
houses that the two warlords and their band had made
of every city that had fallen to them had moved fast and
spread the terrible word far and wide. Now, every
walled enclosure within weeks of marching time had
been forewarned and was doing everything possible to
strengthen its existing defenses and had resolutely put
aside any previous thoughts of trying to deal with the
marauders on any near-peaceful basis.

So, although it went hard against the grain, the two
warlords had begun to rein in their savages and even
resist their own natural impulses and inclinations somewhat. They began to deal gently—gently by their
personal lights, of course—with the inhabitants of any
place that opened the gates without a fight or showed a
willingness to treat.

Mainahkos and Ahreekos even took it upon themselves to move against and either recruit or wipe out
numerous smaller bands of their own ilk lurking about
the countrysides. Then they began to recruit from the
tiny garrisons remaining in a few of the larger walled
towns and the smaller cities. Slowly, their howling pack
of human predators began to metamorphose into a real,
more or less organized, savagely disciplined army.

Therefore, by that day, now three years in the past,
that they had appeared under the walls of the ducal city
of Kahlkopolis—the one-time seat of the *Thoheeksee* of
Kahlkos—the few straggling hundreds of ill-equipped,
sketchily armed bandits that they had been in the
beginning were become an impressive and very threatening sight indeed.

All classes of infantry marched in the ranks, fully
armed and equipped. Heavy cavalry rode at head and
tail of that column, with light cavalry on the flanks and
van and riding close guard on the baggage train and the
awesome siege engines, the large remuda and the beef
herd. Only elephants were lacking, and this deficiency
was partially alleviated through the use of old-fashioned
war-carts as shock weapons and archery platforms—the

stout, reinforced cart bodies with scythe blades set in the
wheel hubs, the big mules all hung with mail, the postillions fully armored having proved quite effective at the
tasks of harrying and smashing in infantry lines for long
years before the elephants had been trained for warfare.

The last *Thoheeks* of Kahlkos, one Klawdos, was by
then nearly a decade dead, a casualty of the civil war.
His wife and young son had disappeared during disturbances shortly after his demise, and the ducal city
was just then being held by a distant cousin of the
mostly extinct ancient line. The man was a bastard, with
scant claim to any scintilla of noble heritage and even
less to military experience.

Therefore, when this poseur ordered the gates of the
city to be slammed shut and barred, the walls to be
manned by the pitifully few men he owned to defend
them, those still living of the ducal council of advisers
did the only reasonable thing—they murdered him and
left the city open to the overwhelming force outside.

Since then, Mainahkos had been *thoheeks* in all save
only name; he had seen to it that that ducal council had
all quickly followed their victim into death, by one
means or another. He had been teetering upon the very
verge of declaring himself *Thoheeks* Mainahkos
Klehftikos of the Duchy of Klehftikos and the City of
Klehftikopolis (for, as he and his men had become at
least marginally "respectable," he had adopted the new
surname, and now no man who did not desire a messy,
agonizing and brutally protracted demise ever recalled
aloud the powerful warlord's original cognomen,
Klehpteekos—"the Thief", and riding to Mehseepolis
to demand legal confirmation of his title and lands of
the council of the Consolidated *Thoheekseeahnee*.

He and Ahreekos had both chanced to be out of the
city when the boy, son he claimed of *Thoheeks*
Klawdos, came nosing around, in company with some
tall, arrogant dotard. But they had both been gone
beyond recall by the time the would-be *thoheeks* had
returned, and he had had the fools who had allowed

their escape to be flayed alive and then rolled in salt for
their inordinate stupidity; those tanned skins still hung
in prominent places on the walls of his hall of audience,
a silent, savage, ever-present warning to his followers.

On a summer's day, Mainahkos sat at meat with his
principal officer-advisers and his longtime partner.
Ahreekos had never bothered to change his cognomen,
still reveling in being known as "The Butcher,"
although he was become so fat that he no longer did or
could do much fighting of any nature. The topic of the
discussion around that table was that army which they
had been warned was marching upon them from
Mehseepolis, in the east-southeast.

In answer to a query directed at him by Mainahkos,
the heavy cavalry commander, one Stehrgiahnos—who
had been born and reared the heir of a *vahrohnos*,
though his father had fallen at Ahrbahkootchee and
Stehrgiahnos himself had forfeited title, lands and
nearly life itself in an ill-timed rebellion against King
Fahrkos, the failure of which had seen him declared
outlaw and a distant cousin confirmed to all that which
had been his—set down his goblet and patted dry his
lips, moustaches and beard before saying somewhat
cautiously, "My lord, it might be as well to at least essay
a meeting with the senior officers of this army. After all,
my lord's claim to this city and *thoheekseeahn* should be
as good as that any other might make, for he has been a
good lord since he has held the city and lands, and,
although not related to the ancient but now probably
extinct house, he does own the support of at least some
of the people of Kahlk—ahh, that is to say, of
Klehftikos."

Mainahkos frowned, sniffed, sneezed and wiped his
nose on the wine-and-food-spotted sleeve of his fine
linen shirt, considering the suggestion.

Ahreekos shoved aside what little was left of the
whole suckling pig on which he had feasted, drained off
a half-liter mug of beer, belched thunderously twice,

broke wind just as thunderously, then nodded his agreement with the cavalry officer, giving no more thought to
his grease-glazed beard than he did to the flies that
crawled on and in it and buzzed about his face.

"Stehrgiahnos, he's right, you know, Mainahkos.
From whatall my scouts done told me, that army
a-coming against us ain't one like I'd of cared to face
three, four years ago, when we was at full stren'th. And
they got them elephants, too. My boys see'd three of the
critters, and you know fucking good and well it's gotta
be more of them.

"Look, why don't we send out Stehrgiahnos here and
a couple more fellers of his stripe and let them palaver
with the *strahteegos* of that army some, huh? Ain't no
fucking thing to be lost by that, is it?"

Pausing briefly to lift a bulging buttock and again
break wind, he then continued, "Look, Mainahkos, old
Thoheeks Grahvos and them over there in Mehseepolis
is making new *thoheeksee* and *komeesee* and
vahrohnosee and *opokomeesee* right and left and up
and down all over the place, I hear tell, and like
Stehrgiahnos just done said, you got you about as good
a claim as anybody's got to thishere city and duchy.
Hell, your claim's a fucking lot better nor most, you're
sitting in it, holding it, and you been doing it for three
fucking years, too.

"So it could be, when you look hard at ever'thing, if
you allow as how you'll stand ahind *Thoheeks* Grahvos
and his Council and all them, won't be no battle or war
at all and you'll wind up as the real, legal *thoheeks*. And
if ever'thing don't work out, we can always fight after
we done talking."

Mainahkos sat picking between his discolored teeth
with a cracked and very filthy thumbnail for a while, his
gaze fixed on a blue fly that had wandered into a dollop
of hot-pepper sauce and looked to be in its death throes.
Taking a mouthful of wine from the heavy gilded-silver
goblet, he swished it about briefly, then spat it out onto

the once-fine carpet beside his chair, guzzled down the rest of the wine, and sat rolling the stem between his greasy hands as he announced his decision.

"Hell, you right, Ahreekos, and you too, Stehrgiahnos, ain't no fucking thing gonna be lost by talking with them bastids, maybe a whole damn lot to be gained, if things comes to go right with that talking. But I still want the levy raised and marched out at the same time, too. And I want word sent over there to old Ratface Billisos and Horsecock Kawlos to bring in ever' swinging dick what they can lay claws to from the western and northern *komeeseeahnee*. And tell them to bring all the mounts and supplies and beeves they can beg, borrer or steal, too. If it works out that we have to fight, I wants ever'thing I can get on our side."

It was a long, slow, very frustrating march for the army led by Grand *Strahteegos Komees* Pahvlos Feeloh-pohlehmos. Only three days out, the captain of pioneers died of heart failure after being bitten by a watersnake while supervising the strenghtening of a bridge; the head *eeahtros* reported to Pahvlos that fright or heart failure must have killed the officer, for an examination of the front half of the dead serpent had determined it to not be a poisonous one at all, though a rather large specimen of its kind.

At the next wide river, several very long, massive *krokothehliohsee* were observed by the scouts, and Pahvlos insisted that the dangerous, armored horrors be caught on land or in the shallows and speared to death before he would allow men or beasts to use the deep, difficult ford. One of the scaly monsters was found to be more than seven and a quarter *mehtrahee* long, its tooth-studded jaws and head being every bit as long as the strahteegos was tall. Officers and not a few others pried and cut out huge, pointed teeth for souvenirs, and the white meat from the thick, muscular tails became a part of the evening's rations—a welcome change from bread and beans and stringy beef for those lucky enough to get some of it.

A week farther along the abdominable roadway, the scouts sent back a galloper to report that at some time in the recent years, a colony of beavers had built a long, high, thick dam that had turned a small vale that the road had crossed into a spreading lake. A study of the map showed Pahvlos that if he backtracked for three or four days, he would be able to cut another road that would eventually lead him to a place from which he could reach his objective by way of a cross-country march of seven or eight additional days.

Rather than waste so much more time, he marched on and went into camp on the marshy shore of the lake, then set his pioneers, artificiers and as many common soldiers as were needed to break apart and tear out the beaver dam. When the most of the water had drained away, the hard-worked pioneers probed what had been the bottom muck and marked the roadway so that sweating, cursing companies of pikemen could scoop up and shovel away the stuff to reveal the fitted stones beneath it. This way, the delay was only two days, not twelve.

Farther on, the van had just passed yet another in the seemingly endless succession of overgrown, burned-out village ruins when, from the direction of a slighted hold atop a small, steep hill, a head-sized stone was hurled in a high arc that brought it down squarely atop a trooper, smashing in the helmet and the skull beneath it. The van prudently retired out of supposed range and sent a galloper back to alert the main column. Even as they sat their horses with a small copse blocking sight of the vine-grown, damaged walls, they could clearly hear the rhythmic creaking as the engine which had thrown the heavy stone was rewound.

Then, up the road, preceded by the furious clash and jingle of metal on metal, the pounding of many hooves and the squeaking of leather, came Grand *Strahteegos Komees* Pahvlos, his staff, his bodyguards and a hundred heavy horse. The lancer officer rode out to meet his commander and rendered a terse report of the incident and his response to it.

Pahvlos nodded once. "Good man. I'll remember you. You're certain your trooper is dead, then, up there?" He pointed with his chin at the twisted form that lay on the road ahead.

"He's not moved a muscle since we withdrew, my lord," was the sad reply. "And no man could have survived such a buffet, not even for a minute."

The Grand *Strahteegos* nodded once more, then turned to those behind him. "Galloper, my regards to Lord Sub-*strahteegos* Tomos Gonsalos. Tell him that I want his Number One and Number Two regiments up here at the run." As that rider saluted and reined about, the old man was already snapping out instructions to another galloper, this one being sent to order up several of the lighter engines of the siege train. An officer of the heavy horse was ordered to take a strong patrol in a wide swing completely around the partially wrecked hold and determine if there might be bodies of troops hidden where they could not be seen from there on the roadway. The new-made captain of pioneers was ordered to seek a nearby site for a night camp and begin to pace off and mark the lines of a defensive ditch and mound for it.

Within an hour's time, the two regiments of pikemen were beginning to regain their breath where they knelt or squatted in formation at the side of the road, the snaps of whips and the shouted obscenities and curses of the teamsters could be heard approaching with the wagons which contained the pieces of the dismantled engines, and the patrol of heavy horse had just returned, all red-faced and dusty-sweaty.

Their captain lifted off his helm and peeled back the mail-sewn padded coif as he approached. Drawing rein before the Grand *Strahteegos*, he saluted and said tiredly, "My lord *Strahteegos*, yon's wilderness around here, all of it, not a field's been worked in years, and the only life to be seen the whole ride was deer, wild turkeys and the like."

"What does that pile up there look like from the other side?" demanded Pahvlos. "More damaged or less?"

"Less, my lord," was the answer. "Although vines have engulfed it too, it looks to be sound beneath them, but although I had two men dismount and creep quite close through some dense brush, they could neither see nor hear anything from within the ruined hold."

"Thank you, Captain," said Pahvlos in dismissal. "You've done well."

Chief Pawl Vawn of Vawn chose this time to leave the huddle of mounted staff and ride up until he was knee to knee with the Grand *Strahteegos*. "Lord Pahvlos . . . ? You do mean to camp here and attack in the morning?"

"Most astute, Lord Pawl." Pahvlos nodded. "Yes, that's my intent. It will soon be too dark for accurate engine work, and my experience with night attacks has shown them to be extremely tricky with results that are inconsistent. I think a dawn attack will be best. Besides, in the night we may be able to judge by the number of firelights just how many men may be facing us in there."

"I have a better way than that to tell you how many they are, Lord Pahvlos," said the Vawn. "But it were better to wait until full dark to do it."

"Oh, no," snapped the commander. "You and your forces are too precious to the army to risk even one of you getting killed sneaking into that pile and then out again. It won't be all that difficult an assault in the morning, anyway. Look you, man, there are two breaches in the walls, and those gates look rickety as hell, to me, so much so that we may not need a heavy ram to burst them in, only a light, rope-slung one. With your archers and the engines to keep the bastards down or dodging, the pikemen ought to be able to go up there and into the place with minimal losses, if any."

Vawn shook his head. "Lord Pahvlos, I was not thinking of sending a man in, but rather a prairiecat."

The Ehleen shrugged. "What would that accomplish, man? Yes, the cat might well kill or injure a few of them and so upset the rest as to keep them sleepless through the remainder of the night, but they'd probably kill the beast in the end."

"No, my lord," said the Horseclansman chief, "I can instruct the cat to remain unseen and to not attack unless attacked, to count the two-legs inside and bring that information back to me."

Grand *Strahteegos Komees* Pahvlos still could not bring himself to fully believe even that humans could communicate through the mind only, much less that they could thus carry on two-way conversations with dumb beasts, but he had seen and heard and experienced enough in past months to seriously undermine the foundations of his doubts.

As the dawn was beginning to streak the eastern sky with rosy red and orange, Captain Chief Pawl came to the bustling scene boiling around and about the pavilion of the commander. He was admitted at once and he found the old Grand *Strahteegos* fully clothed and armored and looking as fresh as if he had had the night's sleep that Pawl knew he had not.

Setting down his cup of watered wine, Pahvlos asked, "Well, did the cat return safely?"

Pawl Vawn nodded. "Yes, my lord, Deerbane is in camp once more. He says that there is no recent trace of any save one two-legs in all of that place. He saw that two-legs, watched him from hiding for an hour or more. He says that he limps badly and only has one eye and that there are some strange peculiarities in his mind. Before you order the attack, my lord, why not send a herald? I'll go myself."

"No, you won't," said Pahvlos, with finality. "I went through all this yesterday, as I recall. You Horseclanners are too valuable to me to risk the unnecessary loss of even one of you. Lancers, on the other hand, are expendable; I'll send a lancer officer and we'll see how many nonexistent men he can spot."

A creamy-white silken square rippling from his lance shaft, young Poolos of Apahtahpolis, ensign of lancers, rode back from the hold at a fast amble.

"Well, boy?" snapped Pahvlos. "One at least of the bastards spoke with you, we could hear your voices if not your words. What did he have to say about why he had us attacked yesterday? I hope you've made him aware that we have a full, field force out here."

"My lord," replied the young man, "the man who bespoke me styles himself *Ahrkehkooreeos toi Ahthees* and—"

"The Archbishop of Hell?" asked Pahvlos with patent disbelief. "Do you think you might've misunderstood him, Ensign?"

With a sigh, the young officer replied, "No, my lord, rather I think that the poor man is quite mad. By his speech, he is a nobleman, but he is dressed in rags and old, ill-kept armor, with not even a patch to cover his empty right eyesocket."

Pahvlos turned to glance sharply at Pawl Vawn, who simply smiled.

"How many besides him did you see, Ensign?"

"Not a one, my lord. I . . . my lord, I think that he may be the only living soul in that ruin," answered the lancer officer. "As to why a stone was loosed yesterday, he said that no man could pass through his lands without paying a toll."

Pahvlos overrode the justifiable objections of his staff and insisted upon riding with his bodyguards just behind the second widespread skirmish line of pikemen as they converged upon the battered and vine-grown hold. As they drew nearer, they could begin to see details through one of the breaches in the wall, enough to be able to tell that the interior building still showed traces of the fire that had partially consumed it at some long-ago time.

As they had departed the roadway, near to the site of

the previous day's killing, the slamming of an engine arm against its rope-padded crossbar had heralded the arcing flight of another stone, but this time it was fully expected and, its flight being watched, the men closest to where it looked about to land simply moved out of its way.

After that, the Horseclansmen had maintained a steady drizzle of their black-shafted arrows on the place to make certain that a man would need to risk his life in order to service an engine. And no more stones or other missiles had been directed at the lines of assaulters.

When the pikemen were almost under the very walls, a signal stopped the flights of arrows, then a dozen of the assault troops entered through each of the two breaches, unbarred the splintered gates and thus provided a way for the horsemen to ride into the weedy courtyard.

Aside from an arrow-quilled medium engine, the only signs of man in the courtyard were a small vegetable garden to one side and a line of weathered, yellowed skulls rattling loosely on the rusty blades of as many warped, leaning spear hafts.

"All right," sighed Pahvlos, sitting his warhorse beside the engine, "you officers break up your pikemen into groups of three or four and root that madman out, him and anyone else you can find. Try to take him alive, but don't lose any of my men in order to do it. And be very careful inside that ruin, too—your armor won't help you if a floor breaks through or the roof caves in on you."

But a full hour of thorough searching produced only a trail of fresh blood-spatters leading to a wall of bricks that gave every feel and appearance of being as solid as was any other surface in the ruin. To an offer of one of Guhsz Hehluh's officers to have his men fetch back pioneers' tools and start taking down the stretch of wall, the *strahteegos* shook his white head.

"No, Lieutenant, certainly not. This place is but

barely standing intact as it is; you start tearing away at
the masonry and we'll all have it down around our ears.
I guess we'll just have to give up and leave the poor
lunatic here to tend his pitiful garden and howl. But we
will render that engine useless before we leave."

"Wait, my lord," said Pawl of Vawn, who had
ridden in during the prosecution of the search with a few
Horseclansmen and a brace of the prairiecats. "Let me
send these cats in there—they'll find him and, likely, a
way to get to him, too."

Deerbane and his litter-sister, Hookclaws, moved
cautiously into and through the place of moldy smells
and charred, rotting wood and the aura of old death on
big catfeet, the larger cat leaving his mental imagery of
the previous night's foray into this place on the surface
of his thought to help to guide his sister in the stygian
darkness. Even so, there were several near-mishaps as
rubble loosened from its previous lodgments by the in-
cursions of the pikemen fell and brought more down
with it. Deerbane remembered the scent pattern of the
two-legs that they sought and Hookclaws took it from
his mind and they cast back and forth, up and down,
until, by chance, they found another way to get behind
the wall at which the blood-drop trail had ended; a low
opening, it was, and so situated that a two-legs never
could have or would have found it.

With blazing torches held high and with dirks out and
ready, the small party filed through the section of wall
opened from within by Deerbane's insistent clawings at
the bolt. After only a few short paces along slimy slates
on which could be seen a line of blood spots, they were
confronted by a flight of stairs too narrow for more
than one man at a time to climb, and even that one
needs must climb sideways, his armor often scraping the
stone walls on either side.

When the spiraling way wound past a long bricked-up
arrow slit, Pahvlos guessed that they were inside a
portion of the outer defenses themselves, possibly

within the ancient, original tower keep which had been
the basis around which most present-day holds had been
built.

At a *mehtrah*-square landing by another such
bricked-up slit, a great gout of blood was to be seen on
the floor and the print of a hand was smeared in blood
on the rough granite wall.

From up ahead, Hookclaws, who had preceded them,
mindspoke back to Pawl Vawn, "Chief of Vawn, there
is no danger here in the den of the two-legs. His only
sword has a broken blade and he himself will soon go to
Wind, so if you would exchange noises with him, you
must make haste to this place."

Pawl turned back to Pahvlos and said, "My lord, one
of the cats is above. She says that the madman is there,
but that we are in no danger from him; his only weapon
is a broken sword and he himself is quite near death of
his wound. She thinks he might die, in fact, before we
reach there do we continue so slowly."

The room was not overlarge, though larger than
many of the old-time tower-keep chambers Pahvlos had
seen, and the number of men so crowded it that the
strahteegos sent a half-dozen back to wait on the narrow
stairs. The furnishings were seen to have once been very
fine, but now dust, mold, dry rot, vermin and lack of
care had had their destructive way. The filthy old
mattress, now stained anew with red blood, strained
against the half-rotten ropes that supported it on the
massive bedframe of carven and inlaid fruitwoods, even
the all-but-negligible weight of the skeletal figure who
lay upon it in his rags and dirt and matted hair seeming
to be almost all that the strands could bear.

Where not covered by a nearly white and filth-clotted
beard, the face of the man could be seen to bear hideous
scars, looking less like battle scars than the evidences of
brutal torture. One eyesocket gaped empty, and the
constant ooze from it was thickly caked on the cheek
below it. The arms and legs seen through the verminous
rags were pipestick-thin and also festooned with scars,

one of the legs showing that it had been mangled and had healed crookedly and a bit shorter than the other.

Pahvlos gazed down at the man lying there with the half of a black arrow shaft jutting out beside his neck, just behind his right clavicle, his breath coming raggedly, noisily, his lips and bearded chin all shiny with frothy blood, gobs of the stuff bubbling up from his skewered lung to ooze out between his broken, rotted teeth. The *strahteegos* thought that the man looked to be about of an age with himself. "Poor old bastard," he muttered aloud, "you've really had a rough time of it, haven't you? But you'll not suffer much longer, now."

He was startled, then, for the lid of the remaining eye quivered, then opened to reveal a pupil as dark as his own. The lips moved, but only a gargling, choking noise came forth. With obvious effort, the bony arms got the torso up far enough for the dying man to clear his throat and mouth of the gory mess that clotted it, but he was too weak to spit and therefore had to let it just run from out his mouth and down into his beard.

Fixing his single eye upon the old officer beside his bed, he slowly nodded, saying in the cultured patois of the Southern Ehleen nobility, "Thank God you have come, my lord *Strahteegos Komees* Pahvlos. I'm dying, and it is not good to have to die alone, without family. My family—Mehleena, all the children, even my infant grandchild—all are dead now, no more pain for them. But it is good that you, at least, are here now. You were always as much a father to me as you were to our Pehtros, may God rest his gallant soul and let me see him soon in His heaven."

"Oh, Christ!" Pahvlos gasped, clenching a thick bedpost for support, the names that had issued together from that bloody mouth having told him who, against the witness of his eyes, this must be. "But . . . but you cannot be him! Old man, are you trying to tell me that you are Iahnos Kahtohahros, *Vahrohnos* of Ippohskeera, he who was my youngest son's battlemate and who wed my Pehtros' widowed bride? No, you cannot be!"

Chapter VII

When the dying *vahrohnos* had imbibed of a stoup of brandy-water and had been propped up more comfortably on the old, blotched, moldy mattress, he spoke marginally clearer and in a slightly stronger voice. Ignoring both the old stains and the fresh blood, Grand *Strahteego* Pahvlos sat on the edge, beside this onetime subordinate, and was recounted a tale of pure horror, told of events that plumbed the very depths of human cruelty.

"As you no doubt recall, my lord *Komees*," said Iahnos of Ippohskeera, "my leg never healed properly from that injury I took at your great victory at Ahrbahkootchee, and so—as I was unable to sit a horse easily or securely anymore at speeds beyond a slow walk—it were an impossibility for me to go a-warring as did my overlord and right many of my peers in the hellish years of the interregnum; no, rather did I bide here, at home, and oversee the working of my lands, but rarely even visiting my small city, which task fell to my eldest son, also named Pehtros, in memory of the man I so loved, my wife's first husband, your son.

"It was hard on the boy to just sit out all the campaigning and the glory-seeking that so many of the nobility were just then doing, and so when Zastros returned from his exile and marched through here with his great host, I made no slightest demur to Pehtros taking half the garrison and quite a few boys and young men from the hold and the hold village to sally forth as spearmen for Zastros. The true king was dead, by that time, and I felt then that Zastros would make probably as good a monarch as Fahrkos. But poor Pehtros never reaped any glory; alas, he died of camp fever before Zastros ever was coronated, while still he and his swelling host were marching to and fro about the kingdom. Some few of my boy's men came back here to bring me the sad word and his ashes, the rest were pressed into another nobleman's following. His young widow—a daughter of *Opokomees* Deeahneesos Likeenos of Ehlahkahnooskeera—moved with his infant son and her household out here from the city, that we might the better share our grief, I suppose.

"Then Zastros made himself king and, almost immediately, his officers and their recruiting parties were marching about the lands, taking men for the army he was forming at very swordpoint, leaving behind only the old, the young and the crippled men. They stripped the villages and the city and even this hold, leaving me only some six old or infirm men.

"And so when that great host of bandits swept down on my barony, we were all as a tree ripe for plucking, with precious few to guard. They must have come in from the north or the west, for they fell upon the city, first; we could see the smoke from its burning. It was then that I brought the folk and kine of the nearer village behind these walls here, but it was all for naught, in the end. This pack, my lord, they are not your usual run of bandit hordes, you see, they have all classes of troops and even a siege train.

"They first came marching up the road as bold as brass and called upon me to surrender the hold; well, I gave the baseborn scum the only answer they deserved for such impudence. Next they assaulted the hold in force, but slender and ill-trained as were my own forces, we sent them reeling back with heavy casualties; the wounded cried under the walls for the rest of that day and into the night that followed.

"The second day, they again assaulted us and were again driven off. Then they brought up their engines and began to hurl stones at the walls and pitchballs over them, and me with only two small engines with which to make reply. They so weakened two sections of the front wall as to make them untenable, then three shrewdly aimed engine stones burst in the main gates. That was when they launched their third and final assault, the bastards.

"Mine fought well and stubbornly, to my pride and their glorious memory, my lord. My skimpy garrison, my few servants, the men and women and even the children of the village. Mehleena and my daughter-in-law fitted themselves into armor and fought upon the walls from the very first day, as too did my younger children. We resisted every bit of ground, even when the enemy were within the walls, and we cost them a dear price for what was by then left of the hold.

"But it could not last, there were simply too few of us and too many of them. All too soon, there were only a handful of us left, and I tried to repair with them up here, into the old keep, but the hall was still burning here and there, and the access was therefore blocked. We made our last stand, such as it was, in the northeast tower, and when it became obvious that we must be overrun by them, brave Dohra, my daughter-in-law, knew what to do. She took her babe in her steel-clad arms, climbed to the very apex of the tower, threw him off, then jumped herself, too proud to live as a slave.

"We fought them from the walltop level of the tower up through its height, but so much climbing had weakened my bad leg, and in the midst of cutting down my last opponent, it collapsed beneath me and the subsequent fall deprived me of consciousness, so I did not see the end.

"When my wits returned, my lord, I was lying, tightly bound, in the courtyard down there. It was the screams had brought me around. My wife, Mehleena, had been stripped and was being held down while bandit after bandit took his turn at ravishing her.''

Old Pahvlos gritted his teeth and clenched his fists, but did not interrupt the recountal of the dying nobleman.

''Nor was she the only victim, my lord,'' the *vahrohnos* went on in a gradually weakening voice. ''The beasts had brought in the pitiful, broken dead body of Dohra and were defiling it as well, along with the still-living bodies of two ancient withered crones and three little girl-children from the village. The beasts also defiled the dead bodies of some of the men and boys who had died in battle.

''But rapine was not their only activity there; numbers of them were looting the smoldering wreck of the hall and were stripping armor and weapons from the dead that lay scattered about. Then two men, both fully armored and mounted on decent horseflesh, rode into the courtyard. They had me dragged up before them and demanded to know where I kept my gold. I answered truthfully that I was a country *vahrohnos* and so owned precious little of value save my lands, but of course I was not believed and was put to the strenuous question.

''Under torture, hours of one's agony seem to pass, but I know that it was not so long. At one point, they gave over mutilating me and offered me a place in their ranks, whereupon I spit on them and they had at me again. At length, I suppose they just decided that either I had told the truth in the beginning and there was no gold hidden in what was left of the hold or that they might torment me unto death without forcing the location of any secret hoard from me.

''The merciless swine had me dragged to a spot near the inner gate where an iron ring was affixed into the stonework, and they chained me to that ring. They had pulled down one of the two great iron hooks that raised and lowered the *krehmahoti* and ground and filed a sharp point on it. Poor Mehleena lay as one dead, still

splayed as they had left her, only the slight rise and fall
of her mangled breasts noting that life still remained in
her savaged body.

"The human animals dragged her over to a point that
was just beyond my farthest reach, chained as I was,
and there they—with many callous jests and jokes—ran
that sharp point through her lower bowels from back to
front, then hoisted her up to hang on that cruel hook
from one of the timbers that supported the wall walk.

"That enormity committed, everything that they
coveted or could use having been borne away, they
hacked the heads off all those other poor women still
showing any trace of life and impaled them on the
points of spears. Then they all departed, leaving me to
watch and listen to my dear wife die in unspeakable
agony and me unable to do aught to aid her. By the time
two good commoner men—who had happened to be out
from the village hunting for a lost ewe and seeing what
was taking place had wisely lain low until they were
certain it was over and the last of the bandit horde were
well away—came and released me from my chains, God
had at last granted Mehleena the boon of death, may He
rest her soul.

"They released me . . . but they did not stay, for
some reason. They cannot have gotten far, however, for
they were afoot . . . I think. And that was only a week
ago . . . no, maybe as much as two weeks, but surely no
longer, surely not."

All at once, Iahnos' eyes brightened and he showed
his broken, blood-slimed teeth in a smile, looking at the
door and saying, "Why, there you are, Mehleena, love.
Look who has come to visit us. Go and fetch the
children that little Pehtros may greet his godfather, the
illustrious *Strahteegos Komees* Pahvlos, he has marched
all the way from . . . from Thrah . . .''

Choking, then, he coughed up a great gout of blood
and shuddered strongly for his entire length. A groping
hand found Pahvlos' and he gripped it weakly, his one
eye open but obviously unseeing any living person. His

gory lips moved, but Pahvlos had to lean very close to hear the words spoken.

"Ah, Pehtros, my dear friend, how handsome you are, you . . ."

And then the life went out of his withered, mutilated body.

Once a pyre had been laid and the husk of Captain of Heavy Horse *Vahrohnos* Iahnos Kahtohahros of Ippohskeera placed upon it, Pahvlos and the rest combed the weedy courtyard until they found the huge, rusted portcullis hook where it had finally fallen when the rope had rotted through and collected all of the human bones left on the ground around it. These, the skulls from off the spears and all the other bones they had found here and there were spread out around the body of him who had been lord here.

As he and the army recommenced their interrupted march westward, the smoke from the pyre still was rising into the clear blue summer sky above the ruined hall.

Another day brought them to the environs of the City of Ippohspolis, and although patent evidences of attack, sack and burnings still were to be seen by the practiced, experienced military eye, it also was clear that folk still dwelt therein. The walls and gates had been repaired; the wink of burnished metal atop that circuit of walls announced that they were defended, and numerous plumes of smoke ascended from within.

When the army's herald announced just who led this force, the gates were opened and, presently, a mounted cavalcade of some dozen men issued forth to greet the Grand *Strahteegos*. Their leader was a one-armed man in battered but sound three-quarter armor.

"My lord *Strahteegos*, I am Gabreeos Pehrkohlis, deputy lord of this city. My lord, you cannot believe just how joyous are we all to see you and a real, legal army in this long-troubled land. Does this mean that the warrings all are done? Do we once more have a king? The few traders who have braved the roads have spoken of one *Thoheeks* Grahvos, who rules not from the ancient crown-city, but from a ducal city named Mehteepolis, or something like that. Is my lord this king's *strahteegos*? Is this his army, then?"

The man's manner was respectful enough, but his speech came out all in a rush that indicated the gnawing hunger for sound news that griped at him and the other city folk of this provincial backwater.

"Lord Gabreeos," replied Pahvlos, "there is no king, nor will there ever be another in these lands of ours. Rather are we to be ruled by a confederation of thirty-three *thoheeksee*, ruling from Meh*see*polis, in the east. *Thoheeks* Grahvos claims no crown; he is but the chosen spokesman of all the others of his peers in civil rank.

"Yes, I have the great honor to here lead the larger part of the army of the Consolidated *Thoheekseeahnee* of Southern Ehleenohee and I am marching west to eject a usurper and his pack of robbers from a distant *thoheekseeahn* and place the rightful *thoheeks* in the place of his fathers.

"The wars between the nobles are done, God grant that such turmoil never again beset our lands and people."

A chorus of "*Ahmeen!*" came from the riders behind the deputy lord.

"Who appointed you deputy lord of this city, Lord Gabreeos?" asked Pahvlos bluntly.

"My lord *Strahteegos*," that worthy replied readily, "I was given the rank in a public ceremony by poor young Lord Pehtros before he rode off to his death with the host of High King Zastros, and I have held it ever since that dark day, doing the best I could with what I had. The city fell once, years back, to a huge bandit army, but even as they stormed in through the breaches their engines had battered in our walls, I was herding most of the still-living people down into the old, secret ways burrowed under parts of the city, so more lived to rebuild the city than might."

"And your landlord, the *Vahrohnos* Iahnos, what of him?" asked old Pahvlos blandly.

Lord Gabreeos sighed and shook his head. "After the bandit army had done with our city, my lord, they marched on the villages to the east and the hold of the *vahrohnos*. We saw the smoke from the directions of the villages, of course, but our circumstances then were simply too straitened to go to aid them or the *vahrohnos*, alas. Then the bandits all marched north, out of the barony, and after some week or so, a brace of shepherds came walking to the city to say that the hold had fallen, been sacked and partly burned, and that the only soul left in it when they had overcome their terror and gone in had been *Vahrohnos* Iahnos himself, chained to a wall. They went on to say that he had been tortured terribly and one of his eyes had been torn out. They had released him, done what little they could for him—ignorant, unskilled herders that they admittedly were, knowing sheep and dogs better than folk—then had decided to come here and seek more and better help.

"I was just then abed, having lost an arm to the black rot, but there then was an old soldier still alive in the city and he took our physician and a surgeon along with his party and made haste over to the hold. But they could never find the poor *Vahrohnos*, search the stinking charnel house the hold was become as they might, from top to bottom and wall to wall. Finally, having seen a distant column of riders from atop one of the towers and understandably fearing a return of the bandits, they quitted the place and came back here as fast as their legs would bear them. In the years since, several parties have gone there, but no living man ever has been found within it. Recently, certain superstitious persons have noised it about that the ruined hold is haunted by the shades of those there slain."

When Pahvlos had told the sad story to the deputy lord of the city, he asked, "Lord Gabreeos, you clearly are of noble blood. What was your relation to the House of

Kahtohahros, now, sadly, extinct in the main branch?''

The deputy lord smiled and shrugged, self-depre-
catingly. "Not very close, my lord *Strahteegos*, a distant
cousin. And I only am half a noble, for my mother was
the daughter of a merchant of this city."

"Well, Lord Gabreeos," growled Pahvlos, "you,
distant cousin or no, are about as close to the ancient
stock as we're like to get, this late in the game. I think
you'd better start getting used to calling yourself *Vahrohnos*-designate Gabreeos Kahtohahros. Deliver up to
me written oaths to support the Consolidated *Thoheekseeahnee* of the Southern Ehleenohee, and when I get
back to Mehseepolis I will see that the documents confirming you to that title and the lands and city are
forwarded to you."

He turned to the rest of the citizens making up the
cavalcade, saying, "What of you all? You know you
need and must someday have another lord of this
barony. Would you rather have a strange, alien nobleman chosen by the council of *Thoheeksee* or one of your
own, Lord Gabreeos here?"

Their near-hysterical cheers were all that he needed to
know that he had chosen aright, in this case. And, after
all, *Thoheeks* Grahvos *had* granted him such authority
to fill vacant titles.

After receiving the written oaths required and
promising that on his return march he would leave a few
dozen pikemen and some lancers on loan to the barony,
Grand *Strahteegos Komees* Pahvlos and his army
marched on in the direction of Kahlkopolis.

In the week that it took them to finally cross the
Lootrah River and so come into the lands of Ahramos'
patrimony at last, Pahvlos' mind was very troubled, and
its boiling thoughts cost him several nights of precious
sleep.

It was not the tragedies of Ippohskeera, really,
although they had a part in it all. No, old Pahvlos was
accustomed—if not really ever inured—to personal loss;
his wives, his lovers, his sons and his daughters, all had

died in their primes, as had full many a one of his
dearest friends, while he lived on to mourn them.
Ahramos, his grandson out of his youngest daughter,
Pehtra, twin sister of Pehtros, was now the only male of
his line left to say the rites over his husk when finally he
went to join in death all of those others who had been so
dear to him.

His first, young, much-loved wife had died in trying
to bear the first child of his loins, and now, after all the
years, he still could hear in his mind her voice, though
he could barely recall exactly what she had looked like.
His second wife had died of a great fever that had swept
the capital one summer long ago; she had left him with
two sons and a daughter, but the pox had taken off the
girl and had left both of the boys badly marked with
"the devil's kiss." That had been when he had resolved
that his next wife would remain in the more salubrious,
rural environs of his *komeeseeahn*, and so it had been,
though he often had been lonely for them, despite the
lovers he had enjoyed in the capital and on campaigns.

Ehlveera, his third wife, had lived and produced a
child per year for eleven years, though of course only
four of them had lived to adulthood; she had
succumbed to a terrible bout of colic while he had been
on that long, hellish campaign in the northern
mountains, against the indigenous barbarians. That
particular campaign had also cost the dear life of his
much-loved eldest son, who had suffered a deathwound
while serving as an ensign with one of three companies
that had held a pass against the foe until the rest of the
army could come up and crushingly defeat them. The
lad's body had still been warm when Pahvlos had
arrived and been informed, but he had only had enough
time to clasp it to his armored breast once and kiss the
pock-marked, so-pale cheeks before he needs must dash
the tears from his eyes and go on to lead his regiments
against the howling barbarians.

His second son had died some years later during a sea
fight against pirates; he had been a lieutenant of fleet

soldiers and had been thrown into the sea from a
catapult platform when his ship was suddenly rammed
by a pirate bireme. Both his third and his fourth sons
had died in one battle against northern barbarians. The
fifth, Pehtros, had died gloriously during the battle that
had put paid to one of the earlier rebellions against King
Hyamos' senile despotism.

Pahvlos' fourth wife, although she had lived long,
and been congenial and an excellent stepmother to his
children and wards, had proved barren. As she had
matured, she had run heavily to fat, as did many an
Ehleen woman, but she still never had failed to be loving
and jolly with her family and the husband whose press
of duties allowed him to visit her and his bucolic domain
so infrequently. At last, bedridden after suffering a
seizure that had left her partially paralyzed, she had
begun to cough up blood and had died a week later.

By the time of his great victory at the Battle of Ahrbahkootchee, of all Pahvlos' onetime family only one
daughter remained alive. This had been Pehtra, wed to
the *Thoheeks* of Kahlkos, with a young son and an
infant girl by him. After her husband's death, certain
occurrences had led the widowed Pehtra to believe that
some of the late *thoheeks'* advisers were inimical to her
and the children, so she and a coterie of still-faithful
servants and retainers had, of a night, carried out a
carefully planned escape from the city and the duchy
that had for so long been her home and fled to the haven
offered by her birthplace.

There they had stayed until a wasting fever had
carried off both mother and daughter within the space
of a bare fortnight, sparing the son, however. By then,
Pahvlos had been living in quiet and cautious retire-
ment, having been dismissed from the army he had for
so long commanded through triumph after glorious
triumph. After wedding the widow of a city-lord, a
sometime vassal, he and his new wife had taken over the
proper rearing and education of his grandson,
Ahramos.

When, some seven months before, his middle-aged "bride" had died suddenly of apoplexy, he had decided that with the new Council of *Thoheeksee* having established at least a modicum of order to the land, the time had arrived when Ahramos should return to the city of his father and claim the lands and the title that were his patrimony.

Yes, the old nobleman knew well loss and its attendant pain, but these were not what troubled his sleeping and waking thoughts, day after day, night after night. No, it was his open, imaginative and creative mind—that flexible mind the easily adjustable thinking patterns of which had given birth to so many stunning strategies and tactics, often on the very spur of the moment and usually resulting in smashing victories over a host of enemies over the long years.

Now faced with things he had for all of his previous life—some seventy years of it—considered ridiculous, impossible tales, he was being forced to admit to himself that these things not might be but must be possible realities.

From the very beginning, he had scoffed at the Horse-clanners' oft-vaunted supposed abilities to read minds, communicate silently with each other and communicate with certain dumb beasts—their horses, their great war-cats and elephants. His certainties had first begun to crumble, however, even before the army had marched, when he had been confronted with the uncanny ability of the barbarian Horseclanner *feelahksee* to put their three pachyderms through intricate maneuvers that he had never before seen even the best-trained and best-controlled war-elephants perform in either drill or actual combat.

He had not objected overmuch to the horse-archers bringing their war-cats along, even though they had flatly refused to either cage or chain them on the march, for certain of the barbarian tribes of the northern mountains trained and used huge, fearsome war-dogs in battle, so he recognized that could the cats be as well controlled, they just might be a definite advantage. Besides, he truly treasured the Horseclanner barbarians' rare combination of military values, and as they had refused to march without the cats, he had acquiesced as gracefully as he could. Nor had he had any slightest cause to regret that acquiescence since, for there had been not even one attack by the felines against men or beast in camp, column, remuda or ration herd. The huge, toothy beasts had seemed quite content to feast on the lights of slaughtered beeves or, sometimes, hunt their own wild meat, never to his knowledge having harmed domestic stock in the lands through which they had passed on the march.

With more than enough plans and problems and worries to occupy his mind, he had let the business of telepathy with beasts slip far, far down into the depths of his consciousness . . . until that queer business at the ruined hold of Ippohskeera had brought it all bubbling up to the surface again and at a full, rolling boil.

There simply was no earthly way that Chief Pawl Vawn could have known that poor *Vahrohnos* Iahnos had a crippled leg, a missing eye and a hideously scarred face and was quite mad. Pahvlos knew for fact that the captain of the barbarian horse-archers had not left the camp that night, not even for minutes, much less for the length of time it would have taken a man to cover the distance between camp and hold and do it twice at that. Nor was there any possible way that the barbarian auxiliary could have known, there upon those winding stairs, exactly what lay ahead, that the wounded, dying man's only weapon was a rusted sword with a broken blade.

Therefore, Pahvlos could not but begin to fully accept the patent impossible as existing fact: these Horseclanner barbarians somehow had developed and fully mastered an eerie talent to join their minds with those of animals and each other. Once his mind had accepted it all fully, Pahvlos enjoyed a refreshing, night-long sleep, and when he awakened, resolved to

question Chief Pawl, Captain of Elephants Gil Djohnz,
and selected others in some depth, then begin to
determine just how these new gifts could be made of use
to him and to the army and to the state.

At last, after long weeks on the march, the army
crossed the Lootrah River and were within the *Thoheekseeahn* of Kahlkos, though still a couple of days' march
from the ducal seat, Kahlkopolis. Because they took the
time to reduce two holds along the way, however, it
took them a full week to reach the capital. Neither of
the holds had been strongly held, but Pahvlos held a
belief that bypassed foes could often present unexpected
dangers at very untoward moments. The reductions had
cost him very little, only a bare handful of casualties,
and a certain amount of welcome information had been
obtained from the survivors of the garrisons before they
had been executed. Pahvlos had never had a reputation
for cruelty in warfare, but he could see no point in
burdening himself with a gaggle of captive banditti;
most had likely owned necks long overdue for the short,
sharp acquaintance with a broadaxe, anyway, that or
the tight, lingering embrace of a hempen rope.

With his rear and flanks swept clear of potential
attackers, old Pahvlos marched his army up to within
sight of the walls of the city held by the ursurper and
began to erect a strong mounded and ditched camp near
the banks of a swift-flowing brook. The pioneers and
artificiers had just felled and dragged in from a nearby
forest a sufficiency of treetrunks to provide lumber for
assembling the larger engines when a herald was seen
riding toward them from Kahlkopolis. The Grand
Strahteegos immediately dispatched his own herald to
meet this visitor from the enemy.

After a few minutes, the army's herald—a *vahrohnos*, one Djehros of Kahktohskeera—rode back at a
brisk amble to salute and report, ''My lord *Strahteegos*,
a gentleman-officer named Stehrgiahnos desires to

come here to the camp and meet with you—he, the herald yonder, and a small attending party."

Pahvlos shrugged and said, "Certainly, I'll meet with him here, just so long as he does not expect me or one of my own officers to return the visit, that is."

As *Vahrohnos* Djehros rode back out onto the broad, rolling, grassy plain, Pahvlos summoned his staff and ordered, "Throw out strong, wide-ranging mounted patrols all around us and hold every fighting man at the ready, full armed. Something about all of this stinks, and am I to be surprised, I want to be ready for it."

The Grand *Strahteegos* treated Stehrgiahnos with every ounce of the contempt that he felt the renegade nobleman deserved, and then some more for good measure. No wine was proffered, not even a chair or a stool. Pahvlos and an assortment of his officers sat behind a table—armed, wearing at least half-armor, their sheathed swords all lying on the tabletop near to hand.

"Look you, my lords," began the enemy officer, "this Mainahkos holds the duchy and city and has held them now for years, with no opposition or even a hint of dissatisfaction amongst the people. He has been a good lord and has been fair in all his dealings with his subjects, you see.

"Now it is widely known that this Council of *Thoheeksee* sitting in Mehseepolis are confirming some unrelated claimants to titles if the original house is extinct, as this one of Kahlkos seems to be. So why should not the Council of *Thoheeksee* simply list this duchy as Klehpteekos—I mean Klehftikos—rather than Kahlkos and confirm the present overlord-in-fact as the legal overlord?

"My lords, I believe that this solution would be far the simplest, least painful and least costly one, for all concerned. Yes, you lead a fine, large, fully equipped army here; pains were taken to show me its strengths as I was conducted through the camp to this pavilion. Nonetheless, I am of the opinion that our army is from a third to a half again bigger than this one, and although you have more cavalry, we have more infantry, which will serve us far better in the event of a siege than will your cavalry serve you then. Nor would such a siege be short, for the city is well provisioned, well armed with a plethora of engines of all sizes and types, and blessed with more than enough uninterdictible sources of pure water in the forms of natural springs and deep wells.

"So, then, my lords, why not send fast riders to Mehseepolis and have our puissant Lord Mainahkos confirmed new *thoheeks*? True, he is baseborn, but then I suspect that the progenitors of more than one of our most noble houses were just such, did we but know the truth."

"I take note that you have not named the patronymic of your own house of origin, Lord Stehrgiahnos," said Pahvlos scathingly, "nor can I say that I blame you, for your shameful service to an honorless bandit chief has dishonored you and degraded your house irrevocably. Indeed, did I suspect us two to be even distantly related, I think that I should fall on my sword in pure shame.

"But as regards your proposal, were the House of Kahlkos indeed extinct, there might possibly be a bare nugget of sense in what you have said. But the house is not extinct; here, at this very table, sits the rightful heir, the *thoheeks* by birth." He nodded his white head down the table in the direction of his grandson, who sat stiffly and blankfaced in his dusty armor and helm.

"Young Ahramos there is the last living son of the late last *Thoheeks* of Kahlkos and is my own grandson. His just claim far outweighs that of any ruffianly usurper, no matter where he squats, aping his betters and aspiring to their place, nor how long he has been there."

From where he stood before the table, Stehrgiahnos eyed the tall, husky heir critically, then said, "Well, there still is a way in which we might avoid a general bloodletting, my lords, a most ancient and an honorable way. That expedient is to arrange a simple, old-fashioned session in arms between Lord Mainahkos and the pretender to the title you present here."

"Cow flop!" snorted Pahvlos scornfully. "In addition to being an arrant traitor to your class, a disgrace to your house, and personally without enough real honor to make an end to your miserable life, you clearly also lack the wits of a braying jackass or even a slimy corpse worm . . . and I warn you, sirrah, if you make the cardinal mistake of actually trying to draw that blade, I'll see you—truce-breaker that you then will have become—lose that hand at the rate of one joint per hour before you leave my camp!

"To begin, now, *Thoheeks*-designate Ahramos, far from being some pretender claimant, is the rightful overlord of the *Thoheekseeahn* of Kahlkos, *thoheeks* by his birth and lineage. As such, he deserves and is being afforded the firm support of every loyal, right-thinking nobleman of this new Consolidated *Thoheekseeahnee*, which is precisely why my army and I are here, since upon the occasion of his first visit to his patrimonial lands and city, he barely escaped with his life from the minions of your precious bandit chief.

"The sort of resolution which you have suggested never applied, even in ancient times, to a situation of this sort. It was thought to be legal and binding only for cases wherein both contenders owned an equal birthright or wherein neither owned such.

"Besides which, no gentleman—no *true* gentleman—of my army is going forth to meet a common, baseborn criminal to fight an honorable duel on terms of a nonexistent equality. I find it indicative of just how far you have descended into the slime that you would even suggest so completely dishonorable a course before me and these gentleman-officers.

"Now, unless you wish to discuss terms of surrender of the city, leave my camp at once and hie you back to your kennelmates; the very sight, sound and stench of you are an affront of my senses. If I should want to see you again, I'll whistle you up as I would any mongrel hound."

Chapter VIII

Some week after the visit of Captain Stehrgiahnos to his camp, the elderly *strahteegos* and his staff were apprised by a sweating, bleeding galloper that a detachment of his far-ranging lancers had made contact—exceedingly violent contact—with an estimated two thousand men, mixed foot and horse, who apparently were proceeding with and guarding a long wagon train, a large herd of cattle and a smaller herd of horses and mules. These newcomers were on an west-to-east line of march that pointed directly toward Kahlkopolis.

Grinning like a winter wolf, the Grand *Strahteegos* dispatched Captain *Thoheeks* Portos with a mixed force consisting of both heavy and medium-heavy horse. As an afterthought, he reinforced the small units of lancers which were ambling just beyond easy bowshot of the city walls, lest someone in there get the idea of riding forth to try to succor this column from the western *komeeseeahnee*—obviously a late-arriving supply and reinforcement column.

At a bit after nightfall, Portos rode back into camp to report most of the foemen dead, the few survivors widely scattered and all running hard, with few casualties in his own force. He also reported that his troopers were bringing in all of the wagons and the horse herd, but that the Horseclansmen who had been a part of his force and were vastly more experienced at moving cattle had advised that the beeves be left at the site of the encounter until men on herding mounts rather than warhorses could collect them and bring them into camp.

Three hours after the dawning of the following day, *Vahrohnos* Djehros Kahktohskeera, with his white banner, mounted on his creamy-white gelding, was sent forth across the plain in the direction of the city. Some two hours later, Captain Stehrgiahnos and a small party issued from out the main gates and rode toward the spot whereon the *vahrohnos* waited patiently, slapping at flies and studying the many engines visible from his position upon the walls and towers of the City of Kahlkopolis, sketching in his memory their placements and fields of fire. For, expert herald or not, he was first and foremost a military officer, and he just might, someday soon, have to take a part in an assault upon these very walls, with those very engines hurling death at him.

Only the renegade nobleman himself and *Vahrohnos* Djehros were allowed to pass the outer lines and proceed into the camp this time, and Stehrgiahnos was escorted directly to the pavilion of the Grand *Strahteegos*. There, ranged in a line just beyond the hitching rail, a number of peeled wooden stakes had been sunk into the ground, each of them crowned with a livid, blood-crusty head. Paling slightly, the broken nobleman recognized the sharp-pointed nose and the large, prominent, outthrust incisors that had given Ratface Billisos his *nom de guerre* on one of those ghastly trophies and the thick, almost pendulous lower lip and thoroughly pock-marked face of Horsecock Kawlos on another of them. The silent message was clear, indisputable: there now would be no resupply of the city, no additional troops, no remounts, no matter how long Mainahkos and Ahreekos waited.

Pahvlos' words were short and brusque, his tone and manner were absolutely frigid. "Yesterday, Lord Stehrgiahnos, units of my heavy horse intercepted and exterminated the western contingent of your chief's bandit

band. We captured some two hundred head of horses
and mules, a goodly number of big, strong draught
oxen, above fifty wains and wagons loaded with
supplies of divers sorts and quantities, as well as so
many cattle that we had to leave the most of them
running loose around the site of the skirmish.

"If you exercise any influence over your chief's
decisions, it were wise that you urge him to come out of
the city and bring his forces to battle without further
undue delay, for he will not now be either reinforced or
resupplied. It would be better for his arms were he to
fight now, while his men still are strong and well fed,
rather than to wait until an ongoing siege has weakened
them through disease and short rations.

"Understand, it is not that *Thoheeks*-designate
Ahramos nor I care a pinch of dried chicken dung how
many bandits, footpads, thieves, ruffians and renegades
of your foul ilk starve or suffer or waste away of the
pox, the bloody flux or siege fever, but we want no unnecessary sufferings to befall the innocent noncom-
batant citizens of the City of Kahlkopolis."

Having recovered from his initial shock, Stehrgiahnos
began, "My lord *Strahteegos*—"

Pahvlos cut him off icily. "Shut up, Lord Stehrgiahnos! You were not whistled over to my camp to talk,
only to see and to hear. This audience is done. Get back
on your horse, ride back to that sounder of common
swine you now serve, to whom you chose to sell your
honor and your soul, and do my bidding.

"I will draw up my battle lines on the plain between
the camp and the city two days hence. If no one comes
out to fight by noon, I will assume that you all are
craven and begin preparation of siegeworks.

"Those are my last words, renegade."

That night, on a meticulously detailed sand table
prepared from the reports of lancers and scouts by his
staff, Pahvlos carefully explained his plans and
projected placements of regiments, squadrons, smaller

units, reserves and portable engines to his assembled captains. After two full hours of briefing, followed by more than another hour of questions and answers, he dismissed them all, staff and captains alike. He, however, sat there long into the night, staring at the reproduction of the city and its surrounding plain, essaying to work out in his mind any and every possible reverse and pre-plan and what his reflexive actions must be.

"Hmm, that scheme that Lord Pawl proposed for the use of those war-cats was brilliant. That'll be one thing that those bandit scum can have no way of foreseeing or expecting in advance; they've never faced such a threat before, hell, no army in these lands ever has.

"Ahzprinos' ideas, now, they're impossibly hide-bound. The man just cannot seem to get it through his thick head that amazingly as these elephants we have can perform, they still are only three cow elephants, with only some year of war training behind them, not a dozen towering bulls. There're just not enough to do this the old-fashioned way, the way Ahzprinos would have us do it. No, I know that my way is best, the only way to make best disposition and utilization of what we have.

"Of course, can we believe what was wrung out of the prisoners taken from that relief column, this Mainahkos owns no elephants at all, only some score war-carts of the antique design. Not that those, if properly employed, can't be dangerous weapons in their own right, but I think I have the answer to scotch them if they are only used as mobile archery platforms, rather than to burst apart infantry lines.

"Naturally, if they do try to break up the pikemen with those carts, Bizahros and Captain Hehluh will know what to do; neither of them are puling babes, comes to open warfare. Open up lanes in the formations wide enough to pass them through to the rear area, where the engine crews, mounted lancers and dartmen will make short work of the bastards. When other than at the gallop, those carts and their crews are terribly vulnerable; that's why they went out of use even before elephants were adopted to serve the same general purposes. I wonder just who got this pack to fabricate them and start using them to begin with? Likely that renegade or another of his unsavory ilk.

"Now our forebears, who invaded and conquered these lands, were no fools, nor anxious to die, either; so I've always figured that the only possible reason they started using those suicide wagons to begin was because they had to have mobility for their warriors and lacked enough horses or mules to mount any large number of themselves as proper cavalry. Why did our arms continue to use them for so long? Why did places like Kehnooryos Ehlahs still use them within living memory, then? Probably because of kings and *strahteegohee* of mindsets similar to Ahzprinos'—'Whatall was good enough for my great-grandsire is good enough for me!' Ridiculous!

"Elephants themselves are far from invulnerable, really rather delicate, all things considered. But they're far more maneuverable than a war-cart, their height gives those mounted upon them a bird's-eye view, and their very bulk and speed—even of these smaller cows —is daunting to those standing to receive their charge. Only the most veteran, best-trained, most strictly disciplined men have what it takes to stand firm before such a charge, then open ranks at the last minute, let the creatures through, surround them and hamstring them or wave blazing torches in their faces.

"Ahzprinos has got his big nose out of joint now, after hearing my battle plans, but he'll just have to accept it and live with it. Had he been willing, as Bizahros was, to modernize his regiment—give his pikemen armor pieces and body-shields and secondary weapons—then I might've made one of the others the reserve regiment in this engagement. As it is, though, I

have to place my best-equipped men on the forefront in
the center of the line, for they'll be the ones who will
take the brunt of an enemy charge or drive home any
charge I hurl, and it's not as if he's been entirely cut out
of the battle line, no, I've taken half of two of his
battalions for the wings of my line, and he knows full
well that he and the rest of them will be sent for should
any gaps appear or any serious overlapping of my lines
occur.

"I think those thieving bastards will get an unpleasant
surprise or two from my placement of my Horseclanner
barbarians, too. Using them on the wings of the main
battle line will give me the lancers, who would occupy
that place in an old-fashioned Ehleen battle, as an extra
maneuver element, along with the heavy horse.

"Best of all, the spot I've chosen gives me a definite,
though far from obvious, advantage for the kind of
battle I mean to fight. I rather doubt that there are
enough command veterans with that hodgepodge army
of theirs to be able to realize that fact, however, until it
has become far too late in the game to break off the
action. They could always try to withdraw back to the
city, of course. I pray God that they try just that.
Heheheh."

He smiled and rubbed together the calloused palms of
his hands. "Damned baseborn poseurs! *I'll* teach them
the folly and the deadly dangers of playing at soldier."

Within the City of Kahlkopolis itself, there had really
been no choice in the matter of which of the partners
would lead out the army against the grim Grand
Strahteegos Komees Pahvlos the Warlike and which
would stay behind to hold the city, for although he had
been champing at the bit like the old warhorse that he
was, Ahreekos the Butcher had been unable to find in
all of the city a panoply that would come anywhere close
to fitting his overcorpulent frame and shape; moreover,
the warlord found that he tired very easily these days, he

frequently had difficulty in getting his breath, and any strenuous exercise—especially of a sexual nature—bred severe pains in his chest, shoulders and arms, and at the base of his throat.

Mainahkos was not entirely pleased with the force he had on hand to lead out. He sorely missed Ratface Billisos and Horsecock Kawlos; both had been good subordinate officers, Ratface's highly innovative tactics having saved the day more than once for the bandits over the years; he also sorely missed the horses that the two had been bringing in from the west, for lacking them, the would-be *thoheeks* was going to be unable to mount all of his cavalry, and he was short of cavalry to begin. Moreover, without the wagonloads of seasoned pikeshafts which had made up a part of the now-lost supply train, Mainahkos would be unable to arm all of the spear levy of the city.

Nonetheless, the two partners, Stehrgiahnos and the other bandit sub-chiefs had done everything that they could: every house and every stable had been scoured of usable weapons and horseflesh of any and every description, age and type; straight, well-cured timbers of the appropriate lengths had been commandeered, even if doing so meant the partial razing of homes and other buildings, then impressed crews of carpenters, turners, joiners and even cabinetmakers had been set to rendering them into hafts to which pikepoints could be riveted, and the craftsmen were kept at it day and night at the points of swords where this was found to be necessary, though it seldom was, for the surviving citizens of Kahlkopolis were, after three years of occupation by the savage, brutal bandit horde, now virtually devoid of leadership and thoroughly cowed.

This exercise did turn out a goodly number of pikes—although but precious few of the hafts were of the preferred ash or oak, rather were they of elm, maple, pine, cedar, hickory and too many others to name or enumerate—but with few exceptions, they were short pikes, only eight to ten feet long, but Mainahkos knew that they would do, they would have to do.

The search for cavalry mounts, however, was far less successful, so few acceptable mounts being actually turned up that he gave over planning on putting former troopers up on a horse and decided to use them afoot or to crowd a couple into each war-cart, instead, to hurl darts alongside the archers.

Even so, the would-be *thoheeks* was able to march a force of some respectable size out of his city on the morning of the day of battle. To the roll of the drums came something over thirty hundreds of foot, about a third that number of horse and some fifty war-carts, each of them with six or eight missile-men, plus two armored postillions.

Screened by two files of mounted lancers whose orders had been to deliberately raise as much dust as possible in their progress, Captain of Elephants Gil Djohnz and the elephant Sunshine led the way toward the position assigned them for the opening of the battle, now looming close ahead. The three cows, Sunshine, Tulip and Newgrass, were all clad in most of the protective armor they would wear in battle, but their huge, distinctively shaped bodies had for the nonce been almost completely shrouded in long, wide sheets of dust-colored cloth, while the heavy, cumbersome archer boxes of wood and leather had been all dismounted and were now being borne in the wake of the pachyderms by the archers who would occupy them and some of the elephant grooms.

After the third or the fourth time he slipped and stumbled on the broken, uneven footing, his boots not having been designed for ease of walking anyway, Gil found himself steadied and easily lifted back onto his feet by the powerful but infinitely gentle trunk of Sunshine.

"I will say it once more," came her strong mindspeak, "you are silly to try to walk, man-Gil. Why your poor little feet will be sore beyond bearing by sunset.

Those men yonder are all astride their own small, skinny-legged beasts, so why do you three not ride Sunshine and her sisters, brother?''

Gil sighed. Sunshine could be as stubborn as any hardheaded mule when she chose to so be. He beamed in reply, "It is still as I have said ere this, sister-mine: high as you are, if I should take my place upon your neck, anyone watching from the other army will then know that at least one elephant is in this area, and it is the plan of the Grand *Strahteegos Komees* Pahvlos that they gain no knowledge of just where we are until the time comes for us to attack them. Please try to understand this time, dear sister."

"Silly, silly, silly!" Sunshine mindspoke dispargingly. "Two-legs are surely the very silliest of any living creatures! Fighting is surely the silliest of all two-leg pastimes, and Sunshine is herself silly for deigning to take any part in such ultimate sillinesses . . . she only does so because it makes her brother happy and she dearly loves him, man-Gil."

Even as man and elephant communicated, seven huge long-toothed felines were but just arrived stealthily in position a short distance behind the cavalry reserve of the bandit army. They crouched, unmoving as so many statues, only the respiration movements of their sleek, wiry bodies denoting that life resided in them. In a tiny copse they lurked, the agouti bodies blending well with the dead leaves that here thickly littered the ground.

One of the prairiecats—for such they all were, having come as part of the Horseclans force—meshed his mind with those of two others of his kind to gain sufficient mental projection for farspeak and then beamed out, "We are where we were told we should be, Chief Pawl. The horses cannot smell us. Not yet, but if the wind should shift . . . ? If they do smell us before you want them to, Chief Pawl, will we still get to fight? It has been so long since we were allowed to fight." There was a wistful note to the last comment.

* * *

Pahvlos found it necessary, at the onset, to alter his carefully laid-out and planned battle line. With the bandit army forming up into position some hundreds of yards distant in clear sight on the verdant plain that lay between his camp and the walls of Kahlkopolis, it was become painfully obvious that was his center to not be overlapped by the more numerous enemy center, he must either stretch his lines of armored pikemen to a thinness that would be patently suicidal or he must commit to the battle line the unarmored pikemen of Captain Ahzprinos, and for the umpteenth time he fouly cursed the old-fashioned, obstinate, obtuse officer and his stubborn failure to emulate the Freefighter regiment as had Captain Bizahros.

At length, the Grand *Strahteegos* made what he felt to be the very best of a singularly bad situation. He grudgingly extended the fronts of Captains Hehluh and Bizahros in a depth of only four pikemen, then he took the two battalions of the unarmored men from off the wings, rejoined them with their reserve regiment and used them to back the armored pikemen all along the battle line. He realized that there still would be some slight overlap, but it was the best he could do under the circumstances.

Of course, these rearrangements left him damnall reserve—one battalion of the old-style pikemen, the engineers, pioneers and artificiers who could be thrown in in a real emergency, the headquarters guard of heavy horse and a scattering of lancers—but it would just have to do.

Nor was he formed back up any too soon, for out from behind the battle line of the bandit army came the war-carts, moving at a slow walk until clear of their own men, then gradually increasing the pace of their big, barded draught mules to a fast canter. As soon as they were safely away, the entire enemy line began to advance, in formation, at a walk, their shouldered pikes standing high above them like some long, narrow forest

of wind-slanted saplings, the silvery points all aglitter in
the sun. Their form of advance told him exactly how the
oncoming war-carts would be used, at least in the
opening segment of this battle. He sent a galloper to the
captain of engineers notifying him of the walking
advance, that he might reset the torsions and tensions of
his engines for the shorter range.

Only a mere two of the oncoming war-carts were
struck by the volley of stones and spears hurled by the
engines before they were reset, but even this was
remarkable and lucky in the extreme, considering that
the targets were moving quite fast and could not be seen
by the men who loosed off the engines. Pahvlos had
been told that Captain of Engineers Teemos was the
best of the best and that he numbered among his
company some real artists at the tricky skills of handling
light engines; now the old *strahteegos* believed it, every
word of it.

Barded to the fetlocks as the mules were, there was no
way for Pahvlos to determine just how heavily or fully
the draught mules were armored, it was only safe to
assume that they were. Between six and eight men stood
in the bed of each jouncing, springless cart, mixed
archers and dartmen from the looks of them; on the two
nearside mules, fully armored men with sabers or axes
were mounted, so none of the missile-men need worry
about guiding the mules. He noted that the carts consistently kept a goodly distance one from the other, lest
the long, cursive steel blades projecting from the wheel
hubs become entangled with another set or, even worse,
cripple a mule.

Even if the slow advance of the enemy infantry lines
had not told him, Pahvlos would have known as soon as
he saw just how few of the armor-plated war-carts there
were that they were too few to tempt even such an
amateur *strahteegos* as the bandit chief Mainahkos to
send them head on at a hard gallop against the massed
pikes and hope to get more than a mere handful of them

back, for anyone with a grain of sense would realize that
the cavalry in the rear areas could ride rings around such
relatively slow, cumbersome conveyances, deadly rings,
in the case of the horse-archers that the bandits knew he
owned as a part of his army.

That left only a couple of alternative uses for the
archaic carts. One of these would be an attempt to drive
between wings and center and thus take the pike lines on
the more vulnerable flanks; the other would be to make
a series of passes across the front while raining the
pikemen with arrows and darts.

It was to be the latter choice, Pahvlos saw. In
staggered lines, the war-carts were drawn, clattering and
bouncing over the uneven ground, the full length of the
formations of pikemen, expending a quantity of arrows
and darts for precious few casualties against the
armored front ranks. As the leading war-carts reached
the end of that initial pass, however, and began to wheel
about, they received an unexpected and very sharp taste
of similar medicine to that which they had been seeking
to so lavishly dispense to the static lines of infantry.
Captain Chief Pawl Vawn of Vawn, commanding the
left wing, treated the carts and their mules and postillions to such a pointblank arrow storm that nearly a
dozen were put out of action then and there. Nor did the
hapless crews of the carts receive any less from the half-
squadron of Horseclansmen under one of Captain
Pawl's sub-chiefs, on the other wing, which eliminated
more of their number, almost halving the fifty that had
set out to begin.

With it patent that the war-carts were doing no significant damage to his front, Pahvlos dispatched a
galloper to carry his order to Captain *Thoheeks* Portos
and his heavy cavalry. Out from the rear area they
came, taking a wide swing around the right of their own
lines to end in delivering a crushing charge against the
mixed heavy and light horse on the left wing of the
bandits' battle line. That charge thudded home with a

racket that could be heard by every man on the field and even in the camp and the city, walls or no walls.

Portos' heavy cavalry fought hard and bravely for a few minutes after the initial assault, their sharp sabers carving deeply into the formations of opposing horsemen, even penetrating completely through, into the skimpily armored ranks of light-infantry peltasts who flanked the pike lines. But then, abruptly, a banner was seen to go down, and with cries and loud lamentations they began to try to disengage and withdraw in the direction of their own lines.

Sensing a victory of sorts within grasping distance, the entire left wing of the bandits' army—horse and light foot alike—quitted their assigned positions to stream out in close pursuit of the retreating heavy horse.

And no sooner had they left the flank they had been set there to guard than up out of a brushy gully filed Sunshine, Tulip and Newgrass. With practiced speed, the cloth shroudings were stripped away, the last few pieces of armor put on and the heavy, unwieldy metal-plated boxes were lifted up onto the broad backs and strapped into place. As the archers clambered up into the boxes, Captain of Elephants Gil Djohnz and the other two *feelahksee* were lifted by the pachyderms to their places just behind the armored domes of the huge heads and those men still gathered about on the ground uncased the outsize swords—six feet long in the blades, broad and thick and very heavy, with both edges ground and honed to razor sharpness—which the behemoths would swing with their trunks in the initial attack. All of these last-minute preparations had been well rehearsed and so took bare minutes in the accomplishment. Once fully equipped and armed and out of the gully in which they had hidden, the three huge, fearsome-looking beasts set out in line abreast at a walk which the trailing and flanking lancers had some difficulty in matching for speed over the uneven terrain.

Now, much of Mainahkos' "infantry" was no such

thing, save by the very loosest definition of the term. Rather were the most of them just a very broad cross-section of male citizens who had been impressed in the streets of the city at the points of swords and spears, handed a short pike and hustled willy-nilly into an aggregation of fellow unfortunates, then all marched out to add depth and length to the bandits' pike lines. To these, the mere distant sight of the three pro-boscideans fast bearing down upon them, swinging terrible two-*mehtrah* swords, their high backs crowded with archers and a horde of mounted lancers round about them, was all that was needful to evoke a state of instant, screaming panic.

Bandit army veterans strode and rode among the impressed men they chose to dignify with the term "citizen spear levy." With shouts and with curses, with fists and whips and swordflats and spearbutts, they tried to lay the panic, get the untrained men faced around to try to repel the flank attack, all the while cursing the peltasts and heavy horse for so exposing the flank and profanely wondering just when Lord Mainahkos would get around to sending the reserve cavalry to replace those who had ridden off to who knew where.

Of course, they could not know that a few minutes before, Pawl Vawn of Vawn had farspoken but a single thought: "Now, cat-brother!"

With bloodcurdling squalls, the seven mighty prairie-cats had burst from out the tiny copse and sped toward the mounting cavalry reserve. All of them broad-beaming mental pictures of blood and of hideous death for equines, never ceasing their cacophony of snarls, growls, squalls and howls, the muscular cats rapidly closed the distance between the copse and the horses and men.

Within the City of Kahlkopolis, things were not well. Ahreekos, frantic for a better view of the battle, one not partially obscured by folds of ground, high brush or copses, had decided on the city's highest tower as an observation point and had led his followers in the climb up to its most elevated level. However, less than a third of the way up, he had gasped and fallen on a landing, jerking and beginning to turn a grayish blue in the face.

His followers had almost ruptured themselves in bearing his broad, corpulent bulk down the narrow spiral stairway, only to find upon finally reaching the first level that they had been carrying a fat corpse. Ahreekos was dead.

Leaving the body precisely where it lay, pausing only to strip off rings, bracelets and anything else of value from it, in the way of their unsavory ilk, the followers departed and began to make ready to leave the city, for what they had already been able to see of the progress of the battle had not been at all encouraging. It would seem that overconfident Mainahkos had finally met his match in the person of this white-haired eastern *strahteegos* and his small but very effective army, and the personal slogans of all of those who had for so long followed the two warlords had always been "He who fights and runs away lives to run away another day." They were, after all, not warriors but opportunists, and so could desert without even a twinge of shame.

The condition of Mainahkos' main battle line was not at all pleasant, for all that there had not as yet been any contact with the enemy for the front ranks or the right flank. Numerous small engines, apparently situated just behind the enemy center, had been hurling stones and long, thick spears in high arcs to fall with effect both devastating and deadly among their close-packed ranks, reducing the depth as rear-rankers needs must advance to plug the gory gaps. But it suddenly got worse, far worse.

At almost the same instant, three towering war-elephants crashed into the left flank and began to roll it speedily up, while elements of their own cavalry reserve slammed into the rear of the right-flank formations, and the panic of those horses, for some unknown reason, spread like wildfire among the horses of the heavy cavalry guarding that flank as well.

In the space between the two opposing battle lines, the harried, now-wounded commander of the war-carts just stared, astounded. Like Stehrgiahnos a broken nobleman and the man who had persuaded the two warlords to build and fit out the carts to serve the functions of the elephants that they did not have and never had had for the bandit army, he had known his full share of formal warfare in better days, but even then he had never before heard of such a thing as this.

Leaving their secure, unthreatened position, the entire length of the enemy pike line was advancing, moving at a brisk walk, their lines still even and dressed, their pikes at high-present—shoulder height—an array of winking steel points that projected well ahead of the marching lines. It was an unholy occurrence, thought the renegade; the miserable infantry simply did not advance against armored war-carts. It was unthinkable!

For him, it was truly unthinkable. Basically akin to Captain Ahzprinos of the opposing force, a less than imaginative or creative man, he did then the only thing of which he could think to do. He signaled and led a withdrawal back to whence he and the others had come, back to their own lines.

But before the carts could reach the left wing, their own infantry lines suddenly surged forward, looking less like a formation of men than like a cylinder of raw dough pressed mightily at both ends. The boiling press of men thoroughly blocked the way of the carts.

Deeply contemptuous of the common footmen at even the best of times, the commander led his force directly into the infantry, carving a gore-streaked path through them up until the moment that a wild-eyed, terrified man smote him across the backplate with a poleaxe and flung him to the ground at just the proper time and place to be raggedly decapitated by the sharp,

blood-slimed, whirling blades projecting from a wheel
hub of his own war-cart.

Portos' squadron of heavy horse had continued their
"panicky withdrawal" until he judged that the enemy
horse and peltasts had all been drawn far enough out
that they could not easily or quickly return to their
assigned positions and that the way was thus clear for
the elephants and supporting lancers to assault the left
flank of the bandits' pike lines. Then, abruptly, the
"fallen" banner was raised high again and flourished,
and the squadron reined about and began to fight, not
flee. They had hacked a good half of their erstwhile
pursuers from out their saddles before the survivors
broke and fled, scattering the peltasts before them.

At that juncture, Captain *Thoheeks* Portos halted his
force, reformed them and directed them against the
nearest protrusion of the roiling, confused mass of men
that had formerly been the center of the bandits' pike
line. But that projection had recoalesced back into the
main mass by the time the heavy horse had come within
fifty *mehtrahee* of it, so quick-thinking Portos led his
force around the broil into the howling chaos that had
but lately been the rear area of the enemy army. After
detaching half the squadron under a trusted subordinate
officer to see to it that as few horsemen as possible escaped back to the city, the grim-faced Portos led the
other half in a hard-driving charge upon the rear and
flank of those units still more or less coordinated and
functioning as flank guards on the enemy's right. His
half-squadron struck only bare moments before those
same units were assaulted all along their front by Captain Chief Pawl Vawn of Vawn and his Horseclansmen.

When the war-carts so precipitately withdrew from
the field, Grand *Strahteegos Komees* Pahvlos ordered
the drums to roll the chosen signal. At that sound, the
pikemen dropped their shields from off their backs,
lowered their long, heavy pikes to low-guard

present—waist-level—position and increased their pace to a fast trot, although they all maintained their proper intervals and formation up to the very moment that their hedge of steel points sank deeply into soft flesh or began to grate upon armor or bone.

The pursuit and slaughter continued for some hours more and the executions of the captured bandits went on for days, both outside and inside the city. But the charge of the pikemen had really ended the hard-fought battle at Kahlkopolis.

Pahvlos had, at first, decided to simply hang the most of the captured bandits and convert the less dangerous ones to slaves of the City of Kahlkopolis, granting the captured renegades their choice of hanging with the rest or being beheaded. That was before the signet of the late *Vahrohnos* of Ippohskeera was found among loot in the personal quarters of Mainahkos in the ducal palace of the *Thoheeksee* of Kahlkos, which find he took to mean that it was this particular pack had committed the atrocities the dying man had detailed.

Consequently, the executions were savage. None were kept for slaves; rather were all of the bandits, excepting only the chief and the three renegades, tied onto crosses stretching all along the part of the trade road that ran through the *Thoheekseeahn* of Kahlkos, many of them after having already been subjected to torture and mutilations.

The three onetime noblemen were manacled heavily and thoroughly, thrown into a wagon-mounted cage and set off on their journey to Mehseepolis to there be judged and sentenced by the Council of *Thoheeksee*.

The Grand *Strahteegos* had Mainahkos' fingers crushed, one by one, then saw him impaled on a thick, blunt stake of oak, most of it with the rough bark still on.

Chapter IX

As he stared into the dark contents of his winecup, swirling to the motion of his hand, *Thoheeks* Grahvos reflected, "Six years now. Six years tomorrow since we few moved the capital from Thrahkohnpolis to Mehseepolis here. Although I tried to project to the others sincere confidence that our aims would, could, do no other but succeed, I didn't really feel that confident, not at all. But it worked, by God; it has succeeded. We are once more three-and-thirty *thoheeksee*, ruling over all of what was for so long the Kingdom of Southern Ehleenohee.

"Most of the lands are once again under lords, they're being planted and harvested, crops are coming in . . . and taxes, too; why, Sitheeros and I were even paid back a little of the monies we advanced Council, they voted the amounts to us at the last meeting and there was even talk to the effect of either buying Mehseepolis outright from me or at least paying rent for the central government's use of it and the lands used by the army. And that's a sign of maturity, that, an indicated willingess to begin to undertake the discharge of responsibilities.

"Speaking of responsibilities, *Thoheeks* Mahvros is doing every bit as good a job as ever I did as chairman of the Council; even Bahos, who wanted the chair himself, has had to admit that we chose well in selecting Mahvros. Besides, neither Bahos nor Sitheeros nor I is any of us getting a bit younger, and while wisdom is required in council, a young, vibrant, vital hand on the reins is needed, too, on occasion.

"The next order of business, I think, is going to have to be the reorganization of a naval presence. The raids of those non-Ehleen pirates on the far-western *thoheek-seeahnee* are getting beyond bearing, more frequent and in larger and larger force. And I just can't see begging the High Lord for help until we've gotten to where we can at least make a token payment of the reparations for Zastros' folly. I must remember to bring that up in Council next time, too.

"I do miss blunt, honest Chief Pawl Vawn." He sighed to himself. "But it's understandable that he had to get back to his clan and his family; after all, he'd been down here for around five years, and some several months away on campaign in Karaleenos before that. I had so hoped, however, that we could convince him to take a title and lands here, bring down his family and become one of us.

"But at least a few of those Horseclanners stayed here. Rahb Vawn was granted the right by Chief Pawl to found a full sept of Clan Vawn here, and Pawl agreed to tell of the fact to his clan and allow any who wanted to come down and join Rahb to do so.

"Gil Djohnz and most of the other elephant Horse-clanners, too, are staying. So, too, are some dozen more of the younger unmarried men of Pawl's squadron. Tomos Gonsalos has agreed to stay on here, at least until the High Lord sends down or appoints a commander to succeed him, which last is a blessing, for our Grand *Strahteegos* couldn't do all that's necessary with the army all alone.

"There are many, especially in the army, who wish Pahvlos would retire, and maybe he should; after all, he's pushing seventy-five . . . though he'd die before he'd admit to the fact. Ever since he executed that victory at Kahlkopolis, the old bastard's been marching the very legs off the army, hieing them north, south, east and west, cleaning up the tag ends of the chaos that preceded this government. Those on Council who criticized him, berate the expenses of his constant campaigning, just don't or won't realize how very much the old man and that very campaigning has done and is doing for this government and for our lands and folk.

"That business last year, for example, now. He not only drove the damned mountain barbarians back across the border, retook all the lands and forts they'd overrun during the years of civil war, then moved his columns up into the very mountains themselves, but so decimated and intimidated the savages that no less than nine of the barbarian chiefs have signed and sworn to trade treaties and nonaggression treaties and sent down hostages to be held against their keeping their words. Yes, it all cost some men and supplies and the like, but real peace is ever dear, and I can't see why certain of my peers can't get that fact through their thick heads.

"*Thoheeks* Tipos, in particular, from the moment Council voted to confirm his rank and lands, has proceeded to balk at anything that was for the common weal. Were it up to him alone, we'd have taxes so high that we'd shortly have a full-scale rebellion that would make that first one against King Hyamos look like little boys at play. Nor would there be any army to put it down or at least try, because he would've disbanded the army entirely, the taxed funds thus saved to go toward rebuilding ducal cities, roads, fords, bridges and the clearing of canals, none of which would do him or any of the rest of us any good were internal discord and the constant threat of invasion by the barbarians staring us in the face, but the stubborn bastard, his brain well pickled in wine, refuses to see plain facts directly under his big red nose.

"And then there's *Thoheeks* Theodoros, too; what a precious pair of obstructionists those two make in Council. At best, Theodoros is but the dregs of a vintage the best of which was of questionable merit.

One would think that he might have learned something from the examples of his sire and his elder brothers, but he is every bit as despotically minded as were any of them. His latest brainstorm was to suggest a law which would forbid, under penalty of enslavement to the state, the ownership of bows or crossbows by any man not in either the army or the employ of some nobleman or himself a nobleman, which is pure poppycock to any rational man.

"But worse than that, he visibly cringes at the mention of monies to be spent on the army and its needs. And he seems to be of the opinion that were we to surrender all of the border marches to the barbarians, they would leave us in peace forever. Had he ever been a warrior, I might think that he'd taken one too many blows to the helm; as it is, I'm of the mind that his wet nurse must have dropped him on his head.

"The one, saving grace is that neither of them is a spring chicken. Theodoros is almost my own age and Tipos is a good ten years my senior, so they won't—God willing—be around to bedevil Mahvros for too much longer. Mayhap their heirs will be of sound mind, though in the case of Theodoros, I much fear that it's in the bloodline of his house.

"Tipos, now, lacks an heir of direct line to succeed him. I would imagine he'll name his young catamite, but Council is in no way bound to confirm that young man. Perhaps he has a nephew or a grandnephew or two of unselfish nature and open mind. We'll see.

"But back to thinking about those who had soldiered here and have then been persuaded to stay on, I consider it a real accomplishment to have gotten Guhsz Hehluh not only to accept a *vahrohnoseeahn* in one of my duchies, but to also take to pensioning off wounded men of his regiment in others of my lands and cities and towns to seek wives and establish crafts and trades and businesses, few of them seeming to be inclined toward agriculture or animal husbandry. But with the way the

mountain barbarians are flocking in at the offer of free
land to farm and the way the Horseclanners who've
stayed here all seem dead set on a life of breeding cattle
or horses or sheep or, in the cases of Gil Djohnz and a
couple of others, elephants, we'll probably have enough
folk to till the lands and produce beasts for us, shortly.

"And those pensioned-out Middle Kingdoms men are
doing really great things for us all, producing items that
have never before been made here, things that we've
always had to buy at vastly inflated prices from the
traveling traders. Not only that, they're developing,
introducing new ways of doing mundane things, easier,
more economical ways. Their coming has put new
vitality and drive into every trade and craft and business
in my lands.

"Naturally, they haven't made the more old-
fashioned native tradesmen and craftsmen any too
happy, but it's just as I told the deputation of them—if
they want to stay in their chosen fields, they'll just have
to ape the practices and quality of products of their new
competition. And that damned *Kooreeos* Ahndraios,
who came to me blustering and issuing veiled threats
because the Middle Kingdoms men who have taken to
lending money here and there are offering it at better
terms and lower interests than the Holy Church ever
has; well, he may have, like the month of Mahrteeos,
come in like a lion, but after he'd heard my thoughts on
the matter, he left like a cross between a lamb and a
well-whipped cur-dog, soaking his oiled beard with his
tears. The Church has never had even a scintilla of
competition in that field ere this, and if he and the
Church intend to stay in the profession of usury, they
are just going to have to match or better the terms and
rates now being offered by these newcomers, that's all
there is to it.

"Moreover, I promised the sanctimonious old fraud
that should he sic any of that pack of ruffians he
dignifies with the name 'Knights of the Ancient Ehleen

Faith' on his new competition, I and the Council will do
with them and him and all the other *kooreeohsee*
precisely as High Lord Milos and King Zenos did with
their like in the other Ehleen provinces of our Confederation—disband the 'Knights' (I've always thought
the Church bullies called that because nighttime is when
they ride to do their worst, being ashamed or afraid to
show their faces in sunlight), round up the *kooreeohsee*,
declare them all to be slaves of the state and put them to
work on the roads or the rebuilding of city walls.

"But when I mentioned that I thought it was high
time that agents of Council have an in-depth look at the
tally sheets and books of records of all of the
kooreeohseeahnee, throughout the realm, I then
honestly thought that the old bastard was going into an
apoplectic fit, then and there. Hmmm, maybe it might
be wise to do just that. I'm sure that for all their holy-
mouthing, these priests and *kooreeohsee* are as crooked
as any other set of thieves in all the lands, and the
amounts of illegally earned gold and silver that the High
Lord and King Zenos were able to reclaim for their
treasuries would surely be of great value to our own
more modest one.

"I think I know just the man to put to the job of
finding out just how much Holy Church is hiding, just
how many fingers there are in just how many pies, just
how many businesses of how many differing kinds are
being funded with Church monies; and I think that this
man will undertake this particular mission as a labor of
love, too, for he has scant reason to love the Church and
more than enough to truly hate it and all its clergy."

Stehrgiahnos Papandraios had been so ill when he
stumbled, filthy, bearded, long-haired and miserable in
his heavy, clanking chains, out of the cage in which he
and his two fellow unfortunates had been borne all the
weary, dusty, bumpy miles from Kahlkopolis to
Mehseepolis that he was not even put up for sale with

them, because everyone thought him to be dying, and he very nearly did do just that.

Deep in fever as he then had been, he recalled only bits and pieces of someone's having come into the slave pens, sought him out where he lay shivering and moaning, with his teeth chattering, and carried him out and away. He recalled only snatches of being bathed, shaved from pate to ankles, then bathed again and thoroughly deloused. Under skillful and careful nursing and feeding and care, he slowly regained his health, and that was when he began to wonder why anyone had taken such interest, invested so much in a state prisoner sure to be soon condemned either to a quick, relatively merciful death or to a longer and far less merciful one slaving away on road-building projects; that was where his two cagemates had been taken.

Then, of a day, when the last of the fever had departed and the worms had been purged from out his intestines, he was decently if rather plainly clothed and led from the spartanly furnished bedroom through a succession of corridors, up stairs, down stairs, and into and out of richly decorated rooms to finally find himself standing before a late-middle-aged nobleman seated in what looked to be a small study and writing room. While the seated man studied Stehrgiahnos with a pair of piercing black eyes, the slave studied him every bit as assiduously.

What he saw was a stocky, powerful-looking man of a bit over middle height for an Ehleen. From his facial looks and his frame, he was most clearly of pure Ehleen stock, from his dress and bearing a nobleman, probably a high-ranking one—at least a *komees*, maybe even a *thoheeks*, thought Stehrgiahnos—and from his scars and the little bits and pieces of him missing here and there a veteran warrior. His black hair and beard were now heavily streaked with grey, wrinkles now furrowed his brow like a well-plowed field, and brown age spots were beginning to make their appearances on his muscular forearms and the backs of his big hands.

One of the two guardsmen who had brought him in shoved him rather ungently to his knees—not a difficult thing to do, that, for just then Stehrgiahnos still was more than a little weak from his long siege of illness—saying, "Who do you think you are? Only freemen may stand before the lord *thoheeks*!"

The seated nobleman then waved the two out. When they seemed loath to leave him alone with the tall, younger slave, he airily waved a hand and said, "You forget, my good man, I'm a soldier, too. I'll know what to do in the event he misbehaves himself." He smiled, patting the hilt of the short, broad-bladed dirk cased at his belt.

When the two spearmen had grudgingly closed the door behind them, the nobleman said, "Get up and seat yourself on that stool yonder, Stehrgiahnos." When he had been obeyed, he went on, "I strongly doubt that you remember me, for when you and the other two renegades were dragged up to confront and be judged by Council, you were swooning and raving with fever. I am *Thoheeks* Grahvos, just now your owner. I bought you from the state at a very reasonable price, since everyone else thought you dying."

"You did not, my lord master?" asked Stehrgiahnos.

The nobleman frowned. "When we two are completely alone, as at this time, Stehrgiahnos, you may get away with it, but if ever you speak without being asked to speak when others are about, you will have to be made to suffer for your impertinence. Remember that well, for I do not ever make false threats toward anyone, slave or free.

"But, in answer, no. You struck me as a survivor, a basically tough man, who could live out the fever and the parasites infesting your body if anyone could do so, just as you had survived your many wounds, as attested by your scars. It was those very war scars, in fact, plus what I learned of you from your two companions, from Grand *Strahteegos Komees* Pahvlos and from certain others of his officers that set me to thinking that there might be a far better use for a rogue like you than slowly grinding his life away at the bestial labor of road-building and suchlike.

"You were born and bred into a noble family, an old and respected Ehleen family, and you know the customs and usages of that world. You were once a lord of lands and a city, which means that you know that world, as well. You were a noble officer, at one time, and this fact gives you yet another sphere of in-depth knowledge. Then, for years, you ran with outlaws and bandits, lived cheek by jowl with the lowest scum of our lands—thieves, burglars, footpads, ruffians, rogues, rapists, slave-stealers, horse- and cattle- and sheep-lifters, cutpurses, highwaymen, kidnappers, professional bullies, abortionists, tomb robbers, army deserters and God alone knows what else and worse. This fact, which many would and do consider disgraceful, does, however, add to your possible value to me for my purposes.

"In my capacity as chairman of Council, as well as in more personal businesses, there are times when the covert use of an intelligent, educated, thoroughly un-principled and honorless rogue who owns an ability to move easily and knowledgeably in many strata of our society could be of some use to me. He must, of course, be a survivor, a strong, ruthless, shrewd man, skilled at prevarication and at acting parts in everyday living. From all that I've learned of you, I think that you are just that sort of man.

"Of course, Stehrgiahnos, the ever constant, ever present danger of employing such men as you in any capacity at all is that of making certain that their baser instincts do not lead them to forget their loyalties to their employer or patron—or, in this particular case, owner and master. However, I think that I have come up with the best solution to maintaining your firm loyalty and fervent support.

"You are an officially registered slave, and you will shortly be undergoing a branding, though on a very unobtrusive part of your body; so long as you behave yourself and remain useful to me, you will not be fitted with a slave collar, only an easily removable bronze bracelet bearing my seal, such as all my personal retainers—slave, free, common and noble—wear while in service to me.

"Should you ever try to run away, or give me strong cause to suspect you of having done so or be seriously considering so doing, I will make of you a gift to the state and you will then be gelded and put to work alongside your two fellow renegades, assuming that they still live at that point. State slaves just do not seem to live long at the tasks of building roads and walls; perhaps the loss of their testicles lowers their masculine vitality.

"Also, should you ever forget who owns you and allow yourself to become disloyal to my interests or those of Council, if it is for it that I then have you working, I will consider that disloyalty to be your prelude to an escape attempt and deal with you appropriately, as earlier detailed. Do I make myself quite clear to you, Stehrgiahnos?"

The old man assuredly had made himself and his terrifying intentions clear to his newest slave. Even sunk deep in his fever, he still could remember hearing the sobbing pleas and then the hideous screams as his two companions had been thrown, pinned down by strong, laughing men, then gelded, cauterized with one red-hot iron, branded with another, and dragged, sobbing and gasping, from out the slave pens.

At the command of *Thoheeks* Grahvos, he had related all that had befallen him in his life, the good and the bad, the honorable and the dishonorable, telling the full, unadorned truth for the first time in full many a year, omitting nothing.

Stehrgianos Papandraios had been born heir to a city and lands, eldest son of the late *Komees* Zeelos Papan-

draios of Pahtahtahskeera. With the sole exception of
his twin, Hohrhos, he was the only male offspring of his
sire to live past childhood; all their other siblings were
females, so the two boys were brought up like the
precious jewels that their family considered them, and
when the time came to ride off to serve a stint with the
Royal Heavy Horse of King Hyamos, the two had
forked fine riding horses, while their arming-men and
servants had led splendid fully war-trained chargers and
pack beasts laden with the very best of armor, weapons,
clothing and equipment. Both of these new ensigns had
ridden, shortly, into their first battle, a brief war against
the mountain barbarians; during the short campaign,
Hohrhos had suffered a crippling wound and Stehrgiahnos had distinguished himself in fighting bravely
against odds to protect his twin brother and another
wounded officer until a squad had reached him and
driven off the savages. Praise and promotion had been
his reward, while poor crippled Hohrhos, borne back to
his natal hold in a horse litter, had slowly recovered, his
army days now done forever.

By the time that King Hyamos' senile despotism had
sparked a full-scale rebellion led by *Thoheeks* Zastros,
Stehrgiahnos was become a troop captain of the
Leopard Squadron of the Royal Heavy Horse and had
led his men in numerous smaller engagements prior to
the great, crashing battle at Ahrbahkootchee, where the
rebel army was crushed and scattered. In that battle, he
had personally seized the Green Dragon banner of the
rebel leader, and although it had been his commander's
commander who had presented the prize to *Strahteegos
Komees* Pahvlos, that same man had been so impressed
with his subordinate's rare feat that he had, on the spot
and before witnesses, offered the still-young man
command of a squardon at a dirt-cheap price.

Stehrgiahnos, not of course having that kind of
money himself, at once fired off a letter to his sire, not
needing to point out the signal honor of the offer for an

officer so young and lowly in civil rank; almost all commanders of squadrons were at least heirs of some *thoheeks* or other, if not already *thoheeksee* themselves. Some length of time passed, which Stehrgiahnos then attributed to the unsettled conditions in the intervening territory, but then the gold was duly delivered and paid, and he became one of the youngest squadron captains in King Hyamos' army.

And that army was kept constantly busy, riding and marching hither and yon, usually in small units, for years, trying to put down a rebellion that never really died, despite the loss of the flower of its army at Ahrbahkootchee and the flight into exile of many of the rest, including its charismatic leader, *Thoheeks* Zastros. But it then seemed that as fast as one head of the rebellion was severed, two or three more sprang up into full life in as many distantly separated spots around the far-flung *thoheekseeahnee* that made up the Kingdom of the Southern Ehleenohee.

Not only were the soldiers, troopers and their officers all overworked throughout these difficult years, but with conditions in the capital at Thrahkohnpolis in utter turmoil following the death of the old king and the contested accession of his son, the troops were no longer in any manner well cared for, often having to forage the areas through which they marched, even pillage, in order to keep themselves and their animals fed and clothed and equipped, having to strip dead or wounded rebels for arms and armor to replace their own battered or broken gear, taking remounts at swordpoint, war-trained or no, whenever and wherever they could find them in the suffering lands. And naturally in such an army in such condition, desertions were common, with scant hope of replacements.

Then, in a manner often afterward questioned but never yet explained, the new king, Hyamos' son, and his entire family had suicided for no apparent reason, some of them doing so before unimpeachable witnesses, all in a single day and night, leaving no direct-line heirs to take the now-vacant throne and grasp the loose, dangling reins of the kingdom now virtually reeling about in a state of near-anarchy. That had been when a former-rebel *thoheeks*, who had managed to purchase a full pardon of King Hyamos after the debacle at Ahrbahkootchee, one Fahrkos Kenehdos of Bahltoskeera, which triple duchy abutted the royal lands, marched in with an overwhelming force scraped up who knew where and first seized Thrahkohnpolis, then had himself crowned king.

King Fahrkos had summoned all units of the widely dispersed Royal Army back to Thrahkohnpolis and then had set about purging it of any and all officers who had remained loyal to their king and their oaths during *Thoheeks* Zastros' disastrous rebellion, replacing them with a host of rebels. Because of his intemperate, vengeful actions, a large proportion of the Royal Army simply rode or marched away, some in whole units, some piecemeal. Nor did those troops who stayed make any move to stop their old comrades, though they did prevent King Fahrkos' rebel forces from interfering with or interdicting the departures.

Of course, not one *thrahkmeh* of the long-overdue back pay had been proffered or collected by any officer, soldier or trooper, so by the time that Squadron Captain Stehrgiahnos and his few hundred officers and troopers finally rode onto his ancestral lands, they were become a force of *de facto* bandits, simply in order to survive the course of the long, hard journey.

Their arrival was timely, to say the least. A relatively small band of rebels were besieging the hold of the *komees*, which hold had been fighting off attacks and slowly starving for some weeks. However, although possessed of slightly larger numbers, most of these rebels were at best amateurs at real warfare, and the tough, professional warriors of Stehrgiahnos went through them like a hot knife through butter, killing or wounding more than half of them, capturing their camp and baggage and loot, and chasing the survivors of the fight like so many hunted deer, coldly butchering those they managed to catch and so horrifying the rest that many of them ran their horses to death or near it, then staggered on until they fell of utter exhaustion miles from the hold they had sought to take, having along the way discarded anything and everything that might weigh them down or retard their flight. Many a man of these wished to have kept at least a spear or a sword when found by the farmers and villagers he and his band had been robbing and abusing during recent weeks.

Stehrgiahnos had entered the hold to find that he now was *komees*, his sire having died of a wound taken in one of the earlier attacks, his crippled brother, Hohrhos, and the elderly castellan, Behrtos, having ordered the defense masterfully, despite the many things they had lacked and the few ill-trained effectives they had commanded.

As soon as affairs permitted, he had closeted himself with his twin. "Hohrhos, this was bad enough, but I think it to be only the bare beginning, and it will assuredly get worse as it progresses. That rebel bastard Fahrkos has had himself crowned king, and the army is deserting him in droves for good and sufficient cause. Soon there will be no army worthy of the name in all of the kingdom; then all hell is certain to break loose on us, and this hold is indefensible for long and against any really strong force, especially against one whose commander might know what he is about.

"Therefore, I think we should abandon the hold, strip it of all usable or valuable and move into the city. With my men and the folk already resident, plus those from the countryside who're sure to seek shelter with us, we should be able to hold those walls against most any force we're likely to see away out here in the far provinces. We can start collecting supplies of all sorts, weapons, armor, horses and mules, kine of all kinds. . . ." He noted his twin's frown and asked, "What's wrong with the plan?"

"With the plan, nothing," sighed Hohrhos. "It's the city. We don't own the City of Pahtahtahspolis anymore, my lord brother."

"Have you gone mad of siege fever, Hohrhos?" demanded the new *komees*. "What the hell are you talking about? Of couse we own the City of Pahtahtahspolis, it's part of my patrimony, it's been a part of this *komeeseeahn* since the very beginning of our house, time out of mind!"

"Well, maybe so, but it's not ours anymore, my lord brother," said his crippled twin brother flatly. "The Church owns it now, it and its plowlands and pastures."

Stehrgiahnos had never known his brother to lie about anything of importance, and he just then felt as if an iron mace swung by a giant had crashed against his battle-helm. "But . . . but, how . . . ?"

There was a bare trace of bitterness in the cripple's voice then as he said, "Your damned promotion after Ahrbahkootchee, my lord brother, that's how! Our sire didn't have that kind of money, not the amount you needed, but he was hungry for the honor for you, for him and for the House of Papandraios, so he rode up to the *thoheeks* and tried to borrow it, but the *thoheeks* didn't have it either, and it was he suggested that our sire seek out the *kooreeos*, and he did, ending by mortgaging the city and its lands to the Church for enough to buy you that blasted promotion and outfit you properly for your new rank and status. Even I approved of what he did . . . then.

"But after that, ill luck dogged us. One year, a drought made the crop yields skimpy. The next year, the rains came too soon and too heavy. Then there was trouble on the land, with rebels and bandits—I can't see much difference between the two stripes, if there is any—trampling grain fields and driving off livestock and raping and looting in the villages.

"What it boils down to, my lord brother, is that our sire could not manage to pay the enormous interest on time, much less touch upon the principal, so six months or so back a sub-*kooreeos* and a detachment of hired pikemen marched into the *komeeseeahn*, served our sire with a document signed by the *ahrkeekooreeos* in Thrahkohnpolis, the *kooreeos* of this duchy and our own dear *thoheeks*, then entered the city and occupied it, claiming everything of ours in it."

The three hundred heavy horse of the Royal Army wound down the dusty road to the City of Pahtahtahspolis with the Leopard Banner unfurled and snapping smartly in the wind, the men all erect in their saddles, with polished leather and burnished weapons and armor, the horses all well groomed in the aligned ranks.

At the barbican that guarded access to the lowered bridge across the broad, muddy ditch that the moat became in the dry season, one of the flashy, bejeweled officers rode up to the barred gate and roared in a voice dripping with hauteur, "Open up the gate of your pigsty! We're on king's business, you baseborn swine!"

"Uhhh . . . but we-alls heared the king was dead, my lord," said one of the pikemen.

"Oh, *a* king died, right enough." Scorn dripped from the officer's voice. "But whenever a king dies, you thick-witted bumpkin, a new king is crowned. He's king of us all, and we ride on his royal writ. Now open this gate and signal the inner gate to be opened for us or I'll have you fed a supper of your ears, eyes and nose, you yapping dog!"

The barriers were raised, the gates swung inward, and the column clattered and boomed across the bridge, then through the inner gates and onto the main street, thence in the direction of the palace of the *komeesee*. The sub-*kooreeos* was very easily intimidated, and at his squeaked command, his mercenary pikemen obediently

laid down their arms before the bared swords of the
Leopard Squadron regulars.

With the sub-*kooreeos* reflecting on the state of his
soul in a cell far below, Captain *Komees* Stehrgiahnos
found himself to be in possession of the city, two
hundred mercenary pikemen and their officers who had
been paid for six more months only a week previously
and did not seem to care to whom they rendered that
service so long as they could bide on in the safety and
comfort of the city, his own troops, some pipes of a
passable wine that had been the sub-*kooreeos'* and a
goodly quantity of silver and gold that he had found
after he had smashed open a locked chest found under
the great bed in which the cleric had been sleeping since
seizing the city.

With shrewd use of the treasure, Stehrgiahnos had
been able to add to the static defenses of the city and to
provide and equip it well with provender and weapons,
so it had ridden out the bad years before the death of
King Fahrkos. He had lost his twin during the only
attack that came anywhere near to succeeding, the bad
leg having failed at a time and place that had caused him
to stumble into two men, be suddenly drenched by the
contents of the pot of boiling oil they were bearing and
then to fall, screaming, from off the wall to the cobble-
stones forty feet below. By the time Stehrgiahnos had
time to see to his only brother, Hohrhos' terribly burned
body had already been cold and stiff, his helm deeply
dented and filled with blood and brains that had leaked
from the cracked-open skull.

Then, after long years of absence, the outlawed rebel,
Thoheeks Zastros, had returned to the Kingdom of the
Southern Ehleenohee and had marched around much of
the kingdom for months, fighting here and there, his
following burgeoning to intimidating size as he went
and fought. He had not come near to the lands of
Komees Stehrgiahnos, of course, but word of him, his

return with a Witch Kingdom wife and his recent exploits traveled far and wide, along with the measure of order that he had brought to the troubled realm.

When he had marched, finally, against the usurper, Fahrkos, he had triumphed, Fahrkos had suicided, and Zastros had been coronated High King of the Southern Ehleenohee. After announcing his firm intention to invade and conquer the lands to his north, to make himself High King of all Ehleenohee and every barbarian people from the borders of the Witch Kingdom to Kehnooryos Mahkedohnya and possibly beyond, he had sent out military units to scour the lands for troops to make up his great, formidable host, to be of a size not seen on the face of the continent since the time of Those Who Lived Before—more than a half million fighting men.

At length, a force of royal officers and lancers had arrived under the battered but still sound walls of the City of Pahtahtahspolis. Upon being admitted, the officers had proclaimed the new High King's announcement of a general amnesty to all who had deserted the army of his usurping predecessor if they now would return to his service and join him on his path of conquest. Despite the fact that many of them now had wives and families and friends in Pahtahtahspolis, the surviving men of what once had been the Leopard Squadron of the Royal Heavy Horse were stirred like old warhorses on hearing the trumpet calls of war, even *Komees* Stehrgiahnos himself.

Planning to delay only long enough to set his city and lands in good order under a noble deputy, he sent his remnant of a squadron and as many of the onetime mercenary pikemen off with the troops of the new, powerful king, promising to report to Thrahkohnpolis himself within the space of a couple of months.

Due to the still unsettled conditions, when he rode the journey to the hold of the *thoheeks*, he rode armed and accompanied by a few also armed retainers. These men were skillfully separated from him at the ducal residence, and while he was awaiting his audience, well-armed ducal guardsmen disarmed him, led him to a secure if comfortable chamber and locked him in it.

Shortly after he had been fed, he was visited by the *thoheeks*, who came alone and seemed rather embarrassed about this imprisonment of a loyal vassal. "Look you, my boy," he had begun, looking anywhere but at Stehrgiahnos, "I don't like what I've had to do here, and I like even less what certain other men have in mind for you, do I obediently deliver you into their hands. Now what the Church hierarchy did to your sire and house was not right—legal, but not in any way moral—but neither was what you did in taking back your city, clapping a sub-*kooreeos* who was only doing what his superiors had ordered him to do, after all, in a dungeon cell after terrifying him, and robbing him and hiring his troops out from under him.

"Now I know what your defense is going to be. Had that sad specimen of supposed masculinity stayed in ownership and control of the city, it would've fallen to the first warband that came along and would today be a charred, broken-walled ruin as so many others are now. But even so, you broke civil laws and your intemperate actions drove the previous *kooreeos* into such a rage that he suffered a fit and died on the same day that he heard the news. Therefore, his successor means to see you charged with and tried by a Church court for murder in addition to a plethora of other crimes. That trial will only be a mere form, of course; they consider you guilty of everything and mean to burn you or crucify you, after suitable torments and maimings and mutilations."

The *thoheeks* ended by giving *Komees* Stehrgiahnos back all of his effects, adding a small purse of old, worn, clipped coins, plus a warning to ride far and fast and keep clear of the lands that had been his patrimony and, above all, to not allow himself to be taken alive by the Church or its agents. He regretted it, he said, but in order to maintain important relations with the Church, he would have to declare this son of his old friend outlaw and himself lead out a fast pursuit of him within days.

Only some week into his flight, the broken, outlawed *komees* found himself confronted by a dozen armed men as he rounded a brushy curve in a road. Without thinking twice, he snapped down his visor, unslung his shield, drew his sword and spurraked his horse into a startled lunge, determined to take as many of the bastards as possible down into death with him. He had cut down two and incapacitated yet another when a crashing blow of a mace hurled him down, out of his saddle, unconscious.

When he regained his senses, he was lying on the ground and looking up at an ill-matched pair of warriors—one thin and wiry, the other big and beefy, Mainahkos and Ahreekos by name. When he realized that his captors were bandits, not agents of the Church, he admitted to his recent outlawry and ended by being offered a place of command in the sizable force led by the two warlords. Stehrgiahnos had accepted.

Chapter X

Over the years, Stehrgiahnos had done what little he could to influence his commanders as to the merits of treating the inhabitants of places they did not have to take by storm and force with less than their inbred savagery. This did not, however, apply to Church-owned communities; on the evidences of what horror had taken place at a rural school for the training of priests, its farms and walled town, the renegade nobleman had been afforded evident respect and a generous degree of comradery by Mainahkos and Ahreekos, certain from the bloody signs that he could be naught save one of them, a true brother of the soul if not of birth or background.

His military training and vast experience had proved of inestimable value to the two warlords; the strict discipline that he and some few other once-noble officers and veteran sergeants had enacted and very harshly enforced had rendered the heterogeneous mob with which they had begun into a relatively more reliable and dependable force of troops.

Stehrgiahnos' strong, compact, wide-ranging corps of dedicated sadists had marched from place to place, deliberately seeking out only Church properties, towns and cities, storming them without offering to treat, and visiting upon the miserable survivors of the stormings the ultimate in depraved atrocities. Then, after all of value or interest had been plundered, they invariably burned the places to the ground, with such few of their

187

human victims as by then still lived left helpless to roast alive.

So many Church places fell to Stehrgiahnos' corps that all of the as yet untouched places felt constrained to desert their smaller, less defensible habitations and join together in a few larger and stronger if less comfortable spots, not beginning to return to their holdings until the authority of the Council had begun to make its steel-clad presence felt throughout the former kingdom.

But when he had marched against the city that once had been his, the broken *komees* had been keenly disappointed, finding both it, his natal hold and the ducal city and hold to have fallen to some other band at some earlier time and become but sacked, smoke-blackened, ghost-haunted ruins.

When he had heard the entirety of the sorry tale from the lips of his newest slave, *Thoheeks* Grahvos had sat in silence, staring hard at Stehrgiahnos for a long while. Finally speaking with a gruff gentleness, he had said, "There's an ewer over there on that commode, along with a brace of goblets, Stehrgiahnos. Pour for both of us, then take the chair yonder. I had thought that I had ferreted out everything about you and your past; I was wrong and I freely admit to the fact. You've had a hard, bitter time of it, haven't you, lad?

"A man of your military antecedents would be of some great value to our army, but of course that's out of the question so long as our Grand *Strahteegos* and *Thoheeks* Portos remain fixtures of it. Our old Pahvlos was bitterly disappointed that you weren't at the least hung up on a cross; Portos would've had you crucified with an iron pot of starving mice strapped to your belly.

"However my feelings toward you have altered now, Stehrgiahnos, little else of what I earlier told you has; some of it cannot, like it or not. You still are a slave; I cannot free you, that was part of my purchase agreement, you see, nor can I sell you, though I may give you to anyone I wish if no money or goods or services are bartered for you. I'll not be having you branded, but there will be a mark cut into your flesh; however, it will be so shaped and placed that it will pass as an old wound scar to the scrutiny of any who don't know exactly what to look for and where to look for it.

"I'll still be using you as my clandestine agent in certain matters for me and, through me, for Council. Between such assignments, I think you'll be a body servant and bodyguard; in such a capacity you'll not only be able to dress like the gentleborn man that you are, you'll also be able—indeed, expected—to go armed. Anent that, before you leave this room, choose a sword that suits you from that rack over there; the dirks and daggers are in the drawer above. When you've regained your energy and strength, I'll expect you to start exercising regularly with the palace guards, both ahorse and afoot, with and without armor. As I'm certain you know, you won't be the first slave bodyguard; indeed, some noblemen will have no other kind."

The Stehrgiahnos who responded to his master's summons on a certain blustery winter day looked the part of a gentleman-retainer to the hilt. His ease of movement warned knowledgeable observers that he had worn a sword for many a year and presumably, therefore, could be expected to know well its use.

Stitched between the layers of his suede-trimmed, half-sleeved, satin-brocade gambeson was a shirt of fine, light, very expensive mail, and his soft-looking felt cap incorporated a steel skullcap. Like these items, none of the other bits and pieces of protective armor scattered about his body in vulnerable or sensitive spots were openly displayed, nor were the highly visible sword and short dirk the only weapons on his person, or even the most incipiently deadly ones.

He had burnished his service bracelet until it gleamed

like the gold-and-garnet finger ring that had been presented to him after the first occasion on which he had saved his master's life through the expedient of forcing a would-be assassin to take some inches of blued steel to heart. The other, more massive, ring was of chiseled silver and set with a piece of dark-blue *kiahnos*-stone; that one he had won dicing in the barracks of the Council Guards.

Upon hearing the words of his master, Stehrgiahnos had frowned briefly, stared into his goblet of mulled wine, then brightened and declared, "A begging monk, my lord! They're under the control of no one, really, not their order, not any *kooreeohsee*, yet any Church facility will welcome one, for right many commoners consider such to be far more holy than any other stripe of churchmen. They're allowed to wander about, poke into just about anything, and other Church folk behave and converse as if the begging monks were inanimate objects or livestock."

Thoheeks Grahvos pursed his lips and nodded. "It sounds good, yes. But could you carry it off? Remember, it could be your very life if you're found out, my boy."

A grim smile lingered momentarily on Stehrgianos' scar-seamed face. "I've done such before, my lord, back when I was scouting out ahead of my corps of bandits, determining the richest, least-protected places to attack. The first few times, I went in with and under the tutelage of a real begging monk who was also a bandit, but after he was killed in combat, I did it alone for some time with never a bit of trouble.

"You see, my lord, all that is required is a fluency in Pahlahyos Ehleeneekos—the ancient tongue of our forefathers, which I happen to own, since my own sire was something of a scholar—appalling personal hygiene, a fair knowledge of Church ritual and the ability to give the impression that one is more or less mad.

"The man from whom I learned all of this was indeed mad, mad as mad could be. He was like three entirely different men inhabiting but a single body. The begging monk, *Ahthelfos* Djooleeos, was a meek, gentle toper who was never quite sober. There was also a noble priest of exquisite manners and gentility, a most devout and caring man, but he was never much seen, and then only briefly; he was called *Pahtir* Leeros. Then there was Rawnos the Blood-drinker, a true berserker in battle, murderer, rapist, sadist, arsonist; he was vicious, grasping, a bully and braggart, a user of hemp paste and leaves, callous and greedy to unbelievable limits; he would never have been tolerated in any aggregation of men other than the bandit army. But there was many a madman and sociopath in that army."

"What exactly will you need to prepare yourself for this mission?" inquired Grahvos.

Stehrgiahnos shrugged. "Not much, my lord—a hooded robe of unbleached wool with a length of rope to girdle it, a traveler's wallet and brogans of hide, a wooden alms bowl, a stout staff of ash or oak, flint and steel, a couple of knives, a brimmer hat. None of these things should be new, if possible; the more signs of long, hard use they show the better."

"When can you depart?" asked Grahvos.

"Not for at least four to six weeks," was the reply of his slave. "I must stop bathing, let my beard grow out and my hair lengthen; I should acquire a modest colony of parasites, too. But, my lord, it were far better that I prepare in some private place well away from the city, where I can weather my skin naturally, hike about and let the brogans and robe and hat acquire stains, dirt and filth enough to be convincing. Can my lord trust his slave beyond supervision?"

Sub-*strahteegos* Tomos Gonsalos had been more than willing to stay on longer with this army he had had the largest part in forming for the Council of *Thoheeksee*, in large part because all that he had to which to return in Karaleenos was lands and cities; his father, mother and siblings all were dead, and his young wife had died of fever while he was on campaign with his cousin King Zenos, against the then foe High Lord Milo Morai, and her still carrying his unborn child in her belly.

For years, this army had been both wife and child to him. Around a nucleus of the troops loaned by the High Lord—a regiment of Freefighter pikemen, a squadron of heavy cavalry and one of Horseclansmen—he and *Thoheeks* Grahvos had gathered first the private warbands of the earliest members of the Council, then the flotsam and jetsam of units and individuals streaming back south from Zastros' disaster in Karaleenos. As a blacksmith drives impurities from the iron by way of heating and hammering, reheating and hammering harder, so did Tomos and his cadre slowly rid their battalions and squadrons of the unfit, the undersirable, the criminal elements that had permeated the ranks of Zastros' host, so that when finally Council had found a Grand *Strahteegos* to their liking, Tomos had been able to deliver into his thoroughly experienced hands virtually a finished product, needing but to be slightly altered, custom-fitted to the personal lights of the new commander.

Tomos had gone on more than one campaign in the capacity of a subordinate officer to Pahvlos, but he had spent most of his time since the old warhorse had assumed command of the field armies in the sprawling, permanent encampment below Mehseepolis, supervising the training of new units and replacement personnel for existing ones, as well as commanding the permanent garrison of the Military District of Mehseepolis, plus overseeing the supply and remount commands.

It had been more than enough work for any one man, and he had been far too busy to be able to find much time to be lonely. He received many more invitations to private homes and public fuctions within the city than he could ever make the time to accept, and he generally used the excuse of the press of his duties to decline almost all of them as a matter of course—the public bashes ran from dull to tedious, and the private dinners too often devolved into drunken orgies that left a man too shaky of the following mornings to get any work done.

The private dinner parties he liked most, which he tried very hard to not miss, were those of *Thoheeks* Grahvos' Council faction—*Thoheeksee* Bahos, Mahvros, Sitheeros, and a few others. At these, the food was from good to superb, the wine was well watered, the conversation was stimulating, the entertainments were subdued; sex—in the form of well-trained slaves of both genders—was available for any guest so inclined, but said guests were expected to enjoy themselves in privacy in the guest chambers provided for the purpose.

He and his servants had lived quite comfortably in the oversized house that had been constructed along with two others for the higher-ranking commanders of the army who did not choose to live in crowded Mehseepolis or the settlements building up just outside the city walls. Occasionally, *Thoheeks* Sitheeros would come to stay for a couple of days, bringing quantities of foods, wines, spirits, cooks, servants and two or three young women, the number dependent on whether or not Captain of Elephants Gil Djohnz was off on campaign with the Grand *Strahteegos* and his hard-worked army.

So it was on the occasion of the thirtieth anniversary of Tomos' birth, Sitheeros and Gil Djohnz having but days before returned from a month at Iron Mountain. While the servants were unpacking a wainload of comestibles, a half-pipe of wine, a keg of brandy and other items, Sitheeros and Gil kept Tomos outside his home in spirited conversation. When, at last, the newcome guests moved on into the house, Tomos' surprise had been arranged by carefully instructed servants.

In the middle of the first room they entered stood a

girl Tomos knew he had never before seen, and he knew
that he would have remembered this one had he seen her
before, for her beauty was striking—long, long blond
tresses from which the sunbeams picked out hints of
red, a face as freckled as his own, but heart-shaped,
holding almond-shaped blue-green eyes, a narrow nose
and the reddest lips he had ever seen. She was clearly
nervous, and the tip of a red-pink tongue darted out a
couple of times to wet those lips. Her clothing, though
obviously in the barbarian mode, was elegant and richly
embroidered, and the jewelry, if it was real, looked to
be worth a good part of the ransom expected of a
vahrohneeskos, anyway.

When the three men entered the room, the girl
hesitated momentarily, then, with downcast eyes, she
made her way to the trio and sank to her knees before
Tomos. As she raised her head and looked into his dark-
blue eyes with her own—which, he noted, were
swimming in unshed tears, which fact he found most
unsettling for reasons he could not explain to
himself—she also lifted her two hands, revealing that
her wrists were encircled by brass cuffs connected by a
length of gilded-brass chain.

Wetting her lips yet again, she parted them and spoke
haltingly in an obscure dialect of Mehreekan, one he
had never heard before, but close enough to that of his
mountain-born mother's to be understandable to him.

"Wilt not my master remove these fetters and free his
handmaiden? She comes to thee a pure maiden; wilt my
master not deign to render her a woman?" Her voice
was soft and a little throaty; the words were a bit
slurred, in the manner of the indigenous barbarians of
the western mountains.

The wristbands, he saw, were fitted with catches, and
the girl could have easily unsnapped and removed them
herself, so he decided that this must be some variety of
barbarian ritual, of which they seemed to have more
than did the Ehleenohee.

With a smile and a shrug, he unfastened the bands

and then glanced at Sitheeros. "Well? What's the proper form now, my lord?"

The *thoheeks* grinned. "Take both her hands in both of yours, raise her to her feet, then bend and kiss her lips. Difficult, what?"

Tomos did as instructed, then started back from the girl, for it had felt when his lips touched upon hers as if some force of power had passed from her being to his. Had these jokers brought down from those mountains some ditch-witch to play tricks, then?

Before she could speak, however, Sitheeros had embraced him and was slapping his back and kissing his cheeks. "My heartiest and most sincere congratulations and felicitations, my old friend. You now are, by barbarian rites, wed to the daughter of one of the most powerful chiefs among all of the barbarian tribes, Chief Ritchud Bohldjoh, of the Tchatnooga Tribe. May you both live long and have many children."

Gil Djohnz had taken and gripped his hand firmly and said soberly, "We felt you needed a woman to care for your needs here, my friend. It is not good for a man to live for too long alone, you know." He grinned and chuckled. "It is said to lead to such afflictions as a permanently stiff . . . ahh, neck."

Thoheeks Sitheeros had slapped him again on the back and crowed, "Now it is time to commence the drinking that must always precede the wedding feast. Come, take the hand of your bride and come. You must not allow your loving guests to perish of thirst, man."

While Tomos was carefully watering the wine—he recalled how very intoxicated he had gotten at his last wedding feast, so befuddled that it had been impossible to consummate the marriage properly for three days, and although he still was at least half convinced that this all was an elaborate joke of some nature or description, he intended to take no chances—the burly *thoheeks* was worrying the stopper from out the neck of a huge stone jug. At length, the obstruction popped free, and, hooking a thumb through the ring handle and resting the heavy container on his arm, the *thoheeks* splashed a generous dollop of a clear, slightly yellowish liquid into each of three small winecups, filling the room with a strong, sharp odor.

Having looked over his shoulder at just what his guests were up to, Tomos wrinkled his nose at the stink and commented, "If that's a jug of fermented fish sauce, I think the stuff has spoiled; smells that way to me."

When the wine was diluted to his satisfaction, Tomos took his seat and left the dispensing of it to the servants. It was then that Gil Djohnz shoved a cup of the liquid from the stone jug before him. "It's a wedding gift from Chief Ritchud's private hwiskee stock, Tomos—it's something he calls 'danyuhlz,' though it tastes just like any other corn hwiskee to me. The chief swears that it's a special kind of hwiskee distilled carefully to a recipe and methods that are an ancient and an exclusive secret passed down for hundreds of years amongst the Tenzsee Tribes."

Holding his breath against the rotten stench of the stuff, Tomos took a tenative swallow of it. After he could once more breathe and, with eyes still streaming from his strangled coughing, was wondering if the buffets of Sitheeros' big, hard hands had really sundered his backbone and shattered his ribs or if they just felt that way, he was able to gasp, "Off the decomposing hides of what dead animals do they scrape the fungi out of which they make that?"

After a while, when Tomos was feeling more his usual self and when his two guests had ceased to laugh at his discomfiture, he inquired, "All right, now, how much of this is real and how much just one of your elaborate, infamous practical jokes, my lord Sitheeros? Am I really married to that child? Or is she just some new slave girl you two bought and coached and dolled up to cozen me? I'll have a straight answer, and it please you, my lord. To a *kath'ahrohs*, such as yourself, barbarian

rites and customs may seem droll, but to me, whose
mother was a barbarian princess, they are far less so."

Gil answered first, saying solemnly, "Tomos, me 'n
Sitheeros, we rode clear up to Chief Ritchud's hold at a
place called Kleevluhnd, smack dab in the middle of the
ruins of a big city of the old times. We went up for a
different reason, of course; Sitheeros owed the old chief
a visit and he thought I might like to go along and see
the place and the people, and it was an education, I can
say that much. We wagoned up a couple pipes of wine
and some other things Sitheeros knew his old pal
fancied, and we both were treated top-notch by all Chief
Ritchud's folk.

"Then one night, after a feast, when we all of us were
drinking and talking in the hall of Chief Ritchud's hold,
the old chief had little Brandee brought out and asked
Sitheeros couldn't he find some rich Ehleen husband for
her. I think he expected old Sitheeros to take and marry
her himself, is what I figure he had in mind, and"—he
glanced over slyly at the *thoheeks* to ascertain if his barb
sank home—"the way old Sitheeros was panting and
drooling and all, his tongue just hanging down into his
cup and his eyes fit to burst clear out of his head and all,
I was just then of the mind that he might, then and
there."

Sitheeros stared, unwinking, at the captain of
elephants, and remarked in a soft voice, "There are
definite ways to deal with your kind of prevaricator,
Captain Djohnz . . . and I am a past master at the most
of them, and those that I misremember my torturer-exe-
cutioner, Master Peeos, does recall. Remember this
gentle warning in future, captain; it will be to your best
interests to so do." Then, unable to longer hold his very
convincing pretense of cold rage, the *thoheeks* burst
into laughter and threw the contents of his cup of
watered wine at his friend become tease, and took up
the recountal himself.

"Oh, Tomos, I admit, I freely, even joyfully admit,

to the fact that that child's very, very female shape and bearing and appearance moved me . . . well, moved certain parts of me; she is assuredly toothsome. But I then was forced to recall that I have a wife, that the Ehleen Church and customs allow but one legal wife at the time, that my old friend, Chief Ritchud Bohldjoh, wanted honorable marriage for his child and would certainly look askance at mere concubinage of her, and that he could field thousands of mountain warriors did he choose to so do; therefore I drew tight rein on my admittedly libidinous impulses, which, God be praised, I am not as yet too aged to feel to their fullest extent on occasion.

"And then, as if we had shared but the single, solicitous mind, both Gil and I bethought: our dear friend Tomos Gonsalos would not—as, you must admit, would most Ehleen nobles and gentlemen—be at all offended were he to find himself wed to so delightful a young woman. Besides which, he really needs a willing, young, strong, healthy and truly ravishing wife and helpmeet, if anyone does. In his own lands, he is as high a noble as am I in mine, possibly more so, since he is the cousin of a reigning king.

"When once Gil and I had described you—your high civil and military ranks, your charm and gentility, the numbers of warriors under your command, your fierce valor in battle, your handsome good looks, all the simple traits of the simple man you are"—Sitheeros grinned slyly—"Chief Ritchud fairly watered at his mouth and we began the dowry negotiations then and there. He is one of the wealthiest of the Tenzsee chiefs and I knew it and he knew that I knew it, so Gil and I were able—after a few days of haggling and feasting and entertainments and really serious, professional-style drinking—to wring a settlement of truly royal proportions out of the rich old bastard for you, enough to give you good cause to remember this anniversary of your thirtieth year of life. We hope too that you will remember your two good, loving, caring friends who brought it all about for you.''

"And should I decide I don't like the girl and the arrangement, that I'd rather have an Ehleen to wife?" demanded Tomos. "What then, my good, loving, caring, practical-joking, near-alcoholic friends?"

Sitheeros squirmed as if he had unknowingly seated himself on an anthill, frowned and replied, "Hopefully, you won't, Tomos. Man, you could go far toward starting a border war that would make the last one look like a field exercise, that way! Why do you think that the border up above Iron Mountain has been so quiet for so many years, man? It's because Chief Ritchud and I have been friends for just that long. A very fierce, bloodthirsty tribe from somewhere up north and east of him, called the Ahrmehnee, raided his lands in force years back, burned the nearly ripe crops through a wide swath of his tribe's lands and drove off quantities of his kine, killing those they couldn't take and leaving the carcasses to rot or using them to pollute springs and wells. They are truly demons from hell, that tribe."

Tomos nodded knowledgeably. "Yes, I know, Sitheeros. We of western Karaleenos have been troubled by that same tribe of barbarians for as long as we have been in the foothills, hundreds of years now."

"Yes, well, anyway," Sitheeros continued, "I knew that rather than see their folk starve that winter, the Tchatnoogas were certain to mount large-scale raids against my lands and any other border duchies within range, so I counciled with my peers and we collected surplus grain, winnowed through our herds and sent the first of quite a few wagon trains up to Kleevluhnd—that first one under strong guard, of course—where I personally gave its contents to Chief Ritchud, who was a young man then, about of an age with me, and but recently having succeeded to the chieftaincy of the Tchatnooga Tribe.

"That was the beginning, Tomos. There was not a

single raid that year; moreover, when the old king heard what we had done up there, he allowed us to credit part of our gifts against our yearly taxes—you see, Hyamos was not always a bad king; only as he aged and his mind began to slip did his son begin to influence him to his and the kingdom's detriment. Eight years later, when a severe, localized flood ravaged part of my domains and those of *Thoheeks* Djordjeeos Lahmdos of Yoyooliahn-skeera in the early spring after a very bad winter, Chief Ritchud himself came down with above two thousand of his warriors to help us drain the lands in time for putting in the year's crops. Many would've gone hungry that next winter but for the help of those good barbarians.

"Twenty years, almost to the day, after we were become friends, the accursed Ahrmehnee again invaded. That time, three other *thoheeksee* and I gathered our warbands and as much of our spear levies as could be spared from working the lands, took six of my war-elephants and marched up into Tchatnooga lands. Our force combined with that of the Tchatnoogas, and their barbarian allies managed to finally bring those Ahrmehnee to battle and trounce them so thoroughly that, to the best of my knowledge, they never have raided in any force again, not against the Tchatnooga tribal lands, anyway.

"Since the sundering of the old Kingdom of Mehmfiz, years back, there are three paramount chiefs in all of the lands of Tenzsee, and the sire of that girl you just married is one of them, so please, I sincerely beg of you—even if she snores, stinks, wolfs her food and guzzles her wine, spits on the carpets, pisses the bed or burns down the house, please try to like her, for a border war of the proportions that Chief Ritchud could bring about might very well end our new and hopefully better rule of Council rather than of kings before it has hardly commenced."

When the feasting finally was done and the last healths had been drunk, when Sitheeros and Gil, both far too drunk to safely fork a horse, had been tumbled into the wain to be driven back into the city by Sitheeros' servants and cooks, then Tomos—still almost sober—ordered the sunken tub in the bathroom of the kitchen house filled and relaxed in the steaming, blood-warm water while his body servant laved him, oiled his dark-auburn hair and reddish beard, then lightly scented his body.

Wrapped in yards of thick linen sheeting, he walked back over to the house and, in his attiring room, exchanged the sheeting for a soft knee-length tunic, a pair of felt shoes and a quilted cotton robe of dark green. While chewing at a couple of dried cardamom pods, he gave orders to his guards and the house servants that he was to be disturbed only in the event of a full scale alien invasion or the outbreak of a serious rebellion; any and all other matters could and must just await his pleasure.

Then he visited the dining room long enough to place a decanter of watered wine, one of honey wine and a smaller one of brandy in a basket with two silver goblets, and, thus laden, he padded in to his new bride.

When he opened the door of his bedchamber, three girls ran, all grinning and giggling, out. Two of them he recognized as slaves of Sitheeros; the other was a stranger, though marked by her clothing as a mountain barbarian, for all that she was as dark as any *kath'ahrohs* Ehleen, with black wavy hair and flashing dark-brown eyes.

He stopped dead when he took a step inside. His bed-chamber had been drastically altered; gone were his own, narrow bed, his campaign chests and his small desk, and in their places was a large, clearly expensive bed adorned with feather mattresses, satin coverings and bolsters, and semi-enclosed in a tentlike affair of gauzy silken draperies. Low carven tables flanked the massive piece of furniture, and where his plain iron watch-lantern had hung there now was an elaborate lamp of hammered, gilded brass with insets of crystal-clear glass. Tomos could not imagine just when and how Sitheeros' servants and slaves had managed to get the room first emptied and then refurnished without his knowledge of their activities.

In the two outer corners of the chamber, braziers glowed, sending up tendrils of fragrant smoke from the rich nuggets of incense that had been scattered in generous handsful over the coals. His head awhirl, Tomos estimated the total cost of these new furnishings to be at least a thousand *thrakmehee*, if not more. Sitheeros was a more than wealthy man, but . . .

A soft, throaty voice intruded upon his thoughts. "Mah lord husband, Ah feared that Ah would sleep before you came to me." Her Ehleeneekos was slow, stilted and most ungrammatical.

Tomos, smiling, strode over to the bedside and deposited the basket on one of the carven tables, then said in Mehreekan, "My dear, given time, I'll see that you learn our language properly, but for now, let us speak in yours, for I do own a dialect or two of it. My mother was, you see, a daughter of King Rahdnee III of Briztuhl."

She wrinkled her brows. "But . . . but mah daddy said that you were . . . that mah husband would be an Ehleenee duke . . . ?"

Tomos laughed. "I'm that, too, my dear. I'm a hereditary *thoheeks* of the Kingdom of Karaleenos, a land up to the northeast of here, but I'm only half Ehleen, nonetheless. I'm down here to command troops that my king's new overlord has loaned to these Ehleenohee until their own army is strong enough to defend their lands without aid."

Although he conversed gaily, Tomos was become painfully aware of just how Sitheeros had felt when first he had seen this child-woman. She lay propped against one of the bolsters, her flaxen hair now loose and framing her small head and lightly freckled face. Her

body was sheathed from throat to below her small feet
in a nightgown so sheer that he could easily discern
through the fabric the bright red-pink nipples of her
proud, pointed breasts and the red-blond tangle of
curling hair between her upper thighs. Once more, he
wondered fleetingly if Sitheeros' back-poundings earlier
in the evening had damaged his back, for his chest felt
suddenly tight and his breathing was become difficult.

Licking dry lips, he poured measures of the watered
wine into each of the goblets, added a dollop of the
thick honey wine, then proffered one to his bride,
before taking a long swallow of his own. Seating himself
stiffly on the edge of the luxuriously soft bed, he
stretched forth a hesitant and, he noted with a still
rational part of his mind, slightly tremulous hand and
gently clasped it on one of those enticing breasts. All at
once, he was become feverishly hot, he could feel the
salt sweat oozing out his pores and trickling down his
face and his body under the quilted robe, and he knew
that the robe must come off and quickly.

When he stood up to remove it, the girl untied something behind her neck and sat up long enough to pull her
wispy nightgown over her head, at which point Tomos'
breathing seemed to become even more constrained, so
that he found himself to be panting shallowly like a
spent coursing hound at the end of a brisk hunt.

Kicking off the felt shoes, he pulled his own tunic
over his head, not even hearing the gasp that issued
from between the red, red lips of the nude girl. But
when he lay beside her, first placed his arms around her,
he felt her stiff, tensed muscles, felt her slender form all
atremble, heard the ghost of a whimper, a sound of
hopeless terror.

Restraining the insistent demands of his body, he
released her and drew a little away from her, though
leaving one hand in contact with her flesh. "Brandee,"
he said in a voice that quavered only slightly, "you
should have no fear of me. I am your husband, child; I

mean you no harm, now or ever. If you so wish it, for tonight I'll just seek out the bed that was previously here and sleep in that, that you may rest and sleep and compose yourself for the morrow. I have no kin here, nor either have you, so what we two do or do not do in this chamber and this bed tonight is no one's business but ours. Come now, speak your thoughts to me, Brandee, tell me your wishes."

A shudder rippled the length of her body, she sobbed one time, then she began to speak. "Ah . . . Ah'm truly sorry, mah lord husband . . . but . . . but when Ah . . . Ah saw *it*, Ah . . . It's just so . . . so *huge*, so much bigger than Ah'd thought it would be. Ah don't think Ah can . . . that you can . . . Ah know I should be, must be brave, that's what my mothuh and aunts told me, but . . . but . . ." Then she began to cry.

Tomos took her, enfolded her slender body in his arms and held her against his hairy chest, patting her back gently as she cried out her fears and her terrors. At some length, when the sobs had first muted, then ceased, he released her, and, propping himself upon an elbow so that he could the easier look into her swimming, blue-green eyes, he said, "Brandee, bravery is only necessary in the face of danger or of pain. I pose no danger to you and I will not willfully hurt you, so save your bravery for some time when it is needed. Because you still have your flower, there will no doubt be some pain, but no more than you can bear, and soon there will be none at all.

"My first wife, who died years ago of a summer fever, was smaller even than are you—only fourteen hands from soles to pate, and slender—yet we two experienced scant difficulty in doing the things that men and women do together, not after the first few days. Indeed, when she died, she was carrying our child in her womb.

"But look you, my lady wife, you have had a full measure of excitement this day just past, as too have I.

Let us sleep now. We two have the rest of our lives in which to learn to enjoy each other and breed me an heir or three. You must be the one to choose the time for a beginning of lovemaking. For now, sleep you well; I know that I shall.''

Brandee thought, as she felt the scarred, muscular, hairy body lying beside her slowly relax, heard his breathing become deep and regular, "This stranger to whom they have married me, he is so very kind, so thoughtful of me, of my feelings, he is so wise and so caring. Could Daddy have been aware of this? He never met my lord husband . . . I don't think; perhaps the Lord Duke Sitheeros told him. But I am so very glad that they married me to this man and not to that old, fat, toothlessly leering Chief Rahbin of the Nahkszfil Tribe, who is always undressing girls with his eyes and dribbling porridge down his chins and the fronts of his shirts. My lord husband keeps himself so very clean and smells so pretty, while I don't think old Chief Rahbin has had a wash since he left his cradle.

"Yes, I think I could be very, very happy with this man to whom they have married me, this Duke Tomos Gonsalos.''

Epilogue

Despite his ever constant press of affairs, *Thoheeks* Mahvros was quick to grant an appointment—over the strident, almost carping arguments of his staff—to the signatory of a properly drafted letter. However, when the man actually stood before him, smiling, he was much amazed. Save only for certain racial differences— lack of height, a flat-muscled, wiry build, hair and skin barbarian-light—had he not known the m~n, he would have taken him for an Ehleen gentleman from his dress, his manners, his cultured dialect.

"My, you have changed, my old friend," he commented, shaking his head slowly. "Please be seated, there. You will have wine?" He signaled the hovering servant to pour, then waved him from out the chamber.

Once the forms, the polite, meaningless words, had been exchanged, the healths to each other and to Council and to the High Lord had been announced and dutifully sipped from the gilded silver goblets of much-watered wine, Mahvros said, "Now, all of that time-consuming foolishness completed, what can I do for you, Captain of Elephants Gil Djohnz?"

"My lord, I want to leave the army," said Gil flatly.

"Well, surely, Gil, this would be a military matter, it would fall under the jurisdiction of Tomos Gonsalos or *Thoheeks* Pahvlos, not under mine," Mahvros replied.

Gil sighed. "I spoke with Tomos; he agreed, though with regret. But when he sent me on to Pahvlos, the old bastard flatly refused. It would seem that he considers

me to be some variety of military slave, thinks that I and
my elephants are owned entirely by him and his army.
Tomos went over and tried to reason with the hardheaded old fucker, but even he could get no more of a
concession than that as the army is actually the property
of Council and the *thoheekseeahnee*, then Council must
make any decision that would serve to override his."

Steepling his fingers and nodding, Mahvros commented, "He's shrewd, but then we've all known that
for years. He knows full well that so heavy is Council's
schedule of business, so petty a matter might not come
up for years. Besides, Council can seldom agree on any
point, it would seem; I've seen smaller bones of
contention than this one would be promote personal
verbal attacks, physical assaults in the very Council
Chamber, duels and the hiring of assassins, on more
than one occasion. We refer to ourselves as 'noblemen'
and 'gentlemen,' but I have seen more of nobility and
gentility in certain mountain barbarians than in the
persons of certain Councillors. But, nonetheless, there
are ways to circumvent the sure delays and chaos of
Council.

"Who suggested that you come to me? Tomos?"

"No, my lord." Gil shook his head. "Lord Sitheeros
was the first to say that I should, but Tomos agreed
when I mentioned what Lord Sitheeros had said. Tomos
dictated the letter to his secretary and I signed it."

"Heheh," chuckled Mahvros, grinning. "You have
good advisers, Gil, among the best, really. The Wolf of
Iron Mountain and the Karaleen Fox are two fine men
to have guarding your flanks. Of course, they know
what many men do not know: right many matters never
even go to the full Council, for many and varied
reasons. Really earth-shaking decisions, of course, must
be decided by the ayes of at least two thirds of Council;
that's the way that *Thoheeks* Grahvos and the early
Council set it up.

"But matters of lesser importance, and your case

would surely fall into this category, can be approved by
half the Council plus one more vote, nor do said votes
have to be cast before the rest of Council, nor even in
the Council Chamber. Of course, the full Council is
almost never here and assembled together, you know
that—many are just too busy on their lands, some are
infirm, *Thoheeksee* Pahvlos and Portos are away on
campaign for at least two thirds of any given
year—therefore, in order to give full votes on important
matters, most of the *thoheeksee* have given their proxies
to men of like mind who are likely to be here, in
Mehseepolis, more often than are they.

"As chairman of Council, I vote five—my own vote
and four proxies. *Thoheeks* Bahos votes for himself and
for a cousin, *Thoheeks* Gahlos; *Thoheeks* Grahvos has
two votes that are his because his is a double *thoheekseeahn*; and *Thoheeks* Sitheeros, as I'm sure you know,
owns three votes due to his triple *thoheekseeahn*. But in
addition, Grahvos holds and votes two proxies and
Sitheeros has three from as many border *thoheekseeahnee*. So the grand total is seventeen Council votes,
exactly the number needed to approve your request that
you be allowed to leave the army, so you may consider it
done and the matter settled, my friend, and if Grand
Strahteegos Thoheeks Pahvlos doesn't like it, he can go
somewhere alone and cry.

"But, as a matter of purely personal curiosity, I'd like
to know why. Are you getting homesick, then, Gil?"

"No, not me, my lord." The Ehleenicized Horseclansman replied. "It's Sunshine and Tulip, my two
elephant cows. They want to go back to the land where
they were born, want to know once more their own dear
kindred and browse again the forests that fed them in
youth, wade and swim the rivers, be dried and warmed
by the sun of home. They have both served me and this
army well and long, so I think they deserve to be served
equally well by me, and that's why I wish to take leave
of the army. I want to go with them to their distant
homeland. Do you, can you, understand, my lord?"

Mahvros had always owned a deeply emotional streak that he had had to work hard to hide, over the years, and the plain, simple sincerity of the words of Captain of Elephants Gil Djohnz had brought a painful lump to his throat and a misting to his black eyes, so that he had to swallow hard before he could reply.

"Yes, my dear friend, I do understand. Your motives are selfless and distinctly laudable. How else may I help you and your elephants on your way?"

The Grand *Strahteegos Thoheeks* Pahvlos Feeloh-pohlehmos, newly confirmed Lord of Kahproskeera, had sent an officer of his personal horse guards to summon and escort Sub-*strahteegos Thoheeks* Tomos Gonsalos back to his headquarters complex on the other side of the sprawling camp under the walls of Mehsee-polis. The gaze he had fixed upon Gonsalos when he had been ushered into the audience chamber had been as glittering and cold as the edge of a headsman's axe.

Tomos had known damned good and well just what it was all about; therefore he had simply saluted his superior and then stood stiffly and in silence, returning the cold rage blazing from the old man's eyes with bland calmness.

Finally, his rage getting higher than the dike of his control, Pahvlos had smashed the side of a clenched fist against the top of his desk and snarled, "You arrogant, insufferable, insubordinate son of a Karaleen sow! You *knew* that I wanted to, meant to, keep that cur of a barbarian bitch's whelping for the good of my army. I imparted to you my reasons, good, sound reasons; I can now see that I should not have so wasted my breath on such as you, my lord foreigner. My decision has been overridden by a Council fiat, but I doubt not that you knew of that well before they chose to inform me of the outrage. Am I not right, you traitorous bastard, you betrayer of trusts?"

Tomos chose his words most carefully, not allowing a scintilla of his own rage—fully justified, in face of the

personal insults that the old man had hurled at him,
heaped upon him—to show in face or voice or actions.
"My lord *Thoheeks* did, if he will but recall, say that the
case of Captain of Elephants Gil Djohnz's request that
he be allowed to take his elephants and leave the army
be adjudicated by the Council of *Thoheeksee* and—"

"Shut your mouth!" growled the Grand *Strahteegos*.
"Try throwing my words back at me and I'll see you
stripped and well striped in a trice, noble officer or not;
it would just now do me good to see your thin blood and
your alien backbone.

"I meant for the case to go to the Council, right
enough, but before the *full* Council, and you *knew* what
I meant, too. It might've been as much as a year and a
half before the Council got around to the matter, and
my army would've had the full use of the barbarian and
his beasts in the interim. At that Council sitting, I
would've had the right to put forth the reasons why he
will be needed indefinitely, and, finally, I would've been
able to cast my vote and that of *Thoheeks* Ahramos of
Kahlkopolis against the barbarian's foolish request. In a
civilized land such as this, the only use or place for
barbarians of his ilk is my army . . . or wearing a slave
collar.

"But no, you and that brawling, boozing, woman-
crazy, meddling, overindulged fool of a *Thoheeks*
Sitheeros had to disregard my sound decision on the
matter and send that barbarian ape to *Thoheeks*
Mahvros, who's thick as thieves with *Thoheeks* Grahvos
and his crooked clique. Now I just have to sit here and
let that damned barbarian go and let him take the rest of
the barbarians and four of my army's elephants with
him! And I lay the full blame for it on you, you turn-
coat, you renegade, you half-barbarian scapegrace.

"I think the time has come for you to leave my army,
take your skinny, barbarian whore and go back to your
savage homeland and leave decent, civilized
kath'ahrohsee to rule themselves without having to bear

the unwashed stenches of your foul breed. Go on, you pig, get out of my presence before I lose complete control and run my sword through your putrescent body!''

Blankfaced, though with great effort, Tomos saluted, faced about and strode out of the audience chamber. But as he was fitting foot to stirrup, the officer who had escorted him to the place stepped out of the building and signaled him to wait. When they had ridden, side by side, in silence for enough distance to be out of sight and hearing of the headquarters buildings, the officer reined up close and said in hushed tones, ''My lord Sub-*strahteegos* must know that he has full cause to issue challenge to the Grand *Strahteegos*, to meet him in a session of arms to the death. My lord is a *thoheeks* and so too is he, so he can have no slightest acceptable reason to decline a challenge from my lord. I heard all of his insults and I will so swear before the chosen seconds.''

Thinking he might be scenting some trace of a trap of some obscure nature, Tomos said in a equally low voice, ''Man, you're an officer in his personal bodyguard! Will he not consider such an action to be a betrayal?''

''Was what my lord did in advising the captain of Elephants truly a betrayal of the Grand *Strahteegos* and the army, as he so stated?'' asked the officer.

''Of course not!'' snapped Tomos. ''I'm only attached to his army; my loyalty is to my men, my king, his overlord and to your Council, in that order; I try to cooperate with the Grand *Strahteegos*, but I never have considered myself to really be his subordinate officer in the command structure of this army.''

The officer nodded once, then said, ''My lord, my own loyalty is to my men and my comrade officers, the rulers of my land—the Council of *Thoheeksee*—and *their* army. This senile old man is ill serving Council and is weakening the army through mistreating and abusing and alienating the officers and men under his command.

212   *Robert Adams*

It is my understanding that he refuses to step down and retire to his *thoheekseeahn*, so it would seem that the only way to remove him is to kill him, nor am I the only man who so feels in this army. So, should my lord decide to issue challenge, please remember Captain *Vahrohnos* Djaimos of Pleenopolis.''

Deeply troubled by all the captain had said, Tomos did not return to his own headquarters, but rode directly up into Mehseepolis and to the onetime ducal palace. He was afforded the opportunity to release some measure of his pent-up anger on two bureaucratic types who would have—completely aware of just who and what he was—prevented him from seeing *Thoheeks* Mahvros without an appointment. When he thought them sufficiently terrified, he stalked past a quartet of grinning guards and sought out the chairman of Council without a guide.

He found *Thoheeks* Mahvros conferring with a couple of men he did not know, but clearly both civilians. ''My lord,'' he said curtly, in a no-nonsense tone, ''I'd advise you to get these two out of here and hear what I have to say privately. You'll probably regret it if you don't.''

At a look from the *thoheeks*, the two civilians rolled up and gathered up a number of what could have been drawings or maps and bustled from the room, giving hard, hostile stares from beneath their eyebrows.

With the doors firmly shut and latched, Tomos led his friend to the corner farthest from those doors and quietly related all that had happened at the army headquarters and after.

After a few moments of digestion of the hard words, Mahvros asked quietly, ''Are you going to call him out, Tomos?''

''Would you?'' was the response.

Mahvros sighed and shook his head slowly. ''I'm not at all certain just what I'd do under the same circumstances, my old friend. He's completely in the wrong, of course, any fool could tell that, and I wonder if the word used by that guard officer doesn't tell us much about the entire kettle of vipers—'senile.' Senility could well be the reason for much of Pahvlos' recent, hardly explainable behavior.

"The captain is right, you know—no, maybe you wouldn't, you don't have all that much contact with the field army anymore. Pahvlos has recently been far more demanding than he has needed to be, stayed almost constantly on the march and insisted on rates of march that were completely unnecessary, considering the circumstances. The best officers, many of them, have resigned and gone home; among the common soldiers, the rates of desertion and rank insubordination have climbed to fantastic figures, and Pahvlos' punishments have been no less than savage—men who deserved no more than perhaps a dozen stripes have been whipped to death on his orders, that or crippled for life; he has had tongues pegged or torn out, fingers and hands and toes and feet lopped off, leg tendons severed, joints sprung loose—he is become a monster to the men of this army he chooses to call his.''

Tomos shook his head slowly. "No, I've only known that the army has been going through with remounts almost as fast as we can train them, pack animals, draught mules, supplies by the mountainload, and is always crying for men from the training units, but I was unaware just how bad it was. Why in hell hasn't Council relieved the man?"

Mahvros snorted. "He's too powerful, that's why, with far too many supporters on Council, men who remember the *Strahteegos Komees* Pahvlos-of-old and will not believe the enormities he now commits and orders, or who swallow his bland excuses hook, line and sinker. His relief of command is a matter of sufficient importance as to require a two-thirds favorable vote of the entire Council, and the last time that the matter was broached to them, there was a real brawl in the Council

Chamber, guards had to be called to finally break it up, two duels grew out of it all, and shortly thereafter there was an attempt to assassinate Grahvos.

"Did I think that it would do anyone any good, I'd say go ahead and call the old bastard out, for that captain is right: he'll never step down and retire, and with matters as they are on Council, there's no way he can be forced out, so the only alternative is going to be his sudden demise, however done or by whom.

"And, were it up to Pahvlos alone, I believe he'd meet you, he was never known to harbor one cowardly bone in his body, and of course then that would be that, you'd cut him down. But naturally, so simple and straightforward a solution to the problem he presents will never be allowed to come to pass. His seconds are certain to cite his great age and insist that you meet and fight a surrogate, no doubt the biggest, fastest, strongest, meanest heavy horse or guards officer they can find. So, no, don't bother challenging him. Have you thought of an assassin? Satisfaction privately enjoyed would be preferable to none at all, perhaps."

"No," said Tomos, "no assassins."

"If it's simply a matter of money, Tomos . . ." began Mahvros.

"Thank you, but no," was the quick response. "If I can't do it myself, I'll not hire another to do it for me; it's simply not my way, Mahvros."

"So then what will you do, Tomos? Just do as he ordered you, take your wife and household and go back to Karaleenos?"

Tomos sighed. "No, I was ordered here by far higher authority than a doddering, sadistic old man. No, I now will do something that I had hoped I never would have to do.

"You will immediately send someone to fetch Grahvos; that someone will tell him to bring with him the sealed red leather tube sent to him by High Lord Milo, years back. Call an immediate meeting of as many of Council as you can lay hands upon, including *Thoheeks* Pahvlos, by all means."

Thoheeks Grahvos worked a thumbnail under the thick seals and thus loosened them enough to snap off the leather tube, its bright-red dye having faded somewhat in its years of dusty storage. "High Lord Milos' letter, that accompanied this, mentioned that one other here would know of its existence and contents, but that person was not named. It was you, eh, Tomos?"

When he had removed the lid, he used a finger to fish out the roll of vellum and opened it. After reading it, he hissed softly between his teeth, passed it to Grahvos, then lifted the tube and upended it over his opened palm; then he extended his hand that both of the others might clearly see the half of an old, worn silver coin, cut in an odd zigzag along its middle.

Wordlessly, Tomos took from about his neck a silver chain from which depended another halved coin and fitted it to that piece on the *thoheeks'* palm to show a whole ten-*thrahkmeh* piece of some archaic High Lord of Kehnooryos Ehlahs, its worn-down date showing him to have reigned nearly a century before the great earthquakes of three hundred years now past.

The dozen and a half *thoheeksee* of Council filed into the wide chamber, dutifully racked their swords and other weapons, then took their accustomed places at the long table. Last to make appearance were Grahvos and Mahvros, accompanied by Tomos Gonsalos. At sight of the nonmember, *Thoheeks* Pahvlos' thick white eyebrows went up and he frowned and began to loudly crack his big knuckles, growling under his breath.

When Mahvros took his place, Pahvlos immediately demanded, "Were we all summoned here simply to hear the yappings of that half-breed puppy out of Karaleenos?" He looked around the Council and added, "He's living with some mountain slut to whom he claims to be married, has the unmitigated gall to refer to the baggage before civilized men as 'his lady wife'! All that I can say is that he never asked or got my permission to marry."

"Why, pray tell, my lord, would he need your precious permission to wed?" asked *Thoheeks* Sitheeros, adding, "And, as that girl's sire is an old and very dear friend of mine, you'd best balk up your prize insults when I'm around."

"Yes," Pahvlos said, smiling coldly, "everyone here knows your perverse love for barbarians, female and male, nor are your peculiar tastes admired, only tolerated because of your wealth and power. But in reply to your question, my lord, this Karaleen was an officer of my army—"

"It is not your army," snapped Mahvros. "It is Council's army and, through Council, a part of the army of the High Lord Milo, who now rules over us, Karaleenos, Kehnooryos Ehlahs, the Isles of the Ehleen Pirates, the *Arhkeethoheekseeahn* of Kuhmbuhluhn, the *Komeeseeahn* of York and the *Komeeseeahn* of Getzburk. You overstep yourself, my lord, but then you have been so doing for some little time."

The old man grinned mockingly. "Going to make motion to take my army away from me again, you young shoat? Remember what happened the last time, don't you?"

"My lord, please, I beg you," said *Thoheeks* Portos, "it is our Council's chairman you are addressing."

"Oh, shut up, Portos!" snarled Pahvlos. "When I want shit out of you, I'll squeeze your malformed head."

"No, Pahvlos, you shut your sewer mouth!" ordered Grahvos. "Keep it shut or I'll summon guards, see you roped into that chair and gagged. If you don't believe me, try me and learn to your sorrow."

He stood up, holding the red leather tube prominently in his hand. "My lords, some years after we had moved the capital from its old location to Mehseepolis, I was recipient of certain dispatches from High Lord Milos. If those who were then members of Council will recall, we then were not at all certain sure that we would be able to rebind the lands together under us and ever take our place in the Confederation ruled over by the High Lord, and I had communicated this to him in a letter.

"His replies were several, but one of them was a letter in a tube that also contained this tube—then firmly sealed. The letter that was within the outer tube recognized the enormity of the task we few then were undertaking and praised our bravery for trying to do it at all in the face of seemingly overwhelming odds, so much opposition from so many quarters. The High Lord went on to say that I should keep this tube sealed and keep it always near to hand, and should all appear lost, the situation either hopeless or completely out of hand for whatever reasons, I was to break the seals and open this red tube, seek out the man who had the other half of the coin therein contained, and follow his instructions to the letter, recognizing him to be the full surrogate of the High Lord.

"It did not work out quite that way, of course, my lords. We have succeeded . . . after a fashion. But now crass politics and a controversy centering around a stubborn, petulant old man in his second childhood through senility is threatening the stability that we have but recently achieved at great cost of effort and time, sweat and gold, blood and worry.

"Although we each of us swore and attested powerful oaths to ever lend our full and unqualified support to the aims and aspirations of our Confederation of Consolidated *Thoheekseeahnee*, its governing body—the Council of *Thoheeksee*—and the larger entity which it serves and to which it owes pledged fealty—the Confederation of Eastern Peoples—many a one of this present council has proved himself to be completely unwilling to sacrifice even a single one of his purely personal interests to the common weal; indeed, members of Council have time and again fought like cur-dogs over a rotting bone within the precincts of this very room, have later drawn each other's blood in senseless duels and have, I am dead certain, hired common assassins to dispose of peers and brothers of Council.

"This can in no way be construed or considered an orderly government, for all that the strenuous efforts of a very few of us have kept most of the outward appearances of one with little help, no help at all or outright and childish opposition from the remainder of Council. I have right often of recent months thought me of that red letter tube tucked away in my files and wondered and pondered.

"All of you know Sub-*strahteegos Thoheeks* Tomos Gonsalos, here. He is Karaleen-born and truly owes us nothing, yet he accepted the High Lord's commission to march down here following the Zastros disaster and, with a small nucleus of troops loaned by the High Lord for a core, rebuild from the broken, scattered elements of warbands and survivors of the royal armies of the various kings a fine, strong, well-balanced and proven-effective army, so that when the present Grand *Strahteegos* took command, years back, he had only to shape and mold a preexisting army to his personal taste, not organize one from scratch, as might otherwise have been the case.

"After the Grand *Strahteegos* took command of the field army, no one would have thought it at all out of place had this selfless nobleman, his job well done, left and returned back north to his own lands and kin. But he did not, rather he stayed on here, and has since then done the hard, detailed and exacting duties of managing the many-faceted support system without which the field army could not exist and keep functioning.

"The army taken over by the Grand *Strateegos* was strong, disciplined and well organized, owning many fine units raised and commanded by effective and

sometimes brilliant noble officers. The skill and valor
and blood of that army won victory atop victory for
Council and was of significant help in finally reuniting
these lands, clearing them of the scum that had
accumulated here and there in the bad old days and
seating us and our noble vassals all securely in our
places. This army of ours remained that way for a
while . . . but no more, my lords, no more."

"Now, dammit, Grahvos," snapped Pahvlos,
looking and sounding thoroughly exasperated, "do you
intend to get to a point or not? I am a very busy man, I
have many important matters awaiting me back at the
headquarters of my army. I think that this session can
get along just as well rehashing recent history without
me." He shoved back his chair and looked to be in the
act of arising.

"I would strongly advise that you stay, my lord
Grand *Strahteegos*," said Mahvros quietly and coolly,
but with force. "I say this both as chairman and as one
privy to knowledge not yet generally shared by the other
members of Council."

The spare, white-haired officer sank back into his
chair, saying, "Oh, very well. But please, please, get to
a point, Grahvos. I left it that the punishment and
executions of certain military miscreants on tap for
today not commence without me there to witness them,
and the troops all are drawn up in formations by now,
that they may be warned by those examples how I
maintain discipline and loyalty in my army."

"As I was saying, my lords," *Thoheeks* Grahvos
went on, "*our* army, *Council's* army, was still a strong,
a terribly effective, a high-spirited force as lately as two
years ago, but no more. Many of the best noble officers
have taken their units and left the camp; many noble
officers who yet remain are much disaffected and have
made that disaffection known to certain of us."

"Really?" said Pahvlos, raising his eyebrows. "They
haven't said as much to me, their commander, their

Grand *Strahteegos*, the man to whom they would logically speak. A wise man would've put no trust in the babblings of a few troublemakers. But are you wise, Grahvos?''

"Wiser than you think!" snapped Grahvos. "Wise enough to know that you don't hold command of a good army by the harsh, brutal, savage and barbaric ways you have taken to using within the last two years, old man.

"Wise enough am I to realize that you cannot keep an army almost constantly on campaign, year-round, and then not allow them to unwind with wine and brandy and carousing in garrison. You don't have men lashed to death or cripplement for being found drunk in their barracks after a three-month campaign in the mountains, yet you did just that. You don't have a good sergeant's ears cropped and burn his scalp bone-deep with boiling pitch simply because he was a day late in returning to camp from a carouse, either, yet you did, my lord. You don't have the hands of an artificier mangled simply because he somehow smuggled a town strumpet into his barracks, but that is just what you did, *Thoheeks* Pahvlos, whereupon the entire unit of artificiers—officers and men alike—deserted the army, and now Tomos Gonsalos is scratching about trying to organize another artificier corps for the field army.''

"The only thing that settles the insubordination of malcontents is the force of example," said Pahvlos coldly.

"Is that so?" Grahvos said. "So what happened when you sent a full battalion of pikemen out to chase down the artificiers and bring them back to star in another of your gory spectacles? They didn't come back either, only a few of their officers, whom you promptly had hung for malfeasance. Man, one would think that you are deliberately set to utterly destroy our army.''

"I've heard enough and more than enough!" Pahvlos snarled and came to his feet.

"Sit down!" ordered Grahvos.

"Make me . . . if you can," sneered Pahvlos, striding toward the rack of weapons near the door.

Grahvos nodded at Mahvros, who pulled the bell-rope, and abruptly the doorway was filled with guardsmen in half-armor, one of them bearing a coil of thick rope and a handful of leather straps.

Mahvros waved at Pahvlos, saying, "Captain, please escort the Grand *Strahteegos* back to his place; there seat him and bind him securely into his chair."

Some others of the Councillors muttered, but most seemed too stunned to do even that. The old officer struggled briefly, but there were just too many hands ready to restrain him, so he gave over, allowed himself to be pushed into the chair, with his arms, legs and torso bound and strapped to its frame. He glared rage at Grahvos and Mahvros, but spoke not a word.

"My lords," said Grahvos, "it has been a painful torment to me to watch the dissolution of our army, the strong right arm of Council, but those of you stubbornly set upon allowing the monster that Pahvlos is become with age to continue his misdeeds because he once was a great and good and entirely different man have tied my hands on the deadly serious matter.

"Today, this once-great senior officer had Tomos Gonsalos brought to his headquarters by a fully armed member of his personal guards and there proceeded to curse him, slander him, insult him on many lines, call his wife a whore and his mother a sow, then order him to leave the camp and our lands and go back to Karaleenos, threatening to sword him otherwise."

"Rubbish!" Pahvlos burst out. "Sewer sweepings, all of it! Yes, I ordered him out of the camp of my army; I did so because he had shown clear disloyalty to me and my authority, he and Grahvos' clique having arranged the legal desertion of a unit of my army. If he says any other, he lies . . . but then he is after all half a barbarian, and to barbarians, as we all know, lying is a native attribute."

Grahvos shook his head. "No, my lord Grand

Strahteegos, it is you who lie, in this instance. Members of your headquarters staff easily overheard your shouted insults and slanders and threats against Sub-*strahteegos Thoheeks* Tomos and they quickly offered witness and full support to him, strongly suggesting that he call you out, meet you at swords' points and kill you, as he easily could. If nothing else is disturbing to you, that should be, my lord, for these are the very men who daily and nightly guard your back, watch over you when you sleep, yet they clearly want you dead, if that is the only way that the army can be finally shut of you."

The eyes of the old soldier filled, then spilled over to send salt tears coursing down his lined, scarred, weathered cheeks and into his snow-white beard. He sobbed twice, then shook his head and said in a whining voice, "I am an old man. I've devoted almost all of my life to my armies and my kings and their kingdom. So why am I used so cruelly by you I have tried so hard to serve well? You choose to believe a whoreson barbarian Karaleen rather than me." He snuffled loudly. "It's not fair, it's just not fair, none of it is fair." He then began to sob rackingly, and to moan, his head sunk onto his chest and his hands visibly straining against his bonds.

With looks of pity, the two *thoheeksee* flanking him, Portos and Vahsilios, set to work on the restraints, freeing first the arms, then the rest of the straps and knotted ropes. With the freed hands, Pahvlos covered his face. But immediately he was completely free and his two benefactors had reseated themselves, he leaped up and ran to the weapons rack. Armed with his sword and a stout dirk, he turned and crowed in triumph.

"Now I've got the edge on you bastards, and a sharp-honed edge it is, too. Those of you who are mine or favor my cause, come down here and arm yourselves, that we may get to the butchering of the swine who sold our kingdom out to the northern aliens. Let's have done with this silly governing of ourselves for some foreign lord and crown a real king to rule over us, say I."

Grahvos could only stand and stare when tall,
saturnine *Thoheeks* Portos arose, smiling and nodding
agreement to the ravings of the old *strahteegos*. Striding
down the room, he plucked his saber from where it hung
and fitted its case to his belt-hook before drawing
the cursive blade with a sibilant hiss from its sheath. He
plucked a dagger at random from the smaller weapons
on the table and shook off its scabbard, one-handed,
then took his place to the left of Pahvlos and slightly
behind him.

Others, following Portos' lead, had begun to push
back their chairs now, and things were looking rather
tight and sticky for the unarmed Grahvos, Mahvros and
Tomos Gonsalos. Mahvros thought it high time to pull
the bell-rope, but his hand hardly had touched it when
Pahvlos' hard-flung dirk sank deeply into his shoulder.

It was while the old *strahteegos* was fumbling on the
table behind him for another weapon that he suddenly
stiffened, rising onto his toes, his eyes wide and bulging,
his mouth wide as well, but no sound other than an odd
gurgle emerging. Then, abruptly, he collapsed all in a
heap, with the hilt of a dagger jutting up from just
under his left shoulderblade.

Thoheeks Portos picked up the saber he had quietly
laid aside and sheathed it, saying to the room at large,
"It had to be done—you all know that for fact if you'll
just think on it. He was no longer the man we all once
loved and respected. I know that he would have chosen
this sort of quick death by steel. It's the only way for
any warrior to die. We must give him a really fine
funeral; the Pahvlos of old earned at least that much
many times over."

About The Author

Robert Adams lives in Seminole County, Florida. Like the characters in his books, he is partial to fencing and fancy swordplay, hunting and riding, good food and drink. At one time Robert could be found slaving over a hot forge, making a new sword or busily reconstructing a historically accurate military costume, but, unfortunately, he no longer has time for this, as he's far too busy writing.

For more information about Milo Morai, Horseclans, and forthcoming Robert Adams books, contact the National Horseclans Society, P.O. Box 1770, Apopka, FL 32704-1770.